SAD
JANET

SAD
JANET

LUCIE BRITSCH

WEIDENFELD & NICOLSON

First published in Great Britain in 2020 by Weidenfeld & Nicolson
This paperback edition published in 2021 by Weidenfeld & Nicolson
an imprint of The Orion Publishing Group Ltd
Carmelite House, 50 Victoria Embankment
London EC4Y 0DZ

An Hachette UK Company

1 3 5 7 9 10 8 6 4 2

A CIP catalogue record for this book is
available from the British Library.

ISBN (Paperback) 978 1 4091 9866 6

Printed and bound in Great Britain by Clays Ltd, Elcograf, S.p.A

www.weidenfeldandnicolson.co.uk
www.orionbooks.co.uk

For the Janets

If you just broke up with someone, be sad;
if you just ran over somebody drunk driving, feel
depressed. You shouldn't take a pill that makes you
feel okay about terrible things.

—John Waters

SAD
JANET

*

It's eight A.M. on Sunday, and I'm taking a dump at work. Or trying to.

Melissa is waiting outside like a dog, or a child, but more like a dog. She's pretending she needs to go, but she doesn't. She just wants to know what I'm doing. She'd be in here with me if she could, but there's barely enough room for one person, never mind two. My knees are almost touching the door. I could whack my head on the sink at any moment. I could do that.

It's eight A.M. on Sunday, and everyone else in the world is still in bed. In bed is where I left my boyfriend—he's probably masturbating now—and here I am at work, trying to drop a log. Trying to get a little relief in my otherwise hectic, depression-filled days. I always feel better after. Lighter. Like I'm sending some of the shit that makes me feel this way off to a better place.

But shitting with someone right outside the door is like the opposite of relief.

Leave Janet alone, Melissa, I hear Debs say. Melissa laughs nervously and says she needs to pee, but none of us are buying it.

In this moment, I feel sad for us all. This bathroom is basically a porta-potty stuck on the side of the office. Like they built the shelter and then remembered there would be humans inside it and that sometimes humans need to go.

What are the normal people doing right now? I wonder. *How are they starting their days?* Getting ready to go to brunch or some other madness. Going to church. Even church might be better than this.

I feel sad for all of us here, having to spend our Sunday listening to me on the toilet.

I wonder if the first person ever to feel sad mistook it for something else. That they needed the bathroom, maybe, or were hungry, or just very tired. We're all so tired.

Our era will be known as the Greater Depression.

I wonder which came first, happiness or sadness, but I think I know the answer. You assume it was happiness, until something shitty happened and then suddenly, *Hi*, sadness was there. But I think it started with sadness. That was the first feeling. The first human was like, *Wtf is this?* Looking at themselves, the world around them—it made no sense, any of it. Sadness was a big gaping hole inside them. But it was also a hole *outside* them, because human beings hadn't built anything yet, and they didn't like all that emptiness or know what to do with it, so they filled it. And only once it was full did they feel happy.

At least for a while.

1

I'm lying in bed watching TV, and some man on some morning show is telling me there are one hundred and eighty-one days till Christmas. I need to be ready, apparently, like there's a war coming, or a storm. It's both.

I switch off the man and the TV. I have to get up and get myself to work, and I do both those things and feel like a goddamn hero. My boyfriend does the same, but it's no big deal to him, which is annoying. He's annoying.

One hundred and eighty-one days. That's half a year to worry that I won't be able to get it up for Santa, or my boyfriend, or myself even. That's a lot of normal feeling-crappy, with the extra worry that I'll feel crappy at Christmas, when I'd rather feel something else—not happy, god no, what even is that?, but different. I'll probably just feel drunk, and then I won't be able to get it up for anyone, but just let everything happen to me, like most years.

As soon as I get home from work, I switch on the TV, my only true friend, maybe, since my boyfriend's not home. I think he said he was doing something, but he lost me at *doing*. A woman with giant breasts and giant lips comes on the screen. She's at some kid's over-the-top birthday party, and she's saying that life is about being happy. *Why isn't that child in bed?* I'm thinking. My only maternal thoughts come at random times, over random things.

She's from a sex tape. The woman, not the child. She spent all her sex-tape money on this kid's birthday party. It's obscene, the party, but she's happy. The woman, not the child. The child looks crazy. They all look crazy.

I switch off the large-breasted woman and the TV and try to sleep. A hundred and eighty-one days. I need to be ready.

The next day at work I'm supposed to be brainstorming ways we can get more money, because we have none, but I'm mostly thinking about sadness. Melissa is thinking the shit out of ways we can make more money, any money, and Debs is regretting mentioning it. All of Melissa's ideas involve us baking, for some reason, but we're not listening.

I'm thinking about how the world is awful right now, but I think I always knew it was.

For as long as I can remember feeling things, I've felt sadness. Now, for example, I feel sad that we have no money. Also a little mad that a bunch of idiots seem to have it all. But sad, mostly, because I think that's just the way things are, and baking cupcakes isn't going to get us enough money to make our lives mean anything.

But that's not the sadness I'm preoccupied with. Mine isn't one

I can put my finger on. It's an all-encompassing feeling, like my lungs are filled with it instead of air. It's not me, but it surrounds me, so it's become me by osmosis.

You'd think it would feel better to be at one with the world.

People don't like this sadness of mine. They'll do anything to pretend it's not there, that *I'm* not there. If I hadn't chosen to work out here in the woods, at a run-down dog shelter, they would have banished me someplace similar, like an outlet mall.

I'm here, though, just barely. Hi.

There's no word in the English language that properly describes this feeling I have, the one that makes other people uncomfortable. The one that people want me to fix—with makeup, a clean sweater, or a dress, a nice pretty dress, and some girls' shoes, not boots, not men's anyway, as if boots give a crap about gender. As if a man can't wear a dress now. Or a dog.

The Japanese have a term for it: *mono no aware*, the sadness of things.

The existentialists made it a whole thing—literally made the emptiness of life into a movement—but you have to *embrace* the sadness to be in their club. I might consider it, if Sartre hadn't been such a misogynist.

The French call it *malaise*, I think, which makes it sound like a condiment.

The cool kids call it *melancholia*, because of that Lars von Trier movie where Kirsten Dunst sobbed at the moon.

The old people used to say *bone sad*, but I think that was because they were all malnourished and dying of exciting things like rickets and syphilis.

My mother just calls it *moody. Difficult.*

But the Japanese get it. They have fourteen words for it that don't exist in the English language, for this feeling that staying afloat is almost impossible.

I'm fine with all of it, whatever you want to call it.

I'm not a goth, though, so there's hope.

People are really into this happiness thing, though. They really want me to be happy, and I'm really not that fussed. I've dabbled with happiness, I want to tell them, but it never stuck.

I want to say to Melissa, I would fucking *love* to be thinking about cupcakes and shit right now, but my brain doesn't work like yours.

Sometimes I think it's my fault that I let the sadness in. I used to make these crying tapes of sad songs that I'd listen to at night when I was in my bed and supposed to be sleeping but I wasn't, I was crying. Crying for all the shitty things I knew were coming. I wasn't even a teenager yet, but I felt tender and raw and open to all the pain. All those dumb songs about love and heartbreak. I should have been listening to the fucking Muppets.

So maybe I willed it to me, the sadness. And since then I've been storing it all up when I should have been throwing it out. Hoarding sadness like I think there'll be a TV show about it one day and someone is about to come and help me sort my life out.

No one is coming.

Melissa is saying something about a car wash now, and it's gone too far. Like she thinks I'm ever actually going to take my coat off. That underneath this is a bikini body I've been hiding and it's the answer to all our prayers.

A car drives past, and I catch a second of some boy band I shouldn't know but I do because you can't avoid them.

I *should* be happy, apparently. Not because we've just won the war on terrorism, or survived a near-fatal collision with an asteroid, or found the cure for cancer, but because happiness is right there for the taking, if I would only take my butt down to my doctor and then to the pharmacy. Even just a smile might do it.

But I can't find the words for my hollow feeling. What I need is for someone to see me standing here in my giant coat, holding a bag of dog shit, trying to get on with my day, while Melissa talks at me about bake sales and car washes and moonbeams, and to see that I'm not okay with any of it.

Antidepressants are good now, they say. Real progress has been made.

Melissa is on Lexapro. Debs is on good old-fashioned Prozac; she prides herself on being one of the originals. Whoever was driving that car playing the boy band was definitely taking something. Everyone is taking something but me.

My best friend, Emma, started taking Zoloft because she got a free hat. She wasn't a hat person, but she thought she might be if she was happier. She never did, but she did feel better, so much so that she ran away to Ibiza and never came back. I can't even pronounce Ibiza.

On the plus side, there's no stigma now that everyone's medicated. It's a huge relief for a lot of people, and I'm genuinely happy for them. Yay, drugs! It still doesn't mean I want to take any pills.

No one wants to take pills, Debs says.

She's wrong. I've known people who want to take *all* the pills. They think if there's something wrong and there's a pill, then why not? They take a dozen different ones. My mother's one of those people. For her, they're a godsend. I like to remind her that god has nothing to do with it, unless he's actually some creepy dude in a lab throwing money around. He might be, for all I know.

Why does he have to be creepy? she says, and I think the only man she's ever met is my dad, maybe.

My dad's a plumber, but he's not super or called Mario, so no one thinks it's funny. When he's not plumbing, he's watching TV and drinking and avoiding my mother like the rest of us.

During the holidays, when other kids got jobs at the mall, I went and learned how to fix a faucet and unblock a toilet. My father thought I was just doing it to avoid the mall, and my mother thought I was doing it to spite her. She wanted a daughter who would stay home and tan with her, not one who preferred to spend the day sticking her arm down a stranger's toilet. The real reason was that I wanted to see how other people lived. I only saw bathrooms and kitchens, but what more was there? They were the hearts of the home and the people who lived there. I saw a lot of shit that Christmas season.

If my mother had had all these pills when she was younger, she might not have had me and my brother. We were supposed to fill some hole, but we didn't. And yet she still thinks I should have children. It can't hurt, she thinks, forgetting how childbirth works.

My mother worked for the local council all her life, doing something that required her to wear an ugly pencil skirt and uglier shoes. I like ugly shoes, but these were too depressing even for a funeral. Then everyone lost their jobs because all the council's money had been mismanaged and she took some different pills and started teaching Jazzercise. Before that, we hadn't even really known she had legs. Finally, something we had in common.

Neither of my parents had had great Christmases growing up, so they wanted it to be different for us. Which meant they went all out, and we got a shitload of pressure. They thought it was important. More so than our mental health. And the world seemed to agree.

My mother was overcompensating for something— everything, maybe, like everyone else. That was all the holidays were about, filling the void. As a result, Christmas at our house was brutal. Like someone sitting on your chest and punching you in the face repeatedly, but in an ugly snowflake sweater and to the sounds of Dolly Parton singing "Jingle Bells."

You know Christmas, right? You've seen it? It's such a huge, grotesque spectacle. When you're a kid, you don't know any better. It's just what you do at the end of every year. But my mother was ruining it. The pressure to perform was unbearable. To be not just a happy family but a happy person in the world, because it was Christmas. But all her pills kept her from seeing how it affected me. They kept her going and she didn't look back. The world was her enabler. It gave her permission to keep shoving it down my throat. You get on the Christmas train, Janet, or we run you over anyway.

Despite all that, I loved Christmas so damn hard, right up to the moment I didn't anymore. Still, like with all relationships, I kept letting it screw me because I didn't know how to tell it I wasn't really into it anymore.

Of course, my mother isn't the only one. Every December the world spends screaming: The more the merrier! The bigger the better! Everyone trying to out-Christmas one another. If you aren't in a festive onesie, grinning because Christmas, you might as well kill yourself. People go into debt for it. People *do* kill themselves over it. It's too sad.

The whole world is too sad, really, but no one wants to admit it because they made it that way.

Which is why I spend the holidays feeling like an embarrassment. I'm letting them down. Moping around in the woods, hoping it will all be over soon.

At least I'm not hanging around malls or parks or wherever happy people go, weeping in my funeral clothes, reminding people that sadness still exists. I'm just living my life. I'm here at the shelter mostly, where my sadness isn't out of place.

There were other people like me for a while. I think of them as the other Janets. People who couldn't do it. The sad, the bereaved, the lonely. I used to read articles about them, about how awful it was to not feel how they were supposed to at Christmas. But then those articles vanished. It was as if people just didn't want to hear it anymore. People only wanted the happy stories. New articles came along, ones about sad people who went and got medicated and now could enjoy Christmas again. All of it paid for by the drug companies, I'm sure. But I like to think the Janets are still out there, somewhere.

I hope some of them just ran away, like me.

Sometimes, when I'm walking the dogs in the woods, I see larpers. Debs calls them *the fucking larpers*, like it's their family name. Mr. and Mrs. Fuckinglarper. I can be walking along, minding my own business, and suddenly out of nowhere there's a boy dressed as a knight. He'll say something like, Sorry, my lady, then bow and charge off, and I'm left there thinking, *Boys are fucking weird*, but also it's the most romance I've ever had, maybe. Once, a larper came to the door and asked to use the bathroom, and Debs said, If I let you, I have to let all of you, and I don't want to look like I condone what you do. I have kids.

My point is, there are other weirdos in the woods, and sometimes it makes me feel less alone.

I work at a dog shelter, so I know a thing or two about sadness. It's like the exact opposite of Disney World.

Unless you've been in a van with a dog on your lap that you're taking to put down, you don't know sad. I'd been preparing my whole life for this job. All my years of crying myself to sleep were training so that I won't cry when I do this job.

Debs doesn't know this, but before we go to the vet to have dogs put to sleep, we go to McDonald's. It's our little secret. We don't get the dog a Happy Meal or anything; we're not that sick. We just get a plain hamburger and feed it to the dog gently, by hand, and tell him or her—but, to be honest, it's usually a him—he's a good boy.

It started by accident. I was starving, and there it was, on the way to the vet. Should I get him something? I said, half joking. Definitely, Melissa said. She didn't really think we should stop, but I said I'd buy her whatever she wanted. She wanted a little carton of milk, but I refused because that's weird, so we compromised on a shake.

I unwrapped the burger. It was the most pathetic thing I've ever seen. The dog didn't know that, of course. He thought it was the best thing ever. But then so was my crotch. Not even my crotch, but *any* crotch.

I can't believe people eat this shit, I said to Melissa. Melissa and I are both vegans—working with animals will do that—but we're nonpracticing. You want to be better, but it's so hard all the time. It's so sad that you can't be fucked. I'd always wanted to be a vegetarian, but someone told me once that most wine isn't vegetarian. I don't even really like the taste of wine, it's just that when I was a kid, I thought that when I grew up I'd be one of those women who drinks wine alone at night, and I wanted at least one of my dreams to come true.

So I'm sad, and I'm stuck out here with these dogs in the

woods, but otherwise I'm not really that different from everyone else. I have a job, I have people, I eat junk food in my car after taking dogs to be destroyed.

And I take Melissa to McDonald's sometimes. I'm not a complete bitch.

2

I didn't plan to break up with my boyfriend and my family on the same day, but here we are, at a party they've thrown me that's actually an intervention. A party in my own apartment, mind you. They thought I'd be okay with it, they say, because I like intervention shows on TV. I like them, I say, happy they know anything about me, but I don't love them. What I love is not having the people in my life ambush and try to medicate me.

At least there's cake. If there wasn't cake I might not be so calm.

We just want you to be happy, my mother says. I would have preferred it if she'd said *thinner* or *prettier* or *smarter*. Anything but the h-word. It's a lie, anyway: what she wants is for me to be someone else entirely.

Just take the pills, for Christ's sake, my brother says, and I want to say, Please don't bring Christ into my home, he always causes arguments, but I don't because I'm too busy trying to focus all my thoughts on the cake and not murdering my family.

He is only saying that because he has taken the pills, the good son. He's like one of those before-and-afters. Before he started taking pills, he barely gave a shit about himself. Now he's somehow convinced some poor woman to marry him and have his child. I have to admit they worked for him, the pills. They take the edge off, he's always saying. People are always saying this, like edges are bad, but really where would we be without them? Ask Bono.

But then I've seen his edge like no one else has. Like the time he came at me with a fork one night at dinner. He hasn't come at me with cutlery since he started taking the pills, so I guess you could say they work, if not stabbing your sister is the goal.

I like my edges like I like my hip bones. It helps to know what you're dealing with. No use pretending the world is soft all the time when it's really a giant rock.

The pills work for my brother, but it's not like he wants me to take them so I can get married and start pumping out babies too. He's just here because he wants our mother to stop nagging him about me. My mother is a different story. Finding a husband and pumping out babies is *exactly* the reason she wants me taking the pills. Couldn't I just get a boob job? I want to say. I hear men like those more than medicated ladies. But I know that's not true, some men do like medicated ladies. Remember how we all used to worry about guys slipping shit in our drinks, because none of them could get laid the normal ways, with liquor and dim lighting? Now that we're all medicating ourselves, everything is easier. Now, when a guy asks what you do, you just show him your prescription. You show me yours, and I'll show you mine.

You're upsetting your mother, my father says, because this is his one line. What he really means is, Thank god it's not me upsetting her, so you carry on. Thanks, Dad.

Your brother doesn't want you around his kids like this, my mother says.

Like what? I say. I only see his kids once or twice a year anyway.

How you are, she says.

Miserable, my brother says.

I'm not miserable, I say.

Depressed, then, my mother says, but she winces when she says it, like it's something awful that needs fixing.

I'm not depressed, I say, defiant. I'm sad.

We're all sad, Janet, my mother says.

Just get some help, dumbass, my brother says.

My boyfriend is very quiet, but then we've had this fight so often I can't say for sure that this wasn't all his idea.

I could see him calling my mother up and saying he didn't know what to do with me anymore. Like I was a thing that needed something doing with. All he'd have to say is something about how he might marry me if I was just a bit different, and she'd be in a cab on her way over to him, to start work on a plan to save me.

Of course I do need saving—only it's from them, not from my *dark moods*, as my mother calls them, which I actually like because it sounds witchy and beyond my control, when really my moods are the only thing I do control.

They aren't actually that dark, for that matter. Most days they're no worse than gray. It's a manageable melancholia, which feels chic and French. It's just them that has the problem.

He says you're sleeping more, my mother says, meaning this

is what my quiet boyfriend has been telling her. He says you only seem to go to work and come home. Are you even still sleeping together? she asks. My father and brother look mortified.

I'm not answering that, I say.

It's a slippery slope, Janet, she says. You know, you could take one little pill and you might feel like doing more things.

What things? I ask.

I don't know, she says, but she knows, looking to my father and brother for help. Not the boyfriend. He's no help to anyone.

Normal things, she says.

If they knew me at all they'd know I don't believe in normal things.

My mother is one of those people who maintains that all it takes to feel better is to do some yoga. Of course, she forgets to mention the pills. It's like when unnaturally beautiful celebrities try to sell you a face cream and you know they've had a shit-ton of work done but you fall for it because you need to believe in something, even if it's just a face cream.

My whole childhood was spent listening to my mother showing me studies saying that exercise helps lift your mood. Studies all paid for by a sports company, naturally. There weren't many studies covering the fact that telling your daughter to go *jog it out* might have the opposite effect. If I'd ever read that going jogging was a perfect occasion to run away from home, I might have given it a try.

Finally, I've had enough. Get the fuck out of my apartment, I tell them. And I'm keeping the cake.

Once they're gone, I sit on the floor with the cake and hug my-self because no one else is going to. Later I dry-hump a picture on my phone of some guy from some show and then fall asleep, feeling a freeness in myself that is as close to happy as I'm al-lowed.

I've just lost all the people in my life in one fell swoop, and somehow I don't care. And it isn't just because of the sugar high. It's because they're exhausting.

We've been arguing a lot. Obviously I have been arguing with my family since I could speak—which, to their annoyance, was earlier than most children—but for some time now I've also been arguing with the boyfriend. And not just about how he thought I would be better off medicated, but about other regular-couple stuff, like how he thought that when I told him, *Put the toilet seat down*, I meant both the seat and the lid, so I'd get up in the middle of the night, sit down in the dark, and pee on the lid. Then I'd wake him up to swear at him. He felt this could wait till the morning. I felt it could not.

In the beginning, he'd been like me. On the night we met, we were both trying to escape a party we'd been dragged to. He liked my sad. But then he grew out of his, and I stopped trying to make him keep up with mine.

It's a cliché, but we said we'd never be those people—people who cared about having a lot of stuff, people who cared about happiness. We would live on love. Love wasn't happiness; love was something else, something that transcended all feeling. If anything, it veered toward the sad side.

But then he got a job and a little money and he loved it. He wanted more. I had a job with no money and that was fine. I didn't need stuff. I wanted less.

He wanted to embrace the capitalist world, like he thought it was made for him, because as a white man it was. I rejected it all.

Once he realized that money didn't work on me, he thought medicating me might work instead. But that was only after I stopped being interested in sex.

I can only have sex if it's dark and I've had a few drinks. It doesn't have to be pitch-black, and I don't have to be blackout drunk. Just a little of both, like I'm squinting at my life.

We've had a lot of arguments about sex. I remember him trying to have sex with me on a Tuesday afternoon and I did not want any part of it. Working at the dog shelter, I get one day off during the week, and I was able to spend it doing stuff Janets enjoy, like not interacting with people. But that day he came home early, I forget why, and he had an idea. I wasn't prepared for sex— mentally, let alone physically. The mind needs just as much time as the body. It ended up with him shouting, There are worse things than sober sex in the daylight, Janet!, and I shouted back, Yes, but not many!

When he said, It's not normal, Janet, people want to be happy, what he really meant was, *It's not normal, Janet, you should want to have sex with me.*

Suddenly, we were characters from a nineteenth-century

novel. I wasn't performing my conjugal duties anymore. I wasn't keeping the house nice. I wasn't even happy when he brought home a giant TV, and I love TV.

I'd always been sad, but now it didn't fit his needs.

Finally, to shut him up, I told him I'd go to the doctor. I've known forever that if I ever told a doctor everything I feel, they'd tell me it's all very wrong and try to fix me. I'm borderline so many things. I'm on every spectrum. But I will not have them tell me it's something that needs correcting. Being on a spectrum just means being human.

So when the doctor asked me how I felt, I said I felt overwhelmed and underwhelmed at the same time. He didn't know what to do with that. Then I said I felt sad. That was the mistake. It always is. No one ever hears the bit after, when I say I'm fine with it. That it's how I've always felt.

I half expected him to say, *Your boyfriend says you've lost interest in sex.* I would have answered, *Only with him. I'm just not that into live men anymore. Have you seen the news? They're awful.* And he might think I was into necrophilia, and I'd explain that I meant I wanted an image on my phone, or my hand, something that doesn't talk, and we'd laugh.

I might've asked him if he'd ever woken up to someone masturbating next to him. *It's the first sign of personal apocalypse,* I would have told him.

Only I didn't get to say much. Before I could do any jokes, he was trying to give me a prescription. No, thank you, I said.

When I got home, the boyfriend asked how my appointment went. I told him the doctor said I was awesome.

A few hours after I kick them all out, he comes back like nothing happened.

A more functioning person than I might have thought to change the locks or throw his stuff out on the street, but that would have been so much effort, and I really just wanted to curl up and die a little—only a little, because there was still cake left and I could dry-hump alone till I rubbed myself raw if I wanted, and I did want. You get tired of not wanting things.

He'd been gone three hours, but that was long enough for me to realize that I like my life better without other people and their bullshit. I explain this to him calmly. It shouldn't come as a surprise. He knows I like the people on TV more than real people, for instance, because I tell him so constantly. They don't ask anything of me.

I ask him if he can crash at his folks' place. He says, Probably, but can't I just stay here tonight?, and I say, Fine, but just because it's late and I haven't remembered to throw his stuff out on the street yet.

So we sleep in the same bed one more time, and now I know what heartbreak sounds like, and it's a lot like next door's cat scratching in its litter box. We just lie there like we have all those nights before, only neither of us even tries to sleep. We just lie there in silence, apart from the cat and the sound of all hope dying.

In the morning, I get up before him and leave a note that says, *Please be gone when I get back*, and thankfully he is. Sometimes having a job that requires you to get up at stupid o'clock can save you.

As if that wasn't enough agony for one lifetime, a few days later he has his mum come over and help him get his stuff.

It's hell.

Thankfully she brings her dog, so I can just sit on the floor and play with her while they remove all traces of the life we had. At one point they almost drop a box on us, probably on purpose, which is fair enough.

I was only ever with him for his mum's dog anyway.

The apartment is in both our names. No joint accounts, no joint anything. I wanted my own everything. That should have told us something. It was nice having someone pay half the rent, and a warm body was sometimes welcome, but that was it.

I didn't have my own dog because we aren't allowed them in the building, and I get all the dog time I need at work. I cry into their fur now and then, but I don't have to look at their sad eyes all night, just my own reflected back at me from the TV screen.

I did bring a dog home once, though, a sick puppy that needed help. I hid her under my coat, afraid that someone would catch me, but no one cared. I was so sure I could keep her alive. I could not.

Debs was really nice about it afterward. She said the puppy would have died anyway, and at least she got to go home first. No one said, *You killed a puppy, Janet*.

That was the last time I brought anyone home.

3

I haven't always been against taking pills. There was a time when I was *dying* to take pills, back when it was fun still, when it was my choice, when they were from some girl at school who stole them from her brother. But now everyone's doing it, and I'm not interested. It's the new normal, and who ever wanted the new normal?

Why did everything change? I think people got tired of waiting to feel things, because when they did, it was disappointing. Instead, they started taking pills that promised them they'd feel *different*, at least, and sometimes that's enough.

This is the world now—impatient, even with themselves.

Those clever pharma guys, as they're usually guys, knew exactly what people wanted. Not happy pills, exactly, they were so last century, but everything's okay pills, if it isn't really and never will be. This has made them super rich, even though it's kept us super sad, underneath it all. People wanted to take the pills because they were everywhere, and suddenly it just seemed easier. Resistance is exhausting. And there are so many pills to choose from now. And they do work.

You're just cutting off your nose to spite your face, my mother says. And she gave me this nose, so she should understand.

I'm driving to work like a hero and I see a billboard that says, *Pharmacology! It's personal!* I see it everywhere, so I try not to look up. Even when I'm driving. The *person* in *personal* is in bold type, in case you needed emphasis. *We want you, Janet*, they should just say. The pharma companies all want you to think you're getting a personalized prescription, unique to your needs, but this new company claims they've cracked the code.

I don't have a problem with other people taking their meds. When I was little, my mother would spend long periods of time in her room with the curtains drawn, and my father would say, *Don't bother your mother, she's lying down*, and I would sit outside her door and wait. When she wasn't lying down in dark rooms, she was locked in the bathroom. My childhood was just waiting outside closed doors for my mother, wondering what I did wrong.

After she started taking the pills, she stopped hiding that way. When I was a little older, I used to get them for her. Twice a day I would line up her pills for her and it was exciting. Then it was four times a day and it started to cut into my TV time. Before long I'd moved on to locking myself in my own bathroom, lying in my own darkness.

The world seems split now between those who take pills and those who don't. I'm what's known as a resister. Which makes me sound like something from *Star Wars*, and I'm okay with that.

I'm resisting happiness, they think, because who doesn't want to be happy? Me, that's who.

You'd be surprised at the people who don't care that much about happiness. There are a lot of older folks, people who have lived through things, who know that happiness means nothing. My father was a resister for a while, but then my mother insisted he take something if he wanted to stay married, and he was tired and at his age divorce seemed like a lot of work, so he agreed.

Happiness is not on my radar. I want other things. Like control over my life, my body. Like being able to get through a day without feeling like I'm doing it wrong. I want to *feel* all my feelings, not swallow them, and if they swallow *me*, so be it.

So there are the medicated and then there are the rest of us. The resisters. It's not just angry women like me—but it's *mostly* angry women like me. And we're angry for a reason.

Sometimes just getting to work in one piece feels a win.

I have been happy in my sadness for most of my life. It isn't an overwhelming sadness but one I have grown into. Like a big sweater I'm filling out. I'm not weeping all over anyone, or lying on floors unable to move or eat. I'm not threatening to throw myself off buildings or hurt myself. I am quietly sad, and not just about myself but about the world. Have you seen it? It's a shit-show. If we lived in France I would be fine. I could mope to my heart's content, which it would never be.

I've never been able to stay in those dark rooms for as long as my mother. People always lure me out. Men, mostly. Worrying they've done something, which they have usually. I just need some alone time, some headspace, I say, which is true, though the opposite is also true. Mostly, I shut my eyes and hold my breath and sometimes put my hands over my ears just to stop the world spinning for a second before I start things over, at my will. A tiny rebirth. I don't think my mother did that. Maybe she didn't know how.

I'm not out to make anyone else sad.

I can still smile when it's required, laugh when something is funny. I will still accept a hug and sometimes even give one. I'm not turning up to weddings crowing that most marriages end in divorce, lurking in maternity wards to tell new parents that they're certain to fuck up their child in some way. I've never interrupted a sporting event by shouting, *There are no winners because we all die!* I'm not totally dead inside. I can still get it up when I want to. I just don't want to, most of the time.

The next day, after work, I have a doctor's appointment. His office had called, saying, It's pap smear time, which is the opposite of Hammer Time. And I thought, *Well, no one else wants to look at it right now, so why not?*

When I get to the doctor's office, he's wearing his best smart casuals—golf-ready, I call it, for men who are counting the hours till they can escape their lives to get back to the most pointless activity known to man. When I start undressing, he says, I think I've made a mistake, and I think, This is all too familiar. But then he apologizes and says, Well, you're here now, so carry on. How's life?, and I want to say, *Well, apart from men dicking me around, it's fine.*

The doctor smiles at me and asks if I've tried this new yogurt, and I know then that he and my mother are in cahoots, which is a place I have never been. Next thing you know he'll be saying, *Your mother says you have no interest in getting married or starting a family, even the gays can do that now, Janet, what's your problem?* And before I have a chance to say, *There are other ways to live,* he'll have signed me up for a Facebook group called Barren Bitches.

I hate small talk. Well, to be honest, I hate all talk.

Am I dying? I ask, only half joking.

Ha! he actually says. You, Janet, he says, are funny.

Funny people die too, I say.

Ha! he says again.

I remember the last time I was here. I'd come to see him about not sleeping, and he said I should try to reduce my stress, and I asked him how exactly, and I told him about my job and the state of the world and my mother and my boyfriend, and I think I might have mentioned nuclear weapons. I definitely accused him of being a man and having white male privilege. He isn't holding that against me, though, mostly because he's always thinking about golf. I have never once thought about golf.

What's this about? I say, like I'm an important professional person who has better things to do than this, whatever this is.

I called you here today, Janet, because I have something exciting to talk to you about, he says, rummaging in his desk.

Please, god, don't pull out a yogurt, I think. I know the pharmaceutical people are always giving out samples, and for all I know the yogurt companies use the same people.

He hands me a pamphlet. A genuine pamphlet, like from the

old days, when there was actual printed material and no one told you to just google it. I might be one of the few people left on the planet who still reads actual books, so I take the pamphlet.

I'm still mad at him for making me think I was getting my pap smear—I showered for this?—so I just stare blankly at the pamphlet, like most adults faced with actual reading material would. I think about making a joke, but I don't bother, because he already knows I'm funny.

What's this? I ask.

The answer to your problems, he says, like all men who want to fix me.

As far as I know, I don't have any problems, I say. Other than people trying to medicate me all the time, I don't say, still thinking of my poor unchecked vagina getting its hopes up.

It's a new pill, he says.

I don't want any pills, I say, so thanks but no thanks, and I hand him back the pamphlet, which is probably a mistake because it is most likely the last example of print media I will ever see again and also because I've barely registered the fact that he called it a Christmas pill, which, what does that even mean?

It's not like the other pills, he says. It's not permanent. It's just to get you through Christmas. It was made for you, Janet.

When someone says my name, a tiny neuron fires in my brain that magics me into focus. I'm not proud of this. In fact, it makes me disgusted with myself. Like I'm one of Pavlov's dogs, salivating at the thought of some attention.

Go on, I say, because I am a fan of myself, even if no one else is.

Okay, not *just* for you, he says, but for people like you, and I want to punch him in the nuts. *You motherfucker,* I want to say so badly, but I rein it in. Most of my life is reining shit in. When I finally let it all go, have my breakdown in the grocery store, it will be spectacular.

I know how you feel about being medicated, Janet, he says. Sure he does—I've told him enough—but also I'm definitely on some master list of resisters. I'm sure this whole new pill got started when the list got slipped to some government office, like it was Santa's naughty list. I can just hear Government Santa now: *Ho ho ho, those little fucks aren't getting any toys till they start taking their meds.* Some elf would object—*But, boss, we've tried!*—and Santa would lean down and yell, *Try harder then!,* spitting all over the elf with his whiskey breath. So that's what's behind this pill: a chem lab full of elves fearing for their lives.

But this is a special pill, Janet, he goes on, a pill to get you to Christmas with a smile. Don't you want to be happy at Christmas, Janet? I mean, it is the most wonderful time of the year. Don't you think you deserve a holiday, Janet?

And fuck it, he's right. I do. I want to be allowed to be my melancholy self for the rest of the year, but I could use a day off from my sadness at Christmas. A day off for good behavior, just for going the year without murdering anyone. It's like the doctor's seen inside me, seen what I've always wanted. For a minute I'm feeling pretty good about this, until I start thinking about what this means—that they've probably been monitoring me, and I've definitely done some things I'd rather no one knew about. I'm ninety percent regret at this point. Everyone is always recording everyone now, after all. Every corporation worth its salt has some stupid chip hidden somewhere in your home, just for future lawsuits.

You'll be one of the first civilians to try this groundbreaking pill, he says, as if I give a shit about being famous. But then he says two magic words: Congratulations, Janet. And once again I'm rendered helpless—by the word *congratulations*, which makes me think I've won something, and by the sound of my name. Most people don't even know I have one.

You start taking it in November for eight weeks, he says. It's nothing, he says. He looks like he wants to shake me and say, *It's a Christmas miracle, Janet! It's what you've always wanted!*

Read the pamphlet, he says. Google it if you must, he says.

I must, I say, and he nods. We are all Google's bitch.

Old me would have crumpled up that pamphlet on the way out and made a show of throwing it in the trash, or ripped it into pieces and thrown it at the doctor.

New me, the me who's curious about feeling new things, puts it in my bag and goes home.

Later that night, when I'm looking for gum, I find it. The pamphlet I've already forgotten.

I like to think that, all over the world, girls like me are finding this pamphlet at the bottom of their bags, when they're looking for a tampon, but they can't find one, or the one they find is ancient, and they don't even technically have their period, it's just some brown sludge, to match their mood, and they're tired of it all. Instead they find this pamphlet, a distraction from whatever is going on between their legs but somehow more *inside*, and they don't really even read it but just look at it, easing themselves into the idea gradually. This idea that there are options. Despite the fact that it was handed to them by a white man in an office where the government was definitely spying on them. And they decide to hang on to the pamphlet. They can always use it for some sort of art piece later. Or toilet paper if there's an emergency. So they leave it by their bed, and maybe once in a while look at it again before they go to sleep and then dream of a different life. One where everything is a little softer and there are always fresh tampons.

Only I was never really sure there were girls like me. At school it was always, No one wants to start a coven, Janet! We're tormenting boys and kissing them, and if you're not into that, then you better fuck off to the library. Only I was already there, looking for books that would tell me how to hex them all.

I unrumple the pamphlet and pin it on the fridge amid the takeout menus. It looks like any other pamphlet, but on closer inspection you can see the subliminal image of Santa's face. Unless I'm hallucinating and seeing Santa's face where people usually see Jesus.

They'll do anything to make me take the drugs.

I order Chinese and try not to think about how things might be different.

You can't just sit in your room listening to the Smiths, Janet! my mother used to say, and I'd say, I think Morrissey would disagree, and if she could be bothered, she would say, Morrissey is barely Morrissey these days, Janet, and I would have to agree.

That was before I knew the power of my Doc Martens, a push-up bra, and a few drinks. Before I figured out how to get everyone to look at me, even when at the same time I wanted no one ever to look at me, myself included.

I didn't know how other girls did it, any of it, so I made it up as I went.

These pills feel like maybe a chance to let go for a while, to have someone else make it up for me, and to be honest, do I really have anything better to do?

If enough people tell you that you have no life, you start to believe them.

4

When I started working at the shelter, I was issued Wellington boots and ear defenders and I thought, *I won't be needing these. I love the sound of dogs crying out for love. I can relate.*

How do you bear the noise? my mother always says, and I think, *How does anyone bear anything?*

Dogs make me the closest to happy I've ever been. Not just puppies; they're too easy. Not the ones in stupid outfits; they're too sad. What makes me happy are the old gimmers, the ones missing limbs, the ones with mange—the ones no one wants. I want them. All of them.

Dogs are goofy, so it's easy to assume that people who love them are goofy, but we're not. There's always a sadness there.

My mother thinks the shelter is a front for a meth lab because she watches too much TV. I tell her Debs has a PhD in Women's Studies, but that just makes her think it's a lesbian meth lab.

I like Debs because she doesn't ask anything of me, which is a rare quality in a boss. She says her door is always open, but that's just a joke, because her door is broken so it doesn't quite shut. She means, Don't bug me unless you've got an arm off.

Something bad happened to Debs, more than once. You can smell it on her. She thinks the dog scent masks it, but it doesn't.

Sometimes, when a dog goes out to a new home, I think, *There goes a piece of us*, a piece of our sadness, getting a second chance to be something else, and for a second I feel choked up, like I might break. Then I remember I'm just shards, shards and dust bunnies, and I am thankful for the bunnies.

My sadness wasn't caused by any one horrific unspeakable incident, like my mother thinks it was. It's more an accumulation of tiny sadnesses, ones I've been collecting for as long as I've known the value of pockets. *I'm going to need more pockets* is my *You're gonna need a bigger boat*.

It doesn't matter how you got sad, not to Debs. All that matters to her is that you know a thing or two about it, and you're all right by her.

Debs told me on day one that she doesn't care what prescription drugs I'm on, but she will not tolerate hard drugs. *A little weed I'm cool with*, she added, *as long as you're sharing, but nothing harder.* I told her I wasn't on any drugs and she didn't believe me. Now she knows me well enough to understand that I'm just like this.

Melissa likes telling anyone who'll listen what she's on. She has something on her phone that tells her what to take and when, and when she gets the signal, she tells us, because she is a child. She tells us every time she goes to the bathroom and what she's going to do in there. She likes us all to know when she has her period. She probably hopes that one day we'll all break down and start telling her when we have our periods, but we don't. One time, I thought I might have mine at the same time as hers, and I willed it back in my body, just to keep from being in sync with her. If that had happened, I'd never have heard the end of it.

The day after the ambush, I get up and still feel like shit, but at least I know there won't be another surprise party anytime soon. I spend my life in fear of unexpected parties, but now I have a reprieve. *I might get to watch my shows in peace*, I think, like I'm a hundred.

I don't miss coming home to someone that first night either. I thought I might, but I don't. I'm completely prepared for it to hit me as soon as I walk in the door—the memory of our life smashing me in the teeth, before I could arm myself—but nothing. It's too soon for ghosts, I thought, and if they do come, I'm ready. I don't have to pretend my day was anything but exhausting.

I'd thought we'd agreed that we weren't the kind of couple who kissed each other on the cheek after work and said, *How was your day?*, but I was wrong. Suddenly I realized that he'd been having some sort of quiet breakdown, which is the worst kind. One he didn't tell anyone about. One that meant he was someone different now, only he didn't think he had to tell anyone. One he thought we'd all just go along with. Or me, mostly. *I need more from you now, Janet*, he was saying, without saying it. *I need you to be someone else now, Janet, because I'm someone else now too.* It wasn't fair, his suddenly wanting me to be happy. He knew what he was getting into with me. And let me add that he was never particularly happy either. He just thought his girlfriend should be.

I still don't miss coming home to someone.

One thing I like about working at the shelter is that it never *requires* me to be happy. I don't like being told how to feel. It's the exact opposite of working at the Disney Store. My friend Emma had a job interview there once, and she didn't even get through the first round because she wasn't cheerful enough—and Emma is the most cheerful person I know, probably from the Prozac, but also from knowing her whole life that one day she was going to get the hell out of here. Maybe not to Ibiza, where she ended up; she probably thought she'd run off to Beverly Hills, stalk Luke Perry a bit, then marry some tech nobody. However it played out, she knew she wouldn't be here having to pretend she gave a shit.

Emma never gave a shit, still doesn't, and that's why she's one of my favorite people. She and Debs would get along great, which is why they must never meet, or I'll feel shittier than I already do.

On my way home from work, I get passed on the stairs by a guy in a Christmas sweater. Happy holidays, he tells me, like he thinks he's hilarious and wacky, though really he's triggering to me. Everything is triggering to people like me.

I was looking forward to going home and watching all the TV and maybe masturbating myself to sleep before I had to get up in the morning and do it all again. Not so bad, I guess, as groundhog days go. But no, somebody's having a Christmas in July party. So now my night is corrupted by the faint hum of Christmas music, broken by the occasional *ho ho ho*, and it takes all my strength to stop myself from going up there to ruin their vibe by telling them all about my PTSD.

So I lie awake in bed, listening to those caroling fucks, and I feel like a small child. When I was little I used to lie awake listening to the grown-ups living their exciting nighttime lives, clutching my flea-bitten stuffed animal and thinking, *One day that will be me.* Now that I'm grown up, it turns out that all I want to be is back in my bed with my stuffed animal.

The Christmas in July people are doing a good job of talking me out of their cult, and I love a good cult.

I put a pillow over my head and it helps a little, mostly because the suffocation almost kills me. It's too hot—under the pillow, under the roof of my apartment, under the sun. I would open the window wider, but then I'd have to hear more people.

People assume I must love summer because I work outdoors. Everything is better in the summer, Melissa once said, and I said, Tell it to the polar bears. People act like the sun can save them, when it's killing us, really. People are idiots. I have a T-shirt that says that, but Debs won't let me wear it. It's okay: my arms haven't seen the sunlight for years.

People's brains change in the summer. They go from gray gloop to neon pink, dumb and throbbing like a giant penis. I don't know what I hate more: the sight of all that flesh or all the bad fashion choices. Shorts. Flip-flops. The number of people who think it's safe to come to the shelter in flip-flops astounds me. I'm not even safe in my boots. They all deserve to get their toes bitten off.

People try so hard to get me to like summer. A goth who hates summer, how original, my brother used to say as he headed out to meet his buds at the park, to drink beer and throw something at one another. I'm not a goth, you moron, I'd say, despite the fact that I was sitting indoors in a long-sleeved black sweater, reading, on a ninety-degree day. My mother never said, Don't call your brother a moron, because she knew he was one. She never said, Don't call your sister a goth, because she knew that if she ever dared to comment about my appearance she'd get a lecture on how you shouldn't comment on anyone else's body and she'd deserve it. And the fact that I kept myself wrapped up in sweaters protected her from having to see my boobs, which meant I probably wasn't showing them to boys either, which must have been a relief to her. (She was wrong.)

The heat makes me mad, but there are things I don't mind about summer. I like ice cream, obviously, and nature isn't so bad. Fresh air is pretty rad. I work outdoors, so I don't want it too cold. I don't even mind picnics. I have been to a park, despite what people think. Okay, so it was when I was a teenager, and I went there to drink and get groped by boys, but also when I went back as an adult, having forgotten how annoying park people are.

What I don't enjoy is feeling like I'm going to die. Which is how excessive heat makes me feel. Even when it's not summer, I spend my life avoiding situations where I might get hot and sweaty and uncomfortable. What I really like is breathing—taking in cool, crisp air. So why would I celebrate the season of crippling humidity, here to crush my lungs and brain?

So now it's July, and people are already acting like such dicks.

The sun really does make people stupider. Slow your roll, I want to say, you've got months.

I lie in bed wondering who on earth wants to be thinking about Christmas this early. There's the evil salespeople, of course. They've been planning their attack since the day after last Christmas. And this lady I used to work with, who started planning her holiday party five months ahead of time. This same woman did all her Christmas shopping in the summer sales. She was so smug about it, we all wanted to murder her. Mostly to steal her gifts.

Then there was the old lady in our neighborhood who was always making jams and baking cakes in the summer, but for Christmas. My mother said she froze them, ready to send to the troops. I think she was the only person who hopes we'll always be at war with someone.

I don't want to lie here thinking about some old lady who's probably dead now. But I keep going, boring myself to death with my own thoughts, until finally I'm overtaken by sleep. Death's cousin.

For a while there, I think my mum thought my entire aim in life was to ruin Christmas. Like once I was done at their house, I'd start visiting other houses, like I had a list or something. Which made me the exact opposite of Santa—he bringeth joy, and I taketh it away. No one else I knew could afford a house, so the laugh was on her, I guess.

One Christmas, my uncle asked what was up with me these

days. He just meant what was I studying or watching on TV, but I asked him if he knew about FGM. He did not, so I told him. That's enough now, Janet, my mother said, and my uncle said, It's okay, I read somewhere that women need to speak now.

The first Christmas I was at university, I decided to get extremely drunk, even though I had to be at my parents' house that evening for some lame party. I had somehow survived my first semester at college, and I wanted to cut loose, Janet style—that is, alone with a six-pack of beer. I was trying to be a good daughter, so I planned to be there for the party, but turns out I'm a bad daughter, and the responsibility was too much. I drank enough to make sure I fell asleep on the bus home and ended up not where I live. And I forgot to charge my phone, so no one could call me. My mother called the police, convinced I was dead. I was not. I was just wondering where the fuck I was and why no one woke me up. Of all the times to not get hit on during a bus trip. My father had to come get me—he was glad for the escape, really—but it didn't matter because I'd already ruined Christmas.

That year was all the proof I needed that I wasn't a responsible adult and maybe never would be.

The first time my brother brought his new wife home for Christmas, he asked me if I was medicated yet. I said, You might have a wife now, but your sneakers are still shit. He cared about stuff like that, so it hurt. My mother said, Don't listen to your sister, your sneakers are very nice, dear. His wife just stood there like, *What the fuck sort of family is this?*

Then there was the Christmas my brother's kid couldn't shit. It was traumatic for all of us. My brother and my mother seemed to think it was a medical emergency, and the kid was pretty upset about it himself, but his mother was actually pretty calm. She knew that stress only makes the body hang on to its shit harder. My mother kept saying, It'll scar him for life, being constipated at Christmas. I kept saying, It comes when it comes, which is my motto for everything: shitting, sex, your period, all of life, really. The only thing it doesn't work for is Christmas, because that comes whether you want it to or not, like most men. Finally, just as we were about to eat dessert, the kid takes a massive dump— right there at the table—and then he's so happy he starts stripping off his clothes and running around, like little kids do. It's maybe my favorite holiday memory.

My father had a different reaction. As a plumber, he was used to other people's shit, but on weekends and holidays he really wanted no shit at all. I think that was the year he realized he was going to have to start taking something if this was going to be his life from now on.

When I still lived at home, I remember saying to my mum, Can it not be such a big deal this year? Christmas? And she looked at me like she so often did, like I was shit on her shoe, and said, I work all year for this, Janet. One day you'll understand.

A few years later I had the same conversation with my boy-friend. But it is a big deal, Janet, he said. Get over it. Then he started in with a full-bore lecture on why Christmas was so im-portant, now more than ever, because of how awful the world was. It united people, he said. Didn't I want people to be united? You know, after all the unease? I remember laughing so hard at the word *unease*. Like he could still see that the world was on fire, but he'd decided it was all just a little discomfort, nothing we couldn't manage.

He was on to something, of course. No one wanted to riot at Christmas. The last few years had been hard on everyone. No country was left unscathed by corrupt governments. People didn't even know what they were fighting for anymore, just that they needed to keep fighting until somehow their side won. Christmas seemed like the only thing everyone could agree on. Everyone loved buying shit and eating shit and watching shit, and there was a big fat white man in a red suit and we would forget that one of them had been on the news, arrested for doing inappropriate stuff to the elf-women who worked for him.

Christmas was the only thing we hadn't torn down.

Why would I want to ruin Christmas? I asked my mother one year. I love Christmas.

We always hurt the ones we love, Janet, she said.

5

One morning, a month or so after the ambush, I pull up to work and sit in my car for a few minutes. It's the kind of moment when other girls might put on their makeup or text boys or whatever. I just sit and look at the shelter.

The sign says *Joe's Shelter* in peeling brown letters; there is no cartoon dog, nothing saying *Welcome* or *Hi!*, just the facts. This is us. We're open to the public for two hours in the afternoons on weekdays and all day on Saturdays. That's enough interaction for any of us, let alone the dogs, who obviously want a home but don't want to be manhandled or examined with false hope too often. I feel sorry for the fruit when I do that at the grocers.

People always ask us who Joe is, and we don't know. Are you Joe? they ask, and we say no. Was Joe a dog? they ask, and we just shrug. Melissa thinks we should make up a story, tell them what they want to hear. She can do what she wants, we say, but we'll just continue to shrug.

For a while Melissa kept on about how Debs should change it to Debs' Shelter, which sounded like a lot of work. I finally got fed up and said, Why doesn't Debs just change her name to Joe? That really made Debs laugh, and she never laughs.

Joe's is a dog shelter, but really it's a shelter for women.

When I got the job, my mum thought it was a phase, like a gap year. Years later she's still hoping it's a phase, because according to her I'm too smart to be wasting my talents. I don't know what talents she thinks I have. In her head I'm so different it scares me; I can't even allow myself to think about it. The version of me that I know is trouble enough.

My dad thought I'd never be able to hack it. Working outdoors in all kinds of weather, dressing in shapeless uniforms, going days with almost no human contact. All of which were selling points to me. He thought within weeks I'd crawl back to the world, throw myself at any job that was in a building with a roof and let me wear clothes that didn't have dog shit on them. Don't disappear, he told me as he saw me off. I didn't know if he meant because my coat was so big, or my body was so small, or that he'd read about someone getting eaten by a dog at a shelter like Joe's, but he seemed to sense that this was my way of removing myself from the world, and he wasn't wrong.

My mother gave me a half-hug that day, mostly because my giant coat was too big for a full one, but I know she wanted to cup my face in her hands and mourn for me, her baby, the one she'd lost a long time ago.

When I graduated, no one said, What kind of job are you going to get with a degree in postmodern feminist science fiction, Janet? But everyone was thinking it. Even my professors, who were writing their books, planning their escapes, trying to regain control of their lives that had been spiraling downward the moment they started teaching.

I didn't go to my graduation. I don't like organized activities. Or having to wear a cape that isn't for being a witch.

My parents were just glad I hadn't dropped out. They sent me flowers, but I couldn't stand the responsibility of keeping them alive, so I gave them to my new neighbors. I'd done that before. I'd once made the mistake of telling another neighbor *hiya*, in a bit too friendly a way, and I was so embarrassed that I proceeded to avoid eye contact with her for the rest of our short life together. When I told my boyfriend, he laughed and told me I'd done the same thing to him when we met.

At college I'd wanted to live on my own, in a cave, but there were no caves available. I ended up sharing a house with three girls I failed to bond with, and now I have to lug that failure around with me, with all my others, for the rest of my life.

I had good intentions. But sharing a house with girls taught me a valuable lesson: never share a house. I was the funny semi-goth who only came out of her room to eat and shit, and I did both loudly, so they knew I wasn't a ghost. She's a goth, but she doesn't dress like one, I heard one of them say outside my room. So she's a goth in her heart, the other person said. He was a boy. Boys always got it. For a moment I considered seducing him in the kitchen later that night, but it seemed like a lot of effort.

I did have one friend at school: Agnes. A Swedish girl who was always happy. She thought I was hilarious. Like it was an act. Like I was one of those girls who wants to be French, only I didn't smoke. I say friends, but Agnes and I didn't go shopping together or go on double dates or any of that. We just weren't awful to each other like other girls were. People thought she was weird because she was foreign, and people thought I was weird because I was sad but not pretty enough to be one of those pretty sad girls who sings about it or writes on the internet.

It was Agnes who suggested I see the campus doctor about feeling sad. She told me she'd seen a poster and it reminded her of this sadness of mine. I didn't really think it was a problem, but I went just to be nice. As soon as I saw the doctor was a dude, I knew I should have left immediately, but then I thought of Agnes and how she'd seen that poster and thought of me, poor sad Janet. So I told him how sad life is, and he said he was sad I felt that way and did I have a boyfriend? I told him I had several. He gave me a prescription for Citalopram, but I threw it in the bin. He told me I should talk to someone, and I said I'm talking to you, and he said, Not me, but he meant, Please, not me, my wife is sad all the time and I don't know what to tell her either, so just be a good girl and take the pills. He said counseling would be essential, too, but they were overstretched, it could take a year before I'd get any. I said that suited me fine.

When I got back to the room, Agnes asked how it went. It turns out I'm the right amount of sad, I said, and she said she was sorry for doubting me.

I made the mistake of telling my mother, and she said, Oh, I love Citalopram, but it gave me terrible gas. Then she said I better not depress Agnes and did she know ABBA? I said, They were her parents, all of them, and my mother just made the noise she makes like, *You're so weird, Janet, and you definitely didn't get it from me.*

Then one of the girls in my house, Diane, started Citalopram and she hadn't even seemed that sad. I mean, I'd only seen her from a distance, standing in the kitchen at two A.M. in her underwear making Hot Pockets, coming out of the bathroom in a face mask, stuff girls do. We once had a moment on the stairs when she told me she liked my coat. (I was basically just a coat, even then.) Another time, when she thought everyone else was out, she had sex with her boyfriend in the living room. She didn't seem sad.

I only knew she'd started taking Citalopram because I heard the other girls talking about it outside my room. I didn't want to take them myself, but I was curious about what would happen if someone else did—say, a girl my age living in my house.

What happened was they made Diane paranoid and agitated. She was convinced she was going to be kicked out of school and that we all hated her—even me; I barely knew her—and that her boyfriend, the one I'd seen too much of, was cheating on her. I remember thinking, *Man, did I dodge a bullet.* I mean, I've felt all those things at one point or another, but I didn't have to take a pill to feel them.

If I hadn't started self-medicating with food and alcohol years ago, I would have never gotten through college.

Diane went back to the doctor, but he just doubled her dose and told her to keep going. By Christmas, Diane was a total wackadoo. The girls in the house all got super worried about her. They thought she might try to stab them in the night. Aren't you worried she might stab you in the night, Janet? they said. She can try, I said, which didn't help. I wanted to say, Maybe she should come off the drugs? But I wasn't her doctor. I was just weird Janet, the goth who wasn't a goth. I wasn't enjoying it, watching Diane unravel, but it was confirming what I'd always felt—that prescription drugs are bad.

Because our once happy home was now seconds away from being a horror movie, and they'd always considered me the most likely to murder them all, the other girls welcomed me into their fold. I was the only one who wore Doc Martens, after all, and if Diane needed kicking to death, I'd be the one to do it.

So for a very brief window I was one of the girls, and girls tell each other everything, so I got a front-row seat to Diane's unraveling. I didn't tell the girls anything, but they kept on telling me shit all the time, like they thought, *Oh, Janet is so sad and weird, we can tell her anything and she won't judge us.*

The doctor suggested that Diane add another drug, Mirtazapine, to calm her down. And it did—so much that it took her an hour to crawl out of bed and another hour to crawl to class and she gained a stone and a half in a month and then her boyfriend did leave her and she was about to get kicked out of school.

Finally she got so ill that her parents came and took her home. They asked us all what she was on, and when we told them, they said, Well, it can't be that, she had a prescription, but it was that. I'd like to tell you that the doctor had his license taken away, but he's probably still there telling girls about the rhythm method.

It was archaic, how they treated mental health. Antidepressants, anti-anxiety meds, antipsychotics—none of it had changed since the 1950s, and then, suddenly, *boom.*

It was when celebrities started coming out as sad that the world really took notice. People loved it. *It's okay to feel sad*, these familiar faces said. *I'm just like you, ignore the mansion.* I never understood why no one said, Fuck off, I don't need your permission to feel my feelings. I didn't need your permission to accept my stretch marks, and I don't need it for this either.

It all made me so angry. *I was sad before it was cool*, I wanted to yell. But I wasn't online, so I couldn't.

My second year of college, I met my boyfriend and moved in with him. I'd done the living-with-girls thing, and it had been super fun, but now I wanted to see if I'd be more suited to living in sin.

I quickly learned that living with a boy is not that great. Once that weird spell that makes you want sex all the time wears off, and you have to think about what you're having for dinner for the next million nights, it loses its charm. I thought it was what you're supposed to do, because it *is* what you're supposed to do. The world is full of people doing things they think they're supposed to do, and no one questions it. But I'd made my bed (not literally, I made him do it), and I had to lie in it. Awake mostly. To distract myself from the fact that I was somehow already living in a loveless marriage without being married, I studied really hard. I studied the shit out of weird pointless subjects that would guarantee I would never find a job.

What do you mean I can't get a job? I'm an expert on nineteenth-century homoerotic gothic literature.

I did try working in an office, after graduating, but it did not go well for any of us. I lasted two months, which was two months too long for all of us. I was hired to bring the tea, but instead I brought the doom. If I'd been medicated it might have gone better, which was why I wasn't medicated. I wanted it to go wrong. I wanted the world to know I couldn't do what they did. I did try, and I should get credit for that. Two months is not nothing. But I stopped, so give me credit for that too.

After all that, I wanted a job that would wreck my body the same way the world was already wrecking my mind. I wanted to not think for a while.

When I saw the ad for the shelter job, I didn't even have to interview. I just showed up and Debs showed me around and said, Still want the job?, and I said, Hell yeah, and that was it. It was a shithole, miles out of town, and I'd have to get up stupid early for essentially no pay, but in exchange I'd get to have my thoughts drowned out by a bunch of rowdy dogs and minimal humans. It was exactly what I needed.

I didn't tell the boyfriend this was my plan because he might have asked if my plan still included him, and I wasn't sure I knew the answer.

Today is trash day at the shelter. Exciting! We keep our trash right by the entrance, which I think says it all. Drive by at the right time, and you might see me jumping on it all to flatten the garbage down, so we can cram even more into the bin. It's one of the things I look forward to all week. Melissa said, Maybe we should move it somewhere people can't see it, and we said, But they'll still smell it and we'd have to haul it back out there every week, so we kept it where it was. We wanted the world to see us for what we were.

Melissa pulls up next to me, and I can hear her radio, and it's that boy band again. You don't know you're beautiful, she's singing, and I feel sad for her. Debs doesn't insist that we smile on the job, but Melissa does anyway, no matter how she's feeling inside, and we can't tell her not to because that would make us monsters. Which we are, but mostly when we're alone. All we have to do is to not mind picking up dog shit and maybe getting bitten and sometimes dealing with annoying people, and in exchange we get to be around dogs, who are soft and warm and mostly not assholes.

Melissa started a few weeks after me, so I'm her senior—in my mind, anyway. I think her ex-husband was abusive, but we don't talk about it. She has a kid who looks like him, which sucks for everyone. I don't hate her.

When she sees me, she leaps out and says hi and asks how my weekend was. This is our relationship, nice and small-talky, no real emotional contact. I just want to come in, do my job or pretend to, and go home, where I can make myself feel better having ticked off *functioning enough to do a job* on my list of goals. Then I'm free to spend the evening doing the kinds of things a not-so-functioning person does, like lying on a coach facedown, turning my head now and then to see what's on TV, then turning back to face the cushion.

Melissa always asks about my weekend, and I never know what to tell her. I usually feel oddly defensive about it—people can be so fucking nosy, even sweet people, *especially* sweet people—so I say something like, Good, thanks, and if I'm bored, I'll ask how hers was, because people like to talk about themselves. I'm always waiting for her to say she thought she saw me at the supermarket but then I hid from her, and why would I do that? I have a recurring nightmare that Melissa sees me out in the world and drags me out for something like a coffee when all I wanted to do was buy the largest bag of potato chips I could find, and I have to stab us both with a plastic Starbucks fork.

But today I tell her everything. I tell her how my family and boyfriend threw an intervention and how it didn't go well and now I'm single with no intention to mingle. I happen to know that Melissa has the Christian Mingle app on her phone, which I can't believe is a thing. I know this because I look at her phone every time she leaves it in the break room. If she didn't want me looking at it, why would she leave it around unlocked?

Whoa, she says, her eyes bulging. I don't think she even knew I had a family or a boyfriend, even though we've worked together for years. She probably just assumed I was a spinster, given how I act around the shelter, shushing people and scowling like a grumpy librarian. I once shushed someone in a bookstore and my boyfriend walked off, pretending he didn't know me, though he barely had to pretend.

I didn't mention what the intervention was for. For the drinking? she said. I laughed so hard I peed a little, then pretended I had some important dog business to take care of and ran off.

I couldn't tell her the real answer—that they felt they had to intervene because I wasn't showing any signs I was going to get with the program and get medicated anytime soon. So now I have no boyfriend, no family, just this job, these women, and a bunch of dogs who don't know me from a table leg or a tree. It's enough to make you want to kill yourself, but we're a no-kill shelter.

We have dogs here that are older than Debs's kids, dogs who will probably die here, though not because of us. We do have to put dogs down sometimes, though only if they've attacked another dog, or us, more than a few times. Sometimes Debs gifts those dogs to the police, though, because she thinks the dogs are her kids, and if one shows a natural talent for something—even if that thing is attacking people—she feels it should be encouraged. And the police like Debs, because she's a not-unattractive woman who lives alone, if two kids and twenty-odd dogs is alone. Sometimes they bring us dogs, sometimes we give them dogs; it's the best relationship we have with any men.

I once heard Debs tell a police officer that dealing with dogs is like dealing with human beings: it's messy and people get hurt. I think he thought she was flirting, but I knew she didn't do that shit, as she called it. We try to minimize the hurt for everyone, she said. That's why she lives out here, away from people. They think we're here because of the barking, but really we'd be here anyway. We live in the shadows, I said once when I was a bit drunk and weepy, and Debs said, You don't know shit about shadows, and I went quiet. Debs has that effect on me. She calls me out on my bullshit, and I let her.

6

My every waking thought is about this Christmas pill. I feel like I've been seen and I wasn't ready. Like I've been waiting to be seen for years, and when they finally caught me, I was off taking a dump.

I need to get my thoughts on paper. Make some sense of it. Paper has never let me down. So, on my break, I make a pros and cons list. I'm not sure where to begin, so I start to draw a penis, but then stop myself. Then I start drawing a vagina, but that feels wrong, so I make it a flower, and then I get mad at the world for always making it about the penis. Then I start worrying that Debs's kids might barrel in and see what I'm drawing, and I start to sweat.

Pro: This pill is like a reward. I deserve a reward! Like you'd give a puppy. Only I don't need one every time I pee where I'm supposed to. Just once a year is fine. Then again, my life is already full of rewards. Sleep is my reward. Jerking off is my reward. Pissing people off is my reward. Just because you can't Instagram it doesn't mean it's not a reward.

Con: My days as a bad example would be over. I'd never again hear the words *Things could be worse! You could be Janet.*

I doodle another vagina flower.

Con: Medicating my feelings goes against everything I believe.

Pro: I don't believe anything, not really.

Con: My sadness is something I'll have forever. This is as much of a life as I deserve.

Pro and con: If I don't give in, my mother will never speak to me again.

Con: If I give in, Melissa will be excited. She still gets excited about things.

Con: I work at the most miserable place on earth. I have a right to my sad.

Con: I'll be like everyone else.

Pro: Don't worry, it won't last.

Pro: I won't have to make any more lists, so I can devote my break time to more important things, like eating a Twix.

A week later, my mum phones me up to tell me about this new pill she thinks I would like, like it is a new yogurt she just tried, because she's done that too. (Are you really calling me on the landline to tell me about a yogurt? I said, regretting answering, after it rang and rang till I was sure someone had died.)

I don't tell her that two other people have already told me

about this pill; she doesn't need to know that at least two other people also think I'm a pain in the ass. I don't tell them that my doctor called me in to tell me about it weeks ago.

And I certainly don't tell any of them what I already know: that I'm considering the idea that this pill—this temporary pill— really *was* made for me.

According to the pamphlet, after two weeks of taking the pill, you should start to feel like your edges are coming off a little. They're still there, but they're baby-proofed. When a Christmas commercial comes on the TV, you should no longer want to throw something at it, just calmly leave the room or switch the channel.

By week three you should feel like you can cope with the coming holiday drama. Like it might all be a dream anyway. (If you feel *too* dreamy, tell your doctor at once.)

By week four you should be ready to surrender to the season. You should have accepted its inevitability and be actively making plans.

Week five takes you into December, and it's supposed to be plain sailing from here on. Christmas is definitely happening now, and for once you're an active part of it. You're no longer fighting, you're shopping. You're one of those people who's just happy to be there—on earth, in the store, on the couch.

Secretly, I was looking forward to the surrender.

For years, with the boyfriend, I had to do the two-Christmases thing. It nearly killed me. His family wasn't as bad as some people's—my own, for example—but I couldn't do it, even the years when I did do it. I had to drink to get through it all, which wasn't fun because it meant making sure I was drunk enough not to care but not so drunk as to be rude to anyone or sick on anyone. It kind of spoiled the fun.

I was used to drinking as a way of getting through things—school, meetings, sex—so it wasn't that hard. It loosened me up, got me close to being as comfortable in the world as normal people probably always are. The hard part was pretending I wasn't drunk the whole time—that this was just my natural state. Which was hard when my boyfriend knew that wasn't how I was. But then he liked me drunk; sometimes I think he preferred me that way. I'm surprised he wasn't sneaking pills into my food. Full-on gaslighting me, to save me the trouble of gaslighting myself.

I have a problem trusting people, but my bigger problem is letting people who aren't trustworthy into my life. It's safer to assume everyone's an ass and let them surprise you.

I was the one who led my boyfriend here. Led him astray. I was the one who took his hand and led him to the bedroom, who said, Stay! Forever, maybe! Let's make—well, not a family, quite, but *something*. And we tried. People think I don't try, but I really do. This is me trying.

He's a boy, my mother said when she sensed we were having problems. You need a man, she said, not a boy.

I've had men, I wanted to say. *This is better. Safer.* (I didn't say that, of course; it would have been telling her too much.) But she was right: it wasn't his fault; he was just a boy. How we thought we could do it, I'll never know. I don't know how *adults* do it.

Sometimes I want to tell him I'm sorry for wasting his time. Other times I want him to say he's sorry, for wasting my time. It's okay, I'd say. I would have wasted them anyway.

7

I'm taking my break. Debs doesn't give a shit if we have breaks or not, but there are laws apparently, and she tries to follow some of them to make her feel better about the ones she ignores. So here I am, eating a Twix, reading *Valley of the Dolls*.

The staff room's up behind the office, away from the rabble of the kennels, but you can still hear them all down there, demanding I remember they don't have a home. Sometimes I wear my ear defenders when I'm on break—the only time I don't have to— just so I can read a few pages in peace.

It doesn't always work, though. Such as now.

Melissa pops her head in. Ooh! Is it a horror? she says, eyeing my book.

Yes, I say, because it is. Then she starts telling me about some movie about a doll that murders everyone. I'm Team Doll, I tell her, and she laughs.

No one leaves anyone alone anymore. It's like everyone read the same think piece about the epidemic of loneliness and started bugging everyone all the time—and not just taking their elderly neighbor a casserole either. Is anyone even making casseroles anymore? Does anyone even know what a casserole is?

I'm not supposed to wear my ear defenders if I'm near the office, in case the phone rings. I never answer the phone anyway—at work, at home, anywhere. If a pay phone rang in the street I might, because it would be the most exciting thing that's ever happened to me. At work, it's sure to be someone asking if we have space for another dog. We don't, but Debs won't turn a dog away. She keeps saying we need more kennels, but really we need fewer dogs, which means that what we really need is for humans to be less shitty. No one ever calls to say, Hi, we got a dog from you a while ago and he's amazing, or, Hi, my mum died and left you all her money. Sure, people donate food and treats, mostly at Christmas. They bring us shitty blankets and old dog coats and toys from their dead dogs, and we take them and thank them and then have to boil-wash them to get the sadness out so our own dogs can use them for their own sadness. It's nice, but it's not enough. It just reminds me of the struggle it takes to get us all to Christmas.

I have my cell phone on vibrate. It's a problem. Not for me but for people who're trying to contact me. People need to contact you, Janet, the boyfriend used to say. What people? I'd say.

Oh, sure, in the beginning we would text. I may even have sent him a dumb heart emoji. I most definitely never sexted him, though, or sent him a picture of my boobs or worse. The closest we ever got to having phone sex was when he was away for work and asked me what I was reading.

I do use my phone—I'm not from the Dark Ages. I text, mostly, and I watch videos of Keyboard Cat, the only cat I like, and wonder what he thinks of us all now. I just don't use my phone to call people, in the hope that people will return the favor by not calling me.

Melissa loves answering the phone. Even if it's the school phoning to tell her that her kid is sick or bit someone again, she answers it theatrically, like it might be the queen calling. She would happily sit by the phone for an entire day if there's half a chance someone might call. Her phone has a fluffy case, but it's not pink, so I forgive her. Mine is black, with a lot of scratches and dents, like my heart.

So I'm on my break, and I'm trying to eat my Twix without touching it because I'm afraid I might still have dog shit under my nails from days ago, and Debs pops her head round the door.

Sarah's in the bins again, she says.

For fuck's sake, I say, cramming the rest of the Twix in my mouth and nearly choking, which is an unwanted reminder that I'm not good at blow jobs. I hate that I'm thinking about blow jobs or that they're even a thing. Sarah is in the bins.

Sarah's this overweight black lab with food issues and anger issues, like a lot of us. I quite like her. She waddles around with her big butt, snarling at everyone, like, What you looking at? Sarah has an annoying habit of getting out of her kennel and breaking into the food store, where she then eats everything in sight and keeps eating till she vomits, then just carries on. If you try to approach her, she'll bite your face off, and I get it. We don't have tranquilizer darts, obviously, so we have to use this stick with a hoop on the end to drag her off. Debs had to build her a special kennel that's like Fort Knox, but Sarah still manages to get out. I'm never not impressed.

Melissa was bulimic in college, so she can't deal with Sarah. I think she should be made to, like a weird form of aversion therapy, but Debs thinks I'm just being mean. I'm not, I just don't want to deal with it either.

Debs is mostly pissed because we don't have food to waste like that.

You'd think dogs like Sarah would be lost causes, but sometimes they turn into different dogs altogether once they actually find a home. Turns out dogs hate being locked up—who knew? We all should have understood that, being prisoners in hells of our own making, me and Debs anyway. Melissa somehow still believes she's free, though we constantly remind her otherwise.

My first year at the shelter, I realized that making Christmas for a bunch of dogs is the most depressing pastime humankind has ever developed. That's nice, my mum said when I told her, which says it all.

They think it's cheery, Melissa and the volunteers, because they'd rather be with us for the holidays than with their own families. Even though all the tinsel they string up will inevitably get ripped down and eaten, giving the dogs worse shits than normal. Happy fucking Christmas, Janet.

After the whole Christmas-for-dogs charade is over and the volunteers have all gone home feeling better about themselves, we still have our regular jobs to do. The extra-broken dogs still need their meds and their shit cleaned up, and we have to double-check that no inmates are trying to dig their way out. Some nights I dream about sneaking into the sanctuary after dark and letting them all out. We all want to escape sometimes.

Sometimes when it's quiet and there's no one around I crawl into the kennels and get into one of the tiny dog beds. I curl right up and pretend I'm a dog. Sometimes I let the dogs curl up with me. (Only if they want to—I'm not forcing anyone to do anything they don't want to do.) I squash right in there and the dog gets in there with me and we curl up like this is what our bodies were made to do. Only that dog will know what I need in that moment. I'm supposed to be the caretaker, but the dog knows I'm barely taking care of myself.

Melissa almost rumbled me once. She was looking for me, and I poked my head out of the kennel and nearly gave her a heart attack. I never explained what I was doing in there, and she never asked. Maybe she does it too. I don't know what people do. I don't think she told Debs. It's not like she caught me sleeping or anything. I was just snuggling—but then isn't that way worse? If word got out I was a secret snuggler, I'd never live it down. I spent the next few days after she caught me being a little meaner than normal, in case Melissa thought I was anything other than a pain in the ass.

Sarah is in the food bins, like Debs said. What she left out is that Sarah has already vomited and now she's eating her own vomit. When I approach, she doesn't even snarl at me as usual. She just looks at me like, *We've all got issues, Janet, this is mine.* I manage to get past her and then use my body to slide her out of the storeroom so I can lock it. Once she's away from the food, there's no problem, and she lies down and looks at me like, *What?* I let her rest for a few minutes before dragging her back to her kennel.

Thanks for the memories, I say, locking her in. She looks at me like, *Likewise.*

Some days at the shelter feel like the dogs are trying to teach me something, but I'm done with people trying to teach me things, even dogs. I just want it all to be over.

Not my life as such, but this version of it.

I'm ready to feel different.

8

It was the pill for shyness that cemented my feeling that pills were garbage, that we were one step away from a pill that would make you straight, when all most of us wanted was to be allowed to be crooked, broken, flawed.

That shyness pill broke me. Enraged me.

It might be great, the boyfriend had said, like he too saw my shyness as a disease, something that needed curing. Like he was only with me because he hoped one day they'd find a cure, some proof that I wasn't really ugly, just shy and sad.

We loved the Smiths, and I remember how, when their song about shyness being nice came on, I was blinded by what I thought was love. I didn't even hear the part about how it can stop you. I didn't care if it stopped me, now that I had this boy in my arms. Because I was stupid.

He probably remembers it differently. That's the problem with love, or what you think is love. If I loved myself more, maybe things would be different.

What if someone can't get out of bed because they're so shy? he said.

What if it's not because they're shy? I said. What if they've just seen how pointless life is and can't be bothered anymore?

I can't talk to you when you're like this, Janet, he said, still talking.

He meant when I'm Bad Janet. The Janet who swears at other people's children. The Janet who won't answer the phone in case it's anyone's mother. The Janet who chooses to work in the woods with dogs rather than have more conversations about what's wrong with her and how it needs fixing.

I never used to say, *There's a pill for that*, when he couldn't get it up.

Debs is the only one who leaves me alone, so naturally I sniff around her all the time, wanting her to notice me.

Everyone is taking all the pills, Janet, they tell me, like that's ever worked on me. I'm still wearing clothes from five years ago. If they really want me to take the pills, they should just say, *No one's taking them. It's all super nerdy.* Or, *It's French.* Or, *It'll kill you.*

Debs is always saying she'd be dead in a ditch if she didn't have her pills, and I believe her.

She has her kids to keep alive now, as well as herself, and that's not easy. I get it. Before she was a mom, maybe she could have afforded to be selfish, to see what would happen if she stopped taking them. Now she knows she has to take them forever. She has to think of the children. So she dutifully takes them every day. I'm sure she assumes that one day I'll join her, if I'm ever stupid enough to get knocked up, and we'll sit out on the porch in the evening, not talking about all the things we'd hoped to do with our lives.

I lie awake most nights now thinking about everything that has ever happened to me. I can't switch it off—switch *me* off—but I want to.

I've always been like this. It doesn't matter if I'm alone in bed or not. Stuff that happened today at work, last week, last year, five years ago, it's all just there at the front of my brain when it's supposed to be shelved away, like I've stored it all wrong, like my brain is one of those closets you never want to open because everything will fall out and crush you. My brain is all abandoned board games and broken lamps. Unworn sweaters you were too lazy to return. I worry that if I live long enough, the stuff will be too much and I'll be glad when I start forgetting.

If I lie awake long enough, my mind always goes back to the boy I used to share this bed with, this life with. Some of those broken lamps were his fault.

A young couple comes in to Joe's looking for a dog. I swerve them and hide in the food store. I know just by watching them that they're newly in love, that no crud has formed there, not yet. It reminds me of the day I met my boyfriend.

He had worked in a Tex-Mex restaurant. I asked him to explain it to me, this "Tex-Mex," and he couldn't. It was my version of flirting. He should have known then I was a tricky one.

He rode a bicycle, which I thought was hilarious. Not the bicycle itself, but the fact that he rode one. Like he was from the old days. Or Cambridge.

I had him cycle over to see me after his shift finished at one in the morning. He'd appear on my doorstep, exhausted and dirty, and I'd search his pockets for tips and those tiny umbrellas they put in the drinks at his restaurant. I was obsessed with those tiny umbrellas. To me they represented a sort of pocket-sized joy, where the regular-sized ones represented despair. I was happyish then, as you are at the beginning of relationships, before the crud starts forming—literal crud, because you can't be bothered to clean, just to have sex, but also the crud that forms on your heart from having to defend it all the time.

Agnes and I would show up at his restaurant and order drinks and see if we could get him fired. We wanted him to be free like us—because that's what we thought we were—but already I wasn't free anymore, because of him. That's what love is, even the best versions of it: a weight you carry. Sometimes you want to be weighed down, sometimes not, but you rarely get to choose. I always want to choose.

It was all part of our courtship. Me showing up at his job and being a pain. Him showing up at mine and me being a pain. He didn't know it, but I had chosen him. One day I'd just decided I was bored of myself, dangerously so, and that being part of something bigger might solve that, might fill the hole inside me. Life is all about how you fill the holes. I am all hole, most of the time, a cave of a person.

The boyfriend was in school, but his parents insisted that he work too, because they knew eventually he'd give up one of the two. I was the best thing that ever happened to him, they told me—and told him, over and over again, so he'd know not to fuck this up too. This made me sad, because I knew me, and I was the worst thing that ever happened to me. We clung to each other, probably longer than we should have, because we knew what came next wouldn't be better, only different. I didn't know how to say *Fuck me but don't fuck me up*; it seemed like a paradox.

Everything seems awful and scary when you're young, and then one day you realize that it actually is, so you push through— and sometimes you're pulling someone else along with you. And it can get desperate and messy, especially when you mistake it for love. I'd wanted to be part of something else, and for a while I was. I could tick *relationship with a semi-functioning human boy* off my list, and someday, I told myself, we could just part ways and move on, forget about how it ended or most of what came before. Keep things positive, keep it moving.

And now it's just me again, lying awake.

Later that afternoon, Debs's brother comes to paint the kennels.

I didn't know you had a brother, I say. Yep, she says.

He paints with one hand and smokes with the other, and I can't say I'm not impressed, because I totally am. Like when you see someone standing in the rain outside a restaurant smoking a cigarette. It's a statement, more than an addiction. It says, *Fuck all of you.*

Debs leaves him to it. This is her style of managing. I look over at Melissa and see her staring at him. I wonder if she'll go over and say hi or ask if he wants a drink or try to braid his hair, but she seems to sense that he's someone she should stay away from. We're becoming more like dogs every day. Soon we'll start sniffing people.

Paint fumes and cigarette smoke—you're really spoiling us, I say to him as I walk past. He mistakes this for flirting, because men are stupid. All the other women ignore him, but I make a joke when I see him, so I must be interested.

The men who come to Joe's—the volunteers, those hoping to adopt, and now Debs's brother—have all heard about us. They know what people say, about these women who live out in the woods with dogs. I heard they're lesbians, they say, but really we can't be bothered with either sex. I heard they're witches, others say, and we might be if we ever got our shit together. All women are witches if they can be bothered, Debs has been known to say. The truth is, there are nicer shelters—plenty of them in the city, where the staff wear name tags and goofy smiles and bright-colored sweatshirts covered with paw prints. Shelters where the air smells of flowers and not dog shit, where the dogs are all in good moods because they don't have to live in the woods with us. I sometimes wonder if the people who do make it out to Joe's come because they want to look at us, not just the dogs. Women come too, and some of them look at us like the way they look at the dogs, like they're wondering, *What is wrong with you that you ended up here?* Though every now and then I think I can sense one of them wondering, *Have you got room for one more?*

Debs sees her brother looking at me and shuts it down immediately. Don't waste your time, she says, she's basically a eunuch. Which I appreciate.

When Debs's kids get home from school, she has them sit and do their homework in the break room so she can keep an eye on them. I like seeing Debs with her kids, because I can see her brain switch to mum mode—though it's only ever half-assed, as the dogs are her real babies. I know this for sure because once, when she was a little drunk, she told me that she had a recurring dream where she gave birth to puppies not humans, and she was cool with it.

When Debs does mum stuff, like school runs and grocery shopping and homework, she's just making it up as she goes— and the kids don't notice or care. They don't know yet it's not how other people live. They just think everyone grows up at a rundown dog shelter with a mum who's wondering how a man can leave a dog chained up outside for two days while he goes off drinking, instead of just trying to remember if she washed the school uniforms.

Watching her, I think, *I could do that if I wanted to, but I don't, not really.* People make such a big deal out of having a family, but when it comes down to it, you just do it. You make mistakes, sure, but you keep plugging away.

Debs asks her kid what he had for lunch. He just says something about gorillas. We all do our best.

As I'm leaving work, a van goes by bearing the logo of the local cat shelter. *Things are getting too quiet around here*, I think. *We need a bit of excitement.* So I flip the van off.

If any cat turd turns up on my doorstep, Debs says, you're taking it home.

Sometimes I like to think the lady who runs the cat shelter is Debs's nemesis, or her ex-lover, that they used to do it behind the sacks of kitty litter. I tell myself stories like this to make our little hovel more bearable, to hang on to the idea that even here, among the shit stains and fur balls, some form of love could grow.

The truth is a little more pedestrian. Debs had a husband once, and she still has the kids, the remnants of a more normal life. There must have been a wedding; someone must have bought them fancy glasses. All before my time, but the ghosts are still there. I wonder about her husband, and I'm sure soon Debs will be wondering what happened to my boyfriend. We never mention our missing men, like they're soldiers who went to war, only we hope they don't come back. If they do, they'll find us all remarried but to dogs.

You think I'm joking, but before I can escape for the day, Melissa has cornered us to show us some pictures on her phone of some dogs getting married. I'm sure Debs is about to grab her phone and throw it out onto the road just as a truck is passing, but instead she just says, People are idiots, and goes back to pretending to listen to her kids.

Melissa still has hope for us all, and sometimes that's enough.

9

My mother asks me to come over because she's done something stupid to her computer. She won't ask my dad, she says, because she did the same thing yesterday and doesn't want to look even stupider, and she knows I don't want her to bug him. Fine, I said, but I can't stay. Turns out it was all a ruse to get me to come to the house, so she could see me and kiss me and confirm that she does indeed have a daughter. I am not pleased.

When you leave home, you should insist that your parents move, or at least let you burn down your bedroom. When I come home, I can't stay far enough away from that room and that bed. That bed where once, when I was fooling around with a boy and he told me to get naked and then said, Do something sexy, and I cried, which I know now is the opposite of sexy. Never have sex in your childhood bedroom. It will fuck you up for life.

I'm so proud of you, my mother says, because she thinks that's what we all want to hear, that our parents are proud. When really what we want is to be *accepted*, to feel that their love isn't contingent on anything we've done. That just being us is enough.

Have you thought about the Christmas pill? she says.

I haven't made any commitments, I say.

But you will take them, won't you? I mean, *I* would, she says. This is no surprise. My mother takes so many pills she rattles.

She doesn't realize that I'm not above regressing to my best teenager self by doing the exact opposite of what she wants, just to piss her off. It's been my only consistent joy.

I mean, I love my meds, she says, but who wouldn't want a little extra at Christmas?

Ugh, I say, stop already.

What? she says. I'm just saying.

Well don't, I say, and she seems to get it and she kisses me and says she's proud of me again. She hasn't kissed me for at least ten years. Air-kissed, maybe, but not a proper kiss. *No pressure*, I think. What sort of world is it when parents are proud that their kids are considering getting medicated?

The fact that Christmas is such a big deal tells me that everyone knows life is shitty, and that every so often we really need it not to be—say, a few weeks at the end of every year. It's a necessary release, the world's yearly happy ending.

This is what used to happen at Christmas: The holiday season would start to seep into our collective consciousness in late November. By early December it would be in full swing, enough that even I felt like participating. People would ask me to do stuff and I would, because it was Christmas. Bake cookies? Check. Wrap gifts? Check. Laugh at carolers? Check. Only when I grew up did it all start to feel a little empty. For a while I told myself it was all fine, because it was like that for everyone. Only it wasn't.

So I stopped saying I'd do stuff. And after a while I stopped getting asked. And now, if I say I'll do something, they look at me real hard and say, Really? Are you sure? They don't actually expect me to show up, of course, and I usually don't, but I want to. I really want to. Sometimes I even sit outside in my car crying because I know that if I went in, I'd just ruin it for everyone. Then I drive home to spend the night binge-watching Christmas movies, grieving for all the holidays I'd fucked up and the fuckups still to come.

My Christmases as an adult have always been weird because I made them weird.

For instance, one Christmas Eve I went to dinner alone. The boyfriend had wanted to take me somewhere, but he would have made me shower and change and, you know, talk to him. I loved him, or I thought I did anyway, but I didn't want to talk to him, really. When the time came, I'd forgotten altogether what day it was. Once I realized it, I resolved to eat somewhere besides my car or my bed. I hated almost every restaurant, because of the people mostly, but I liked to eat, so I thought, *Fuck all of you, why shouldn't I be able to go to some gross chain restaurant and eat some nasty cheap food when I want to? It'll give me the shits, but it'll stop me thinking for a while.*

The restaurant I chose that night wasn't a fast-food joint, but it was packed, because it was Christmas Eve, and people were celebrating already. I had to beg them to let me in, even though I was clearly dining alone and possibly from another planet that didn't have Christmas. I stood there waiting by the entrance, my nose pressed up against the glass like some Dickensian orphan, hoping I was invisible in my dirty coat and boots. Isn't she that girl from that place? someone whispered, and I felt the most seen I've ever been.

We wouldn't usually do this, they said, but it's Christmas. They put me in the corner behind a plant, so I wouldn't bum out the other diners. *I should have gone to McDonald's*, I thought, but the thought of being surrounded by fry-throwing teenagers, unaware of the shitstorm that was life coming for them, was too much for even me on Christmas.

My clothes under the coat were vaguely smart for once—I didn't have anything else clean that late in the year—but as I sat down, I realized I still had on my disgusting fingerless gloves from work. I'd cut my hand the day before on one of the old rusty kennels, and the gloves hid my bandage. It was a perk of the job, the tetanus shots. Most of my waking hours then were spent trying not to bleed on things. The hostess, a girl young enough to be my daughter if I'd been a teen mom—which my mother wouldn't have minded—must have thought I was in a rush, and she offered to make my order takeout. *No*, I thought, *it's Christmas. I want to use cutlery.* Besides, the gloves only added to my pathetic spectacle: the girl with the bandaged paw, eating alone on Christmas Eve.

Sometimes a mountain of nachos and a beer or two is all it takes to stop feeling shitty. I didn't care if people stared or looked away; I had my book and enough melted cheese to make the world disappear.

Just as I was almost in a food coma, a waiter came over. I immediately assumed he was going to ask me to leave, or worse, try to take my plate before I was done, but instead he asked me what happened to my hand.

I told him my sorry tale, about how I worked at a decrepit dog shelter and the kennels were all falling apart and I'd caught my hand on something sharp. It was nothing, I said.

But you're safe now, he said, and the combination of his tenderness and the beer and the painkillers I'd necked in the car earlier made me go a bit woozy. I believed, in that moment, that if a crazed gunman burst in, or there was a sudden zombie apocalypse, this waiter would protect me.

Most of the time I go around a little numb, but sometimes I feel things pretty hard, and these flashes of feeling are why I don't want to be medicated.

Once, not long after Emma left for Ibiza, I was a little drunk and I decided to call her. Don't you remember when we used to feel everything? I said. I was grieving our youth. I remember, she said. It was exhausting. That was when I knew I'd lost her. She'd grown up without me, and it was devastating.

But that Christmas Eve, alone in that restaurant, a not-ugly waiter was not only talking to me, he wasn't repulsed by me. I felt like I might be human after all.

When I got home, the boyfriend was playing some computer game where you have to kill everyone. Have you eaten? he said, but not in an accusing way. I said no, because if we spent the night eating takeout, we wouldn't have to talk.

Happy Christmas, he said when it came, trying to clink egg rolls with me like they were glasses.

It's not Christmas yet, I said, and I thought he would try to argue, but he didn't. The two of us not fighting about whether it was Christmas was really quite magical.

Once I've fixed the computer for my mother, I start edging toward the door. Just as I've almost made it, she looks up and notices what I'm doing.

I expect you have to go, she says. Yes, I say. She doesn't get up or try to hug me, just looks at me and tilts her head like a bird, or an alien.

We did have some happy Christmases, you know, Janet. I think she's going to say, Before you children, but she doesn't. She just smiles, and I know a good closing shot when I see one.

When I reach the safety of my car, I close my eyes and just sit for a while. I know she won't be watching from the window; we've already given each other all we can for one day.

She's got me thinking about those happy Christmases.

One of the happiest I remember—besides the one when my nephew took a dump—wasn't a bullshit childhood memory where I got some kind of Sparkle Barbie or saw snow for the first time. I was fifteen, and I had a fake ID, so I went to this local dive bar where all the cool kids from school went. I liked this boy in the year above me who was popular. I already had needs. I was a little drunk, but I knew exactly what I was doing. I went there with the sole intention of seducing this boy. I had a teenage girl's idea of seduction, from what I'd seen in magazines and movies—

I knew I was supposed to look at him, then look away, lick my lips, mimic his body language, laugh at his jokes—but I really couldn't be fucked with all that, so I just wore something low-cut and grabbed him. I dragged him outside and kissed him. I think that's a crime now, but back then it was just what girls like me had to do if they ever wanted to kiss a boy.

Anyway, this boy had no idea who I was, but he went with it because it was Christmas and he was a little drunk too. The kissing was wet and rushed and disappointing, the way things with boys often are, but it was mine.

I stumbled home, but it felt like floating. When I got in, my folks could tell I was a little drunk, but it was Christmas and I was happy, so they let it slide. I gave them both a kiss and went up to my room and lay on my bed and I felt changed. I had gotten drunk, enough to feel invincible instead of my usual invisible, and I'd gone out and gotten what I wanted.

I felt happy that Christmas, in my bubble, for a little while anyway. I believed things could be different, that I finally had some power. Only now that I'm mad as hell do I wonder why my tiny, fleeting joys are always to do with boys. I don't even like them that much.

I wonder if a pill might stop me thinking with my vagina.

My family never visit me at work, and I appreciate it. Why would they? It's not like you can window shop for dogs, and if you were going to, you would go to one of the fancier shelters in the city, one that wouldn't hire me because of my depressing demeanor, not that I would want to work there. They're so bright and shiny. I feel sad for the dogs who don't feel like wagging their tails, and there's a lot of them. We don't ask our dogs to put on a show for the public. If they want to hide indoors and shake a little, that's fine by us.

I once mentioned to my mother that we always need volunteer dog walkers, and my mother said, Isn't that your job, Janet? Yes, but it's one of the nicer parts and I like to share, I said, but she was my mother, so she knew I was lying. I think she thought I was trying to trick her into coming, so I could video her getting pulled down the street by a giant Rottweiler and stick it on YouTube or something. I wasn't planning to, but it was tempting. She said she doesn't have the right shoes anyway. My brother once told me he was thinking about getting a dog, but then he got a cat, so he's dead to me. My father came once to bring me some mail. He said hello to every single dog, even the ones snarling at him. Call your mother, he said. Yes, boss, I told him, because everyone wants to be the boss of someone, even if it's just dogs.

10

People are always surprised at what a tight ship Debs runs. Everything is by the book. My theory is that she murdered her husband and doesn't want anyone snooping around. Maybe that's why she keeps that cop around too. More likely, though, that this is her one shot at not screwing something up. Her kids might have no chance, but these dogs will get saved thanks to her.

A volunteer called Maggie does our home checks, where we visit the dogs' potential new homes. The new owners seem really put out that we do these; they look at how run-down the shelter is and assume they're just doing us a favor by adopting the dogs, which they are. But we like the dogs more than we like them, and we don't want to fuck the dogs up even more by sending them to live with another shitty family when they already think most humans are the worst.

Debs always wishes she could do the home checks herself, because nowhere is good enough for her dogs—which is exactly why she can't do them. Even if we had a corgi and the Queen of England came in her carriage to see about it, Debs would have to go to the palace just to check it was up to her standards.

I won't do them, but for different reasons: I always want the families to adopt me too. I'm secretly jealous of all these dogs who are getting their second, or even third or fourth, chance at life. I'm so exhausted of taking care of myself that I'd happily curl up wherever anyone would have me. I'd be no trouble, really. I just want to be taken care of. When a home check needs doing, I pretend I have more important stuff to do, like clean a degenerate Yorkie's anal glands.

It's a problem. Me wanting people to adopt me when I pretend I don't even like people. I'm not even an orphan; my parents aren't that bad. (Don't tell them I said that.) It's just this feeling I have, that Good Janet might come out in a different setting, that Bad Janet is bad because nothing changes, least of all the feelings.

Which was why I finally gave in to this Christmas pill pressure. I mean, it was made for me. How many of us can say that? Soon, I'm sure, all our meds will be specially formulated just for us—or at least for our star signs, maybe—but for now it's just us, the Janets.

I don't tell anyone about my decision, and no one asks me, which I appreciate. I was sure my mother would be calling me every day to see if I'd come to my senses, but once I'd fixed her computer, I heard nothing for weeks.

The minute I decide this, I feel lighter. As if I might not even actually need the pills now. The decision itself is the change, a shift in my thinking. I am open now, instead of closed. I worry that Melissa will smell it on me and start planning fun activities we can do once I'm too drugged up to fight her off. I picture myself lying on her sofa, unable to move as she and her kid decorate me like a tree and force-feed me novelty cookies till I choke.

Sometimes Melissa is straddling me, forcing a Santa hat on me, saying, *Wear the hat, Janet,* in an increasingly menacing tone, and I am powerless to it all.

I *want* to be powerless to it all. I want to give myself over to Christmas. *Take me, Santa.* I hate how horny I can get about the wrong things. Let's hope these drugs kill your sex drive the way the regular ones do.

I have to tell my doctor the news. Part of me thinks it's all a prank—part of me thinks most things are a prank—but the rest of me suspects he'll get some obscene bonus or something. I make an appointment, feeling smug because for once I'm doing what everyone wants me to do. It's good news for him and capitalism and my mother, bad news for any scrap of self-worth and integrity I was clinging to.

When I walk into his office, I expect him to hug me. Balloons, maybe, a piñata filled with drugs, some sort of celebration. *Congratulations! Welcome to the world, baby girl!*

But there's nothing. As usual, everything is more fun in my head. People think it's all storm clouds and the Smiths up there, but really it's happy storm clouds and the jangly Smiths songs you can dance around to holding a branch.

He doesn't even remember why I'm there, has to look through his records. Oh yes, here you are, Janet, filed under *Beyond Help.* After all those years working on me! Trying to get me to take some pills, any pills. For his sake, for my mother's, for my poor

long-suffering boyfriend's, for the world's. He did everything but
hold me down and force me to take them. Now he just hands me
a prescription, which says:

1 tablet to be taken once a day for 8 weeks starting November 1.

½ tablet to be taken once a day for 1 week starting December 26.

Mandatory group meetings.

I find this last bit most disturbing of all.

What's this about group meetings? I ask, wondering if I can
still change my mind.

I am not a group person. Once I thought I'd join the Brownies,
until I realized it was a front for evil. I think I was hoping for a
coven, but all I got were more opportunities for other girls to
make me feel like shit. I had to be dragged there kicking and
screaming every week. It put me off of church halls for life. The
words *group* and *meeting* have been my trigger words ever since,
along with *five-year plan*.

But my doctor doesn't know any of this. Because he doesn't
actually know me, just that I have janky ovaries and a reoccur-
ring urinary tract infection. He wrongly assumes that I'm basically human, that I must like hanging out. Sure, in parks when I
was fourteen, but not in the last decade.

There's a song that goes *I'd like to hang out but who doesn't*.

I doesn't.

He sees the group-meeting panic in my eyes and dismisses it
with his hand. If he weren't a doctor I'd probably punch him. I'm
trying to start over, and punching a doctor is not a good start to
anything, except a movie, maybe.

It's nothing, he says. When you get your prescription, they'll tell you what to do.

Why can't you tell me? I say, but he ignores me.

The meetings are for your own good, he says, like he's sending me away for a rest cure.

Will you be giving me a pill for my birthday too? I say, only half-joking.

Would you be interested in that, Janet? he says, scribbling something on his pad. If he ends up patenting my birthday pill idea, I want full credit, or blood.

Maybe that's how it will be from now on. Maybe this is the world now and I never saw it coming. Maybe I'll get a pill to take before every occasion that requires a show of happiness: Christmas, birthdays, weekends, sexual encounters. Just to make sure I feel like I'm supposed to. Or to make sure I stop making other people feel bad.

My mother thinks I do it on purpose. A few years ago, I wore my dog-shelter clothes to her wedding anniversary dinner. I had no choice—I was coming straight from work—but she thinks I did it on purpose. I wasn't even going to go, but I had no food at home, and I thought it was better to show up as I was than not at all. I was wrong. On the way I even stopped and bought them a gift—a new pair of kitchen scissors; they'd been needing one—but apparently this was the wrong gift. Symbolism, I guess.

My mother tells me all the time that I'm never appropriately happy. As if there's a list of things in life we're supposed to be happy about, and I forgot to memorize it. Once I told her I didn't really think too hard about when it was okay to be happy, because most of the time I was sad. She didn't like that either.

It actually makes me a tiny bit happy how clichéd my relationship with my mother is. Makes it easier to navigate, like a textbook exercise.

When I was younger, I thought I might want to be happy when I grew up. It was something I might at least want to try, like making my own bread, or a home enema. I quickly came to realize, though, that it's the kind of thing I could never sustain in my regular life, like bangs or a gym membership.

I had a boyfriend once who never smiled, and I never minded. When I asked him about it, he said he tried it once, but it just felt weird and looked weirder and people wanted to punch him when he did. I said I could see how that could happen. So he just stopped. Even though everyone was doing it, and people did sometimes comment on how he should smile more or at least once, it just wasn't for him. I wonder now if I should have tried harder to make things work between us, but turns out sometimes you do need your boyfriend to smile at you now and again, just so you know your outfit isn't too awful or they like how you're touching them or that the food they're eating isn't poisoned.

It's a phenomenon anyway, not smiling. Most women have had some man tell them to *Smile, love*, as they walked by, or some bullshit like that, so maybe he was trying to change the gender stereotype. Or maybe he thought women actually still liked moody tough guys who were too cool for smiling. I have no idea. Boys are weird.

I'm not miserable, not really, any more than the people on all those happy pills are actually happy. We're all somewhere in the middle. But no one wants to talk about it.

The doctor takes off his glasses and rubs his eyes. Janet, he says, I think you're going to do great. That's not so bad, as last words go, so I take the prescription and leave, for once doing as I've been told.

The only thing I can't shake are these mandatory meetings. Like I didn't already have enough problems with Christmas being mandatory. Like that wasn't the *entire* problem.

On my way home, I start thinking of the long list of things I have to do that I don't want to. First I had to go to the doctor, which I avoid doing for obvious reasons, many of them involving having my boob squeezed longer and harder than appropriate. Next I have to go to the pharmacy, which I don't even mind that much; they have plenty of fun stuff there too, like tampons and lip balm and candy. And the people there tend to act shifty, so I relate.

And now I also have to go to *meetings*. Which is what really makes me anxious. I don't like meeting people I know, let alone new people.

That's three things I don't want to do, all in order to do something I don't want to do. It's like someone punching you in the vagina and telling you your jeans are all wrong.

I can already feel my legs turning to lead at the prospect of it all. It's almost worth stepping in front of a car—not to kill myself, you understand, just to cripple myself. But then someone would just wheel me around to all those places, and with my luck it'll be Melissa or my mother, not some hot nurse. So I'll just have to drag my leaden legs there myself.

I thought I wanted to be in control, but now I just want to let go of it all. To have someone else do the work. I feel defeated.

Happy fucking Christmas, Janet. Maybe someone will give me back myself as a gift.

11

We, the Janets, were the first ones they told about the pills. And once we'd signed our lives away, or at least the next few months, the rest of the world was apparently allowed in on it.

Facebook ads, TV and radio ads, bus wraps—all of it popped up overnight. All the usual tricks when they want you to want something. All I ever want is a nap.

Now, everyone's talking about it. Santa's Little Helper, they're calling it on the street. Some are saying it's just ketamine cut with candy canes. Others say it's magic mushrooms and baby aspirin. It looks like any other pill, only this one comes gift-wrapped— because it's a gift. Not for you, though, but for the world, because you'll be less of a miserable fuck, and that's the best gift you can give.

There are several online commercials, all subtly different. One with a girl, one with a guy, and one with someone ethnically confusing who I think is supposed to represent the LGBTQ community. There's one that I'm starting to think was made just for me. It shows a girl who looks exactly like me, but with better skin, shinier hair, more expensive jeans—jeans that fit, that is, instead of what I wear, which are not those newly ironic mom jeans, but the unintentional ones.

In the ad, this better version of me is sitting in her apartment watching TV, just like I am now, only her apartment is obviously much nicer than mine. For authenticity they have a pizza box open on the table, even though this girl only eats seven almonds a week. Her world is black and white, which seems intended as a signal for depression but actually makes her look like she's in a cool French movie, waiting for her cue to say something amazing through the haze of a cigarette (not pictured). She is definitely getting laid. And yet, somehow, we're meant to gather that this girl has, you know, *let herself go*. I'm sure there's a zit on her somewhere, but no one else can see it.

Do you want a happy Christmas, says a voiceover lady, but feel like you'll never have one? Are you currently resisting everyday antidepressants but still want a joyful holiday?

If I hadn't already signed up, I might have dropped my Hot Pocket.

Try it now, the voiceover lady says, and you'll have no long-term serious health problems—and no more aversion to fun, family, and festivities!

On the screen, Model Me is still looking chic but miserable on her couch. I am wondering about the pizza, which she has clearly never touched. What will become of it after the shoot? Will she throw it out? Will the crew get any? I am worried for it.

In clinical trials, the voiceover lady says, seven out of ten people with moderate to severe malaise saw seventy-five percent improvement in their ability to enjoy the holidays and return to their normal disposition with no significant side effects.

At the bottom of the screen, four words flash quickly: *your results may vary.* The pamphlet I was given has a lot of small print like that. It says *Be sure to speak to your doctor* a lot, like he's really lonely.

Now Model Me is getting up to answer the door. She doesn't even ask who it is, just opens the door, and there's a guy there holding a big gift in front of him, his midsection obscured by a big shiny bow. I start to wonder if I've accidentally switched to an adult channel.

The delivery guy doesn't say anything, just hands over the box. She doesn't have to sign for it, doesn't ask if he's even slightly a serial killer. She just takes the box and goes back to the couch, like an idiot. We watch her unwrap the gift, pull out some pills, and react with a kind of glazed wonder. She doesn't even read the label, just downs a pill and smiles. Without any water. Not even a Diet Coke, like I'm sure she has in her model fridge.

As soon as she's taken the pill, her world changes to color. Off we go, subjected without consent to a montage of her doing fun holiday stuff, climaxing with footage of her not just surviving but actually enjoying Christmas dinner with her family. No one gets stabbed with a fork.

Hanukkah and Kwanzaa versions available! it says at the bottom of the screen, even as the whole family is knee-deep in Christmas.

Talk to your doctor today about—, says the voiceover lady,

and I switch off. I don't even change the video, just turn the whole thing off. Thanks for ruining YouTube, I say to no one. This ad is all the proof I need to know they've been watching me—not just watching but *studying* me, and instead of thinking, *Wow, that Janet's so smart, let's hack her stem cells to make a magic Janet elixir,* they said, See, that's a problem, and they made me this pill.

Of course I couldn't keep away from the internet forever, so before long I'd seen all the commercials—all the variations, made for every Janet. My favorite is the one with the sad sexy widower, a hot dad who's worried he can't give his little girls a magical Christmas, because Mummy is dead. But it's okay! There's a pill for that too.

Back in the real world, Debs tells me there's a new dog in the boarding kennels. He was brought in late last night by one of those cops I always think Debs is sleeping with, though really I know she's not because like all of us, she has willed herself to have *vagina dentata* after realizing how disappointing men are.

The dog was found chained up in some man's bathroom, Debs tells me, only it wasn't on the news because it wasn't a missing girl. They were doing a narcotics raid and there he was. He'd been kicked about a bit but mostly ignored. His owner was going to prison, but not for the right reason.

She takes me to see him. He's a surprisingly friendly little guy. A complete mutt, maybe a bit of every breed, scruffy hair, straight out of some dumb movie. The trust he shows us is heartbreaking. Is he like this with men? I ask, because I wouldn't blame him if he wanted to kill every man he sees (I get that way too sometimes), but he'll be harder to rehome (ditto).

He was fine with the cop, Debs says. How were *you* with the cop? I want to ask, but I know better. He could be one of her kids' fathers, for all I know. Instead I ask, What's the dog's name? The cop says the perp just called him *fucker*, she tells me, so she's calling him Tucker. Most of the dogs we get in are called Max, so we're old pros at renaming dogs.

Tucker, I say, and the little fella wags his tail at me, and it's lovely if you forget that just a few hours ago he was chained up in some crackhead's den.

We keep dogs like Tucker up in the boarding block because it's nicer there. People are paying us to look after their dogs, so it has to be nice. The other dogs are supposed to just be glad they have a roof over their heads, even if it's a bit leaky. Truth is, I hate dealing with boarders—not so much the dogs, though they can be pretty spoiled, but their people. You have to accept that people might have to leave a dog behind once in a very long while—if their mum is in the hospital, maybe—but most of these people seem like they're just jetting off somewhere to work on their tan, and that's extra shitty. Part of us always hopes they'll never come back to collect their dogs, so that we can find them a nicer home with people who want to take them away on holiday.

So I go about my business getting Tucker settled in. I'm barely recognizable as a human in my work clothes, and I'm fine with it, even though Melissa's always looking at me like she's planning a makeover for my face and clothes and soul. People so rarely see me out of my work clothes that when they do, it's like some rom-com body-swap hell, with people saying things like, Don't you scrub up well, or We didn't know what was under there. Melissa is always trying to jazz up her clothes, with varying degrees of success on her part and nausea on ours. She tried to belt her waterproof jacket so people would know she has a waist under all that, that she's still a woman, though I don't know what that even means. She says she does it for herself—the hair styles, the lip gloss—but she can't fool us. She still believes someone will come along to save her if they see her. I see her, but it's not enough.

She always looks like she's on the verge of a mental breakdown, and Debs can't deal with it. This is a place of work, Melissa, Debs says in a tone she usually reserves for her kids when they've puked on something.

Melissa's Wellington boots have flowers on them. I only comb my hair if I have to, and I don't really have to.

I have issues with my body like most humans, and I like that my work clothes allow me to forget I even have a body, at least until I need to pee. I was the same way at school. Other kids couldn't wait to get home and change into their play clothes, but I would skulk home, crash out in my uniform, trying my best to play at being someone else. Dressing yourself is exhausting; having to think about your body is exhausting. I don't want to look good, I just want to be comfortable.

Which is exactly what I do next: after working all day without thinking another minute about clothes, I go home and fall into bed, fully dressed, work boots and all, like a hobo. This is a luxury. There's nobody to impress, no expensive jeans to peel off, no phony pizza box to leave a stain. When the boyfriend was still there, I used to come home and hop in the shower, put on fresh sweats, and pretend to be a person, for him mostly. Now I'm free to be a blob, free to be a hobo—free to be anything.

12

I love October. It's a good month. It makes me the closest to happy a month can make anyone. It's always Halloween in my heart.

Christmas is already breathing down on me, though, like a man I don't know in a bar, a man who doesn't know I have a flick knife. The knife is real—I have it for work, and Debs has one too. Sometimes, when dogs come in that have been taken from bad people, the bad people come looking for them, and these two knife-wielding thirtysomething women in fleeces and wellies are *prepared*. I mostly use mine for eating apples because I'm trying to eat healthy while preserving my status as a badass. Sometimes I catch Melissa watching me, wishing she could be that cool, wishing we'd let her have a knife, but we can't risk her turning on us one day. This place will do that. I've seen perfectly good dogs come in and after a week they want to bite your arm off. We don't blame them. We still try to see the best in them, find them a good family that look like they need to care about something.

The pill ads have been getting more intense. This one's a full-on infomercial. In the first shot, a woman in a power suit is walking through a busy mall at Christmas. No one is looking at her like, *Who the fuck does their shopping in a power suit?* No old woman stops her to say, *I haven't seen shoulder pads like that since the eighties and it's bringing back a lot of feelings!* No kids are scrambling around the mall, trying to get in the shot or trip her up.

This time it's a voiceover man, not a voiceover lady, who does the honors:

> *Here at MedsForLife, we know the holidays can be a time of stress, not just relaxation. Whether you love the season or hate it, you can't avoid it! And your brain needs protection. Here at MedsForLife, we've created something wonderful. Something that will allow you to enjoy that time of year again.*
>
> *Life is hard. We get it. Just look at the news. But that shouldn't stop you enjoying your least favorite time of year. You deserve it.*
>
> *You deserve Christmas.*

It's basically a Viagra ad: *We can help you get it up for Santa.*

Then they bamboozle you with science. Scene: a man in a white lab coat obscuring the cages of weeping rats. One of them turns to the camera and says, We've found Christmas in your brain! Hooray! We can fix you now. Whenever you're ready! he leers.

Then there are diagrams and more people in white lab coats, pointing at things with sticks, forgetting that's what Hitler did. Standing oh so carefully before the cages of weeping rats they've tested, forgetting rats don't know what Christmas is, and if they did, they wouldn't give a rat's ass about it, would they? Isn't that where that comes from?

But then the screen fills with facts and diagrams and lots of small print, whizzing up and over the screen. Speak to your doctor about it today! Better still, tell your doctor about your friend who's a buzzkill and we'll medicate them for you! It's that easy. Sign here. And then, in that anxious disclaimer voice: We have nothing to do with the devil, and we can't help if your family are a bunch of racists. But give us your email so we can stay in touch! We're working on a pill for that too.

But that's not all. It's an infomercial—it keeps going. After years of research we've found how festive spirit works in your brain, the man in the white coat says, pointing at a picture of the brain, in case you forgot what that is. Part of the brain is lit up with the word *joy*. The holidays are a time of joy . . . or they *should* be, he says, cocking an eyebrow. And this influences the chemicals in your brain that affect happiness.

You know these chemicals, don't you?

A little cartoon elf pops up. Hi! I'm Dopamine! he says, horrifically. I like rewards and pleasure!

Another elf pops up. Hi! I'm Serotonin, she says. I like self-worth and belonging!

Together we make Christmas cheer! they say, high-fiving.

The man in the white coat is talking again now.

Participants in our study were shown holiday-themed
images, and by studying their brains, we've been able to

identify the most active centers of brain activity. These very areas here!

(He points to areas labeled SENSORY MOTOR CORTEX, PREMOTOR and PRIMARY MOTOR CORTEX, and PARIETAL LOBULE.)

These areas of the brain are related to our spirituality, our senses, and our empathy. In short, we now know how the holiday season affects the brain. But that's not all! We didn't stop there. Many people find the holidays stressful. All that pressure to have the picture-perfect family gathering when your family are jerks!

(He doesn't say *jerks* but I hear *jerks*.)

Under stress, your body releases adrenaline and cortisol, harsh and unkind chemicals that make this trying time of year even more trying. It's hard to imagine the festive period without thinking of your family and friends, but not everyone has good relationships. Maybe you've even lost a loved one?

(I get the feeling his wife definitely left him. Probably because his job is being a drug-peddling scientist on TV.)

But socializing is a huge part of Christmas, he says. It releases the hormone called oxytocin in the brain. Another elf pops up: Hi! I'm Oxytocin! I'm that warm, fuzzy feeling you get when you're with people you love. These are the parts of the brain that our magical new pill targets, the man says, very pleased with himself. Think of your brain like a Christmas tree. Our pill will light it up for you! Which just sounds creepy to me.

Speak to your doctor today! he says. And then the side effects fill the screen.

I should switch off that ad when I see it, but I can't. I'm transfixed. I keep hoping that if I watch it again that it'll somehow make sense, that I'll start believing in science, if not Christmas. But it hasn't happened yet.

As of now, it's still only Halloween, one holiday I'm glad people still celebrate. I've already watched *The Craft* ten times this year. Melissa wants to hang decorations, bats and shit. Debs keeps telling her the dogs don't know what Halloween is, but Melissa says it's for the humans. They have this fight about everything— Melissa reminding her about the humans and Debs shutting her down, regretting ever hiring her.

Halloween is also the last day before I'm supposed to start taking my meds, so really I should go out to some costume party, but I probably won't. I'll just stay in and pretend I'm not home like most nights. I'll eat some candy, but I would have done that anyway. My boyfriend and I used to get invited out to those Halloween parties—*Spooky drinks!* or some such bullshit—but the invites were for him, really, and he knew I wouldn't want to go. But he also knew it would be weird for him to go on his own, so instead of going we would just have a huge fight. I want to go, I would say, and he would try not to get his hopes up. I mean, if I was someone else, I would say, and he would try not to swear for about a minute and then we'd both start swearing together. It always ended up with me telling him he should just go, actually wanting him to go, so I could have some headspace, so that I could decide for myself what I wanted for dinner and what I wanted to watch on TV. But then he would never go. Relationships breed resentment, and toward the end, love is just a string of misunderstandings looping us together, confusing us enough to make us think it's worth continuing for the sake of what came before. Misunderstandings like him thinking I wanted sex in the morning when all I wanted was a sandwich.

You're supposed to start taking the pills at the start of November because they take six weeks to kick in. If those TV ads work, on the morning after Halloween, pharmacies around the world will be full of hungover people like me shuffling in to pick up their meds. Maybe our collective sadness won't feel like sadness anymore? Maybe it will feel like something else, something hopeful? Probably not. It'll still be waiting in line in a pharmacy like we're waiting for death, which we are.

Last Christmas Eve, after Melissa had left for the day, Debs asked me if I had any place to be. I said no, even though I did. She said she had somewhere to go, so I agreed to watch her kids, even though it meant throwing a wet blanket on both her kids' Christmas Eve and mine. I'll be back real soon, she said, in time to do all the Christmas shit, she said, definitely.

Her kids weren't bothered because they had a new computer game, something to do with zombies or war or both. It was supposed to be a Christmas gift, but that whole family has zero chill. If Debs never comes back, this might be my life now, I thought, and I was fine with it.

I used to watch Debs's kids so I could snoop around in her house. Going through people's stuff is one of my few remaining joys, but I know the odds are against me: I've never found anything interesting. Not even a vibrator. That's how joyless we all are. We don't even think we deserve even basic pleasures. I do know she sleeps with a baseball bat by her bed, though, so maybe she hasn't murdered her husband *yet*.

Of course she did finally come back. We were watching *Home Alone* like we'd never seen it before when she swooped in and squished between us on her tiny couch. If it was a boat, we would have thrown the babies out and saved ourselves. We both had a little drink, and eventually the kids kissed me on the forehead with their sticky drooling lips and disappeared upstairs to brush their teeth. When they were smaller, they used to stare at me or hand me wet things—Cheerios, mostly—and I just said thanks. Now that they're older, they mostly climb over me like I'm furniture and I sit back and take it. Sometimes it's nice to be furniture in someone else's home.

Debs said I could crash if I had nowhere to be. I've got many places to be, I told her, but nowhere for me. I heard myself getting singsongy, but I didn't care. I was a little drunk, it was Christmas, leave me alone. Then we all trundled off to our corners, feeling fizzy and festive, me on the couch with dog blankets. Debs shouted at us all to go to sleep and we did, because she's actually, literally, the boss of us all.

The next morning was Christmas. Debs wasn't sentimental, so it was just like any morning but with presents, and the kids got to eat junk for breakfast. There were still twenty rowdy dogs who needed feeding and cleaning and walking, which is a buzzkill every day but also what saves us.

When we got to the shelter, Melissa was there. I was aghast. She said she forgot it was Christmas, but she was lying. Debs had given us both two days off; neither of us was supposed to be there. Trouble is, we're drawn to Debs like moths to—well, not a light, but more another moth, the mother of all moths. She is Mothra.

Eventually, Debs made me leave. Made me go to see my parents. Told me to shower first. Told me to be nice. It's Christmas, Janet, she said, and not just for you. So I did as I was told—okay, I didn't shower, just had a whore's bath—and I wasn't really nice, but I wasn't mean either. I was just there. By the time I got to my parents' house I'd already left behind the best part of myself, with Debs and the dogs at the shelter.

This Christmas is going to be different. This year, apparently, I'm going to be off my head on whatever these drugs are—all so I can *really be there*, which doesn't make any sense. Where is it that I'm supposed to be? Somewhere, anyway. Anywhere but here is fine by me.

Debs is taking her kids to the library like a fucking hero. She tells me I'm in charge, though I know she's only saying it to soften the blow because I can't go along to the library with them. She knows how I feel about libraries.

Once, I stole a library card. It was just there on the ground in the street. Someone else would have ignored it, someone better would have handed it in, tracked the person down. I stole it with the intention of using it fraudulently.

That's fucked up, the boyfriend said.

Why? I said.

You know it's free to use the library, right?

I'd thought about getting my own library card, but I knew that meant going somewhere and filling out forms and having to tell someone who I was and where I lived and that I existed at all, and that all felt like too much. This was better. I promised myself I wouldn't borrow anything risqué, no bawdy Victorian romps or books about serial killers. Nothing they could point to when I did something worse and say, Well, I mean, just look at the books she borrowed.

Stealing that card was the perfect crime. Free books—the

dream! At least until the owner reported it lost and got a new card and my card got cancelled. If I really loved books, I would have murdered him, or just gone and gotten my own card.

Why do you do these things, Janet? the boyfriend would say. You're fucked up, he wanted to say, but didn't because he still had a girlfriend, and I was still fuckable. He was just mad I got off on weird stuff like petty crime more than I got off on him.

When I get home, I want to watch TV, but I daren't. I can't switch it on now without being assaulted by Christmas. Finally I close my eyes and decide to click the remote till I find something I can stand—some weird documentary about crime, maybe—but no dice. There's no escaping it now.

The music channels are the worst. Mariah fucking Carey. Just say the word *Christmas* and she's there, like a dog when you drop a sausage. It's always Christmas in her heart, but also in her house—I know this because I saw it on MTV's *Cribs* when that was a thing—and I wondered why no one thought that might indicate a problem. She said she loves the holidays because it's an optimistic time. Maybe they should have hired her as the spokesperson for our pill, but they probably figured we're just a bunch of goths, and goths don't go in for Mariah much, not in public anyway.

In that case they should have gotten Morrissey. But he wouldn't do it, of course, because he wants us to all be sad. Sometimes I think Morrissey is the only one who understands me, and then I remember he's barely Morrissey anymore, which ruins everything.

I wonder if Mariah is taking these pills. I'm pretty sure no one is making her go to any meetings. I don't care as long as she's okay. My empathy for humans is weird and fleeting.

Finally, I find some dumb horror movie—the girls in these films are still dumb, even though we're supposed to be better now; guess no one told this director or he didn't care—and soon I've stopped thinking about Mariah altogether. Someone somewhere will be thinking about her.

13

I feel like I'm standing in a cornfield and willing aliens to take me. I don't care if they're the probing kind or the cute cartoon kind, I just want them to take me.

For once, I'm doing what everyone wants me to do. I am surrendering, Dorothy. I keep waiting for my boyfriend to leap out of the shadows at any moment and embrace me, tell me all is forgiven, try to move back in as if nothing had happened. I'd have to knee him in the groin and run for the hills. Or the woods, at least—I was going there anyway.

Everything I've worked for, this small space I'd made for myself in the universe—all of this is nothing now, or so I'm being told. I myself am nothing, reduced back to dust, and not even stardust but everyday household dust. Dust I'll have to brush into a pile and reanimate into a Janet, so that people will think I am remade, when really I'm just a dust bunny to be puffed away or vacuumed up.

One little pill every morning for eight weeks. Eight weeks, Janet, my mother says, like it's nothing. Eight weeks, my doctor says, and it sounds like a lifetime. A lot can happen in eight weeks.

Then, bam, it's Christmas. Come the New Year, you wean your-self off: half a pill every day for two weeks, then half a pill every other day for one week, then no pills. I'm already counting the days till no pills.

Meanwhile, of course, I have to get up every day and go to work and pretend this is all normal.

My doctor told me to google the information leaflet, and I goo-gled the shit out of it. This was war, and I wanted to be ready. That it was war against myself I chose to ignore. So I downloaded it and printed it out—am I the only person who still has a printer?—and I sat down and read it. For all I knew, there was a chance they'd test me on it at some point. We might get whisked off to Lapland to meet Santa at his pharmaceutical factory.

The leaflet was pretty standard as far as drug leaflets go. I'd seen enough of them, since childhood, to know what I was in for. I read Emma's Prozac one when she couldn't be bothered. (You're taking your reading thing a bit far, aren't you, Janet, she said. No one reads those things, Janet, she said, they're like the terms of service. Maybe they should, I said, and started reading. When I finished, I went and found her. That had the worst ending ever, I said. Everyone dies. I guessed, she said.)

You must follow the guidelines for the pills to work, I read. *No shit, Shirley.* You must wean yourself off them as directed. No thinking you're smart and together enough to just throw the pills away the second you escape your family.

This already sounds like no fun.

It doesn't say what will happen if you just neck all the pills in one go. I'm guessing death but in a festive way, like you think

you're a reindeer and try to fly but trip on some fairy lights instead and die of frostbite where you've fallen in the snow.

Nowhere does it say that you should avoid getting pregnant,
but I'll avoid it as usual. It doesn't say what you should do if you
do get pregnant, but I know anyway. I do wonder what would
happen if I went through with it, though. Would the baby love
Christmas, like Mariah-level love, or hate it? There are so many
Prozac babies by now, and they don't seem any happier. I think
about things like this a lot, because as a woman I'm hard-wired to
always be thinking about babies even if what I'm thinking is that
I definitely don't want any. Mostly I want to forget I'm a woman
and just be a person, but it's almost impossible.

I stay up late, lying in bed, reading the leaflet like I'm studying
for a test. It says the pills might disrupt your sleep, but I don't
know how you'd know it was the pills and not the parties in your
building, or the drunk Santa in the street yelling about his wife
who left him, or the fact that you fell asleep reading this leaflet in
the first place.

The pills are meant to build up silently in your system—under
the surface, like a fungus, I guess—until wham, you can't do anything but let their effect consume you. You reach for your Frosted
Flakes and you notice that Tony the Tiger is wearing a sweater
with a reindeer on it and you don't know how it happened but it
happened, and somehow you're meant to feel it's okay.

What this tells me is that the world has little respect for people like me, people who need *easing in*. Take this pill, week after
week, and nothing—and then suddenly it's a full-on assault to the
senses. Every single TV commercial is yuletide, every song glib

and festive. It's like you're suddenly in Whoville, which makes me the Grinch, and I'm fine with it.

Side effects may include making your heart grow three sizes.

On November first, I tell Debs I'll be late. She doesn't care as long as I show up, which is just what I want everyone to ask of me. I dig my prescription out from the bottom of my bag, brush the granola dust off—into my mouth, because I'm disgusting—and march myself down to the pharmacy. On the way, I comfort myself that I can always change my mind when I get there and pick up a box of condoms, just to make everyone's day a bit more exciting. I could even leave one on the street, so that people who see it will feel gross but a little bit nostalgic for sex.

Instead I walk in through the sliding doors, shut down a chunk of my brain, and wait in line for the bottle that will change my life. I wish my mother were here to see my sacrifice. She would have come if I'd asked, but who asks their mother to come with them to the pharmacy? Melissa would have come too, would have seized the opportunity to slather me with makeup samples. Debs is the only one with sense enough not to have come. She'd just wonder what the fuck was wrong with me that I couldn't go on my own. I have actual work to do, Janet, she would say.

I try to distract myself by guessing which people in the queue are getting my pill. It's not hard to find my people. I spot one immediately, a guy in his pajamas and a big coat. I feel an urge to salute him, but you can't do that anymore without people thinking you're some kind of overly social Nazi, so I just nod.

There's a girl with super-thick black eyeliner and a cigarette behind her ear, and I want to marry her. I hope she's at my meeting.

There's a cute boy listening to something loud and shouty. He doesn't realize we can all hear it, or maybe he doesn't care. Thinking he's cute makes me mad. I want to punch myself in the ovaries and tell them to quit it. I don't want to meet new boys at the pharmacy, but there they are, taunting my vagina. I'm done with men and families. If I have urges, I deal with them myself, like a grown-up.

My mum would love if I met someone, even if it was at the pharmacy. It would make a good story to tell our dogs: We were waiting for the same meds, I would say. It was meant to be. There should be a dating app for that: You're on this, they're on this, you can talk about your side effects. Your mouths will both be too dry to kiss, but there are dry-mouth lozenges in Aisle 5.

There's a woman with a small child curled round her leg; she keeps peeling it off, only to have it curl back round her like a snake that wants her dead. If the boyfriend was here, he would be making stupid noises and faces at it, like I do to dogs. I keep wondering why she doesn't shake her leg and fling the kid into the tower of cough medicine.

The rest of the customers are regular folks lining up for regular meds. They look at us like we're freaks because we are. Who can't be happy at Christmas? Us, that's who.

I buy candy and condoms because I want to feel young again

and hopeful. The woman at the counter doesn't care, which is a shame because today I only have eyes for her.

All day I can tell Melissa wants to ask me where I was this morning, but she can't because it's none of her business. I almost want to tell her because no one else cares, but I don't. Part of me hopes she goes through my bag. She's not my mum, so I don't care. She stares and stares and finally tells me she's there if I want to talk ever, about anything, by which she means, Please tell me everything because I live to live vicariously through you.

She thinks she catches me taking a pill and asks shyly if I feel anything yet, and I don't have the heart to tell her it's a Tic Tac. Instead I just tell her I've been having cravings for sugarplums, and she thinks I'm being hilarious and not mean. She's like an annoying little sister, even though we're the same age; this probably means I love her but will sit on her and threaten to punch her if she tells anyone.

Debs doesn't care what I'm doing as long as I do my job and don't try to touch her. She knows about the pills because they're all over the news, and she knows I'm part of it because I have to tell her medical stuff, but she hasn't asked anything about it. Just tell me if you feel weird, she says, which is no help because I always feel weird.

Finally I decide to throw Melissa a bone and tell her about the guy at the pharmacy. She goes all moony, as expected, and asks me what he looks like, because that is what daft people need to know to process any information. I wish I had someone I could count on to ask some weird question, like how big his dick looked or how he smelled, just for variety.

To mess with her, I tell her he looked just like some lame actor she likes. Melissa brings out the Bad Janet in me.

Finally, when I get home, I look at the pills. Things are moving quickly. November 1 is almost done.

The pills aren't gift-wrapped, which is disappointing. I feel cheated already. There's no box or ribbon. Just an ordinary bottle of pills.

I pull out the same pamphlet I've seen before, its warnings like the worst slam poetry: *Tremors and shaking. Decreased sex drive. Exhaustion. Loss of appetite. Restlessness. Diarrhea. Increased thirst. Blindness.* Blindness! Happy fucking Christmas, Janet. Not to mention *increased anxiety, aggression, irritability, hostility, worsening of depression, and suicidal thoughts.* Just what every little girl dreams of for Christmas.

The pill is green and red. Of course.

I shake one out in my hand and look at it. *This is some fucked-up shit*, I think, but I admit I'm a little curious about who I'll be if I take it. The dream daughter. The perfect girlfriend. The joyful employee and colleague. *Fuck that shit*, I think. I like who I am. It's everyone else who has the problem.

The pamphlet doesn't say what to do if you change your mind. If you have concerns, it says, talk to the host of your meeting. You must attend every meeting, it says. It doesn't say that it's because these pills haven't really been tested on civilians yet and they need to know we're okay.

I think about that little pill for a long time. I think about how all I have to do is swallow it and I'll suddenly be a happy, carefree person, someone who doesn't see the sadness. I shed a little tear for the sadness. *Someone needs to see it*, I think, *why not me?*

I feel my throat closing, getting sore, and I swallow.

Before I go to sleep my mother texts me. Did you take your first pill? she says. I ignore her. It could be worse. At least she didn't throw me a Daughter's First Pill party.

14

I have my pills and my candy and my condoms. Now all I have to do is go to seven hour-long meetings and I'll be a changed person.

It doesn't say anywhere that I can't be drunk for those seven hours. Or at least a little drunk. I know you're not supposed to mix alcohol and pharmaceuticals, but it's the holidays. If you're not having Baileys for breakfast, you're doing it wrong.

I often had to be a little drunk to get through the school day. Just a little. I kept a bottle of peach schnapps under my bed. I'd take a swig, enough to get me through, especially if it was a gym day or a day when I might have to speak in class. I hate that all I had was peach schnapps, not something cool, but it served a purpose and didn't taste gross like most alcohol. I had a friend who'd bring her schnapps in to school in a thermos. I liked her a lot, as people go. I hope she's still alive.

On the day of my first meeting, I drag myself out the door and drive to the church without turning back, but once I'm safely parked outside I sit in my car as if someone who's never heard of me might come and get me. It feels nice. I could be anyone. I used to walk past this church and think, *At least I'm not in AA yet*. Yet. And now here I am anyway.

In the back of my head, I hear my mother saying, You want this, Janet, or you wouldn't be doing it. In the front of my head, I see Debs holding her hands like she's pointing a gun at me, saying, So long, Janet.

Inside, the building smells like life and death and piss. People use the doorway as a bathroom because they hate Jesus, and I don't just mean the bums but drunk regular people. The smell wafts through to the hall where my meeting is. It's the opposite of that fresh donut smell stores pump out to lure you in.

I'm the last to arrive, it seems. I'm tempted to say, Well, actually I was just sitting in my car deciding if you're all really worth my time, but instead I clam up and take the last empty seat. I leave my coat on. There are ten of us in the room, and seven are women. There is no hot widower, like the commercials promised, so I instantly feel cheated. But then someone might look at me and say I'm nothing like the Model Me on the poster and I'd have to say touché.

Across the room, I see an official-looking guy sitting by the door making notes. I don't think he's there to stop us walking out—running out, in my case—but I bet he'd try. Maybe stand up, at least, put his notebook down. But he's definitely from the pharmaceutical company. Men medicating women—just as it's always been. I once took a class on the history of women and the mind. Or, as I called it, How Men Have Fucked Women Over for All Time, but my professor threatened to fail me if I didn't stop putting that title on my exam booklets.

Karen is our group leader. She looks like she's never led any-thing, not even a dog. She seems more pathetic than any of us, and for that I decide I'll cut her some slack. She wears clothes that look like she made them herself, like no one ever told her there are stores. Also, she is called Karen, which makes me sad for her. Karen is a sad-girl name, because of Karen Carpenter. I know all the dead sad girls.

Hi, I'm Karen, she says, but she doesn't sound that sure, and no one believes her.

The official-looking guy introduces himself but says he's just here to observe and goes back to his seat by the door. Try to ig-nore him, she says, which sounds like it's directed at me. They just want to know how we're doing, she says, and I remember again that this is all an experiment. We are chimps in Santa hats. I wonder why they didn't just get cameras.

Karen makes us go around and say our names. I really want to give them a joke name, but if I do I'll probably get kicked out. Plus, I really can't be bothered. I wear my apathy like it's perfume I stole from Sephora.

Pharma Guy is wearing a suit, so we know he is at work. Kar-en's outfit is obviously homemade, because it's knitted, which is code for I have a ton of cats. I wouldn't be surprised to find out she was married, but to the Lord.

Then Karen starts telling us about our pill. It's almost like a little play. I wonder if it'll turn into a musical, but it doesn't. If I get bored I'll have to make up my own songs.

They don't have PowerPoint, and we're all thankful, Karen mostly, because I'll bet things like PowerPoint keep her awake at night. I can relate. Being in this room with these people is already softening me, and I don't like it.

Karen tells us what our doctors told us: that the pill was made for people just like us who want to be happy at Christmas. Everything we need to know is in the pamphlet, she says, and then spends ten minutes rummaging around her giant bag to find it. Finally she whips it out and waves it above her head, like, Got it! I'm not completely incompetent after all! I might have more in common with Karen than I thought.

I like how old-school this all is: there is paper, there are actual humans talking—or one, so far—and over by the side there are donuts. There are no weird sci-fi vibes, no giant screens, no signs we're all doomed. It gives me hope, if I can forget they're drugging us all.

By this point, Karen says, we all should have been taking our pills for a full week. How are you all feeling? she says. No one answers, but I see a few people shrugging at one another. No one feels anything yet. Karen senses our disappointment. It's early days, she says. You won't necessarily be feeling anything yet. This only bums people out more. We all want instant gratification. We all want this to be over.

Before this, I used to secretly love stories of drug trials gone bad. Obviously, I felt awful for the poor people who needed a quick buck and thought letting someone test their pharma-grade meth substitutes on them was better than a real job, but who can resist a fairy tale where Big Pharma is exposed as the wicked witch? I could not get enough.

What I'm really obsessed by, though, is where the Christmas

pill idea started: with the pharma boss's wife. The first Janet, that's what I call her. The one my pill was invented for. I read about her online. I'm not stupid; I know origin stories are marketing scams, designed to make us think something profitable was actually created out of love. This one, though, I hope is true. Apparently the boss, whose name was Richard Grossman, wanted to make his wife happy at Christmas, but he didn't know what to get her—until he realized how unhappy she was. And so, instead of setting her free from a loveless marriage, he devised a pill to help her forget about it . . . at least through Christmas.

Surprisingly, the origin story has a tragic ending: apparently the pill made the first Janet a little . . . *excitable*, shall we say, and one day she left Mr. Big Pharma to run off with a sexy mall Santa. But I can't help thinking that was all part of the big sell. Because it *is* part of the big sell, right there on their website. I mean, it doesn't actually say he was sexy, the mall Santa, but he must have been, right, or what's the point? I picture him as a hot felon, not just some overweight, out-of-work bearded guy who gave in and took the gig because he was sick of people constantly telling him he looks like Santa and making no money at it.

I want to know what happened to them in the end. I want to know if they're still together. I want to know if the first Janet is happy. Maybe one day our paths will cross. She might be the only one who understands. It's a lot, to pin all your hopes on someone who probably doesn't exist, but isn't that what Christmas is all about?

I have so many questions about the first Janet, but no one to ask.

I'm actually rooting for her, not her nerdy pharma husband. And if that doesn't say love, I don't know what does.

I had assumed that everyone at the meeting would be like me and feel like this is all a huge inconvenience, that we all have somewhere better to be, but I am wrong. There are at least two people who seem to think this is the most fun ever. I'm worried that one of them is going to reach over and start trying to braid my hair soon. I make a mental note to come in with my hair extra dirty next time, so no one will want to touch me.

We're seated in a circle, and I'm wishing it was a coven, like the one I always wanted to start with Debs—just the two of us making voodoo dolls of all the people who have wronged us, held in a pro-witchcraft bar.

Thankfully, no one calls for us to go around and tell our stories. It's obvious we're all here for the same reason: we're all a giant pain in someone's ass.

I did rehearse what I'd say in the car if they did make me speak: Hi, I'm Janet, and I'm in the business of sad—here I'd tell them all about my glamorous job at the shelter—and I don't really want to take any pills, because life is sad and I don't want to forget that. But maybe a few weeks off at Christmas wouldn't be so bad. I never get the chance, though. Instead Karen starts clapping for us and we just look at her, blank. Read the room, Karen, I want to say. Too soon, I want to say.

A few people leave even faster than me. I like them instantly. A few hang around the snack table, exchanging numbers. I could walk over and give them my number and we could all text one another little messages of support: *You got this, girl*, or *Don't stab your brother with a fork, Janet.* But I don't do that, obviously. Instead I just go back to my car and pet it on the steering wheel— *What a good car, waiting for me so long*—and we go home together.

One day at a time, I tell myself as I try to fall asleep. It's just one day, Janet. Okay, so you had to go to some weird mandatory meeting. Doctor's orders, but you did it.

I wake up crying.

You'd think I'd be used to crying by now, given the shelter and all. In the beginning, Melissa used to cry constantly. *It's so sad, Janet,* she would say cradling a dying puppy, her tears disappearing into its fur. I was sure Debs was going to fire her.

I did catch Debs crying once. Only once, in the whole time I've been at the shelter. In those three years we'd lost several puppies who were too far gone when we got them to recover, and we ourselves had to put three dogs down, but no one had ever seen Debs show any emotion over it. For her it was life, because it was her life. This song came on the radio, and I guess the song conjured up some feelings for her, ones she didn't want conjuring, and then there they were, the tears, and there I was suddenly, lurking in the background, just another person she usually had to be strong for. But it was over as soon as it began, and I knew she'd deny the whole thing, so I never mentioned it again.

People see the shelter in two ways: as a second chance for dogs to find a home and love, or as a prison where unwanted dogs go to die.

It can be either, really, but most days it's just a version of home for all of us.

15

Every day in November someone asks how I'm feeling. My mother, Melissa, the girl in the apartment across from me, a perky woman on TV trying to sell me lady cereal. You deserve to feel this great, she says, almost cycling into a lamppost.

I should block my mother, but then she might come over. Or send my father to say, Call your mother.

I go out without my phone a lot. It's the closest to free I've ever felt. People think their phones connect us all, but mine feels like a weight around my neck.

Debs thinks it's hilarious that Big Pharma came up with a pill for people like me. Who knew there were so many Janets? she says. I still haven't told Melissa, but she's seen the commercials; she knows a target consumer when she sees one.

The girl who lives across from me only knows about the pills because of something that happened one night. Before that, I'd pretty much avoided eye contact with everyone in the building, mostly because they've all heard me have sex and explosive diarrhea, but then I generally avoid eye contact with people if I can help it. Most people are looking at their phones anyway, so no one calls me out on it. Sometimes I look at my phone just to not look at people, and no one suspects a thing.

I get up each day, put my head down, make my way to work, and power through the hours, barely looking up, banging into stuff, mostly making a hash of it. I try to give off the message *I can't stop or I'll die.* I don't need pills to shut down, I did it by myself, I want to say to my mother. I'm just like you but also better, I want to say, which she maybe already knows.

My neighbor is the coolest person I don't know. In another world we'd be friends. Her name is Min-seo. I only know that because I heard her boyfriend shout, *Min-seo, you are such a bitch!* That's how I know we'd get on. *Hi,* I'd say, *I too am a bitch.*

We bonded, or my version of bonded, over Ethiopian food. We both ordered food from the same place a lot, and when the guy showed up, I thought it was for me and she thought it was for her and it was for both of us and it was some rom-com shit neither of us wanted but we went with it, laughed a little, mostly at how embarrassing being alive was. We were both just grateful this guy didn't say, *Hey, you two should hook up.* I might have been up for it, but she probably had other plans.

When the guy left, it was just us standing awkwardly in the hall with our food. It was like when neither person wants to be the one to end a phone call; we just stood there letting our food get cold, unsure how anyone did anything at all.

Then Min-seo said, I thought I was the only one who ate Ethiopian food.

She seemed almost a little mad, like *How dare you, this is my*

thing. *There's so much other food. Don't you dare go making it a trend.*
I liked her thinking I had that power.

Same, I said.

My ex used to say, What the fuck is Ethiopian food? she said.
Like flies and rice and shit?

He sounds great, I said.

Yeah, well, she said. Enjoy, she said, finally going back into
her apartment so I could go back into mine.

We sat in our apartments, eating our food alone, but it was
nice knowing she was there across the hall. Sometimes that's
enough. There's this Shakira song that goes, I'll be there and
you'll be near, which sounds stalkery to me but also perfect.

So that's my neighbor. Min-seo. She's there in the hallway
when I get home that November day. Our whole relationship
takes place in this hallway, this tiny space. People think relationships need space, but I think they might be wrong. This one was
working out great for me.

I nod, like *What's up*, because I want her to know I'm cool.
Min-seo always gives off this cool vibe, like *Whatever*, though at
this point I probably just give off a crazy-lady vibe. She watches
me drop my grocery bag, but she doesn't swoop in to try to catch
it, which I appreciate. A boy might have, because boys always
want to be someone's hero, because their brains have been fucked
by books and movies and the world, and it all makes me tired.

I bend down to pick my crap up and my bag spills out and my
pills roll right across the floor to where she's standing. She picks
them up, not necessarily to help, but because it's always interesting to see what people are on, so you can go, *Oh, right, that ex-*

plains a lot, or, *Same! Pill buddies!* This is a common thing now, apparently—girls everywhere are in these Facebook groups based on what meds they're on and what crystal they carry. My mum loves it when she meets someone on the same meds as her; it's like discovering someone who likes the same brand of coffee.

Min-seo hands me back my meds, but she lets me handle the rest of the mess myself, and I respect it because I'd do the same. I once saw some crabby-looking lady drop a bag of oranges, which promptly started rolling into traffic. Some dude tried to chase one, but he just looked like an idiot. I stayed put. I looked like an idiot already, I had nothing to prove. The crabby lady looked at me, and I thought, *Curse me if you must.* Whatever. I'm so wretched I probably wouldn't know the difference.

It's that white-girl pill, Min-seo says. Nothing gets past her.

I once heard her boyfriend ask if he could call her Minnie. Who the fuck is Minnie? she said. He said, You know, Mickey's girlfriend, the mouse, and she said, Why the fuck do you want to call me that?, and he said, It might be cute, and she did not get it. I was there listening by the door, and I thought, *Who is this guy?* She meant *Don't try to call me anything other than my name or I will cut you,* and I believed her. He's her ex-boyfriend now, thankfully, but I've seen the men who leave her apartment, and some of them look like they have definitely been cut, maybe from weird sex but maybe from rage.

What are you doing for Christmas? she says, to make small talk.

Oh, I say, me? No, nothing. I mean, the old *family obligation,* I say, you know, rolling my eyes.

You can spend it with us if you want, she says.

Min-seo and I are ships crossing in the night, or strangers, or buses, I don't know. I just know she's there and I'm there but we're never *really* there, we're mostly in our heads. I have never seen her at the pharmacy, not even buying tampons. I hear her more than see her. I thought I saw her in a bar once, but neither of us is the type to acknowledge we've seen someone out in the wild, because it's exhausting having to validate people that way.

But now here she is, reaching out to me, extending pity to the pathetic girl in the hall.

It'll just be me and my dad and my sister, she says. You should come. You don't have to be happy, she says, but you don't have to be sad either.

I want to say, Sure, I mean, I've been planning our wedding for months anyway. I haven't, obviously, because I'm not into chicks, or anyone really. If I'm into anyone it's myself, which makes me sound like a terrible narcissist, but in my defense, I never look in the mirror. Anything could be going on with my body and I'd just let it do its thing. Why shouldn't I? The world is reflective enough for me to know I exist. Once I did my hair a different way, pulled it back, and Melissa made such a fuss about it, like I was from some makeover show where they take someone normal and make them look like someone else, someone who's had major cosmetic surgery. I said, It's just hair, Melissa, and Debs said, Leave Janet alone, Melissa, but then she said, Nice hair, to me too, so I made sure I always tied it back after that.

Min-seo makes more sense to me than anyone I've ever met, man, woman, or dog, and she's been living right there across the hall all this time. She could have saved me a lot of time, a lot of feelings. *That'll teach me to be so insular,* I think, which is just another word for snobby, shut off, shut down, unfriendly, sad, lonely, scared of change, of letting people in—even scared of no longer feeling sad, because anyone who's been sad a long time knows that you get so used to it that it's hard to give any other feelings a chance.

I hadn't really thought of it that way, I say to her. It's important to let people know when they've blown your mind, even if it's a tiny mind in a tiny building. Min-seo had blown my mind a little, offering me an alternative. Sometimes we just want options. Until then, I didn't feel like I had many.

My mother wouldn't agree, I tell her. You know, about not being happy. I tell her this so she'll know I have a mother, against all appearances. I even had a boyfriend once, I want to say, but she knows, she heard it all through the wall.

So your mum wants you to be happy? What a bitch, Min-seo says, smiling. I laugh so she knows I'm not completely dead inside. Ha ha, yeah, I say, laughing at my awful or maybe wonderful mother.

In the space of five minutes this girl has pointed out that I'm a spoiled white girl with shitty white-girl problems, yet I still want to marry her and have her babies, if that's possible, which I think it actually is now. We could name the baby something festive, like Carol.

It's no big deal, she says. I mean, my family, some friends maybe. Come if you want, she says.

Don't ditch your pills, though, she adds, starting down the

stairs. I've seen them do great things. You know that guy in 12B? He used to keep throwing himself off his balcony.

But he lives on the ground floor, I say.

Yup, she says. But now he has a job and a boyfriend and a plant on that balcony.

Should I bring anything? I ask. I always hope the answer is no, but you're supposed to ask.

Just yourself, she says.

Not even a little smile? I joke, so she knows I'm not all about the white-girl problems.

If you feel like it, she says. My dad's pretty grumpy-looking, but that's just his face.

She turns back to the staircase, and I panic. My friend wanted me to spend Christmas with her in Ibiza, I say, to keep her from thinking I'm a complete loser. It's not true, of course. Emma has never invited me anywhere.

Ibiza, she says. Lucky you. But . . . you didn't go?

I don't really dance, I say.

They make you dance there? she says, and I can't tell if she's joking or not.

I think so, I say.

Well I'm glad you stayed, I guess, she says.

Me too, I say, and not just because the thought of Ibiza did something funny to my butthole.

When I finally get inside my apartment, I dump my bag on the floor and sit beside it, processing our conversation. Sometimes I feel like I need to do this every time I interact with anyone who isn't a dog.

I will never understand people.

Dog breeders and puppy farmers are scum to us. Debs always says that if she hadn't had her accidents—that's what she calls her kids; she doesn't even say the "happy" part—she probably would have adopted. I can see her at the adoption agency now, trying to convince them that a run-down dog shelter in the woods is a great place to raise kids. It's better than a third-world country, she might argue, but you've got to wonder.

When her kids begged to go to Disney World, like all kids do, even ones raised by crazy dog-shelter feminists who live in the woods, she just told them, This here is the happiest goddamn place on earth—now go pick up that poop out the front before one of you skids on it. And her kids would pick up the poop and only curse her a little, because they knew there was no point cursing the most powerful of all witches.

A spaniel called Lady comes in. I say comes in, but I mean she's dumped on our doorstep. Some days we come in and find a dog just tied up outside. Sometimes I think Debs lets us find them, so we'll know how good we have it. There's no note this time, just a collar, so she has a name at least. Lady is so exhausted she looks to be past caring. She isn't the first one who comes in that way—the dam who gets dumped on us when the owners have got every last drop out of her, when she's too exhausted to breed from anymore. They come to us as husks. You should have seen me back in the day, I imagine them saying. They can barely lift their heads now, their bellies swollen and sagging, nipples sucked dry. The parts that made Lady a lady barely recognizable. She pees all the time. Sometimes from joy, like when we pet her and tell her everything's okay now. She's such a sweetheart. So trusting, even when she has no reason to be. She has this look in her eyes that says, Where are my children? My hundreds of children? Someone took them, I want to say. You're safe now, I want to tell her, though how safe are we all, really?

We'll look after you, we tell her, try to make you as comfortable as we can.

She lasts two weeks.

We called the vet out three times in those two weeks, more than I can ever remember calling the vet for a single dog, but we're all rooting for Lady. Each time he examines her and he shakes his head. She's all sucked dry, he says. Is that a medical term? I want to joke, but I am capable of a modicum of tact.

Debs lets us bring Lady to her house, to breathe her last on a comfortable couch. We carry her in there like she's the queen. I put the TV on. What's wrong with her? the kids ask. She's all used up, Debs says. They don't ask where her puppies are. Everyone seems to know this is one hell of a sinkhole of sadness that has just opened, and we tiptoe around it to keep from falling in.

Once a month, a dog trainer named Fran comes to the shelter. She comes as a favor to Debs. She's an old friend. An old flame, maybe. She brings her girlfriend, who is one of the most beautiful women I've ever seen, like Beyoncé if she ate what she wanted and was a lesbian. Too beautiful, apparently, to get out of the car.

Fran comes to help Debs out with the problem dogs. Really, she comes to talk shit about the girlfriend she's got waiting in the car. That's why she has to wait in the car. Debs lets us visit with her for half an hour, then tells us to fuck off, the grown-ups need to talk. I like to think they're planning some crime. So we all go out into the front office and sit there, in too many clothes, wishing we were a pretty girl waiting in a car.

The dogs get quiet when Fran is here. They know that soon someone is going to make them do shit they don't want to do, like sit on command and walk in a straight line, and who wants to do any of that?

Fran is an old-school butch dyke and proud of it. She scares Melissa. Melissa always makes sure she's next to me when Fran's around, almost hiding behind me. I can hear her trying to slow her breathing so she doesn't say anything stupid, anything at all really. Melissa would be easy prey for Fran in most circumstances, but here it's clear she's one of us, one of Debs's girls, so she must be okay.

She knows I'm cool because on the first day we met I said, So you're the dyke, and she said, And you're the Janet, and we smoked a cigarette until Debs came and told us both off because this isn't the fifties and you can't just smoke over babies, which is what the dogs are to Debs.

It's on visits from Fran that I find myself thinking, *What happened to us?* Nothing, really. Or everything. Men, mostly. If you don't know what I'm talking about, it hasn't yet happened to you, but it will. All the tiny sadnesses will build up until they make you into whatever monster you are that keeps you up at night. They tell you it's under your bed or in your closet, because if they tell you it's going to be inside you, there's no coming back from that.

When Fran's not hovering around Debs, she does spend time with the dogs. They all need so much work, and we do what we can, but it's nice to have professional help.

Like all of us, Fran has her favorites. Hers are the big stupid dogs who are soft as shit, but they're always at risk of crushing some whiny toddler by accident, and their owners tend to get skittish and dump them. She spends time with them, tries to teach them not to be so huge, but it's like teaching elephants how to ballet dance. She doesn't give up on them. If she can get them to walk on a lead without pulling your arm off, to sit when asked and only crush children who deserve it, she's winning. It's all a favor to Debs; she usually gets paid handsomely to fix people's dogs, but we get it for free.

Fran goes away for Christmas. She can't deal with that bullshit, she says, so she takes her girlfriend to some island somewhere. She's with Debs in that she thinks Christmas should really be about Mrs. Claus, and until Mrs. Claus leaves Santa for a woman, she's not into it.

It wasn't always just us three and the visits from the lesbians. Once, even before Melissa came, Debs hired a boy. He lasted two days. Debs was humoring him, I think. Not because the work is hard and most people can't cut it, but because half the point of the shelter is that it's a place where women come to sort their shit out, or to do something that's so exhausting that at the end of the day your desire for sleep leaves no room for the sadness you've acquired. Debs isn't sad, she's angry mostly, but no one knows why. She pretends it's for the usual reasons, but I just know there's something else.

When this boy came, we were open to the idea, but we knew he'd be eaten alive—by us, not by the dogs. We didn't treat him any differently because he was a boy, and that might have been the problem. We expected him to get on with it like we all did. He said he thought the job would be more about playing with the dogs. We all thought that, I wanted to tell him, but instead I just told him to go and pick up the shit in Block A.

That was the end of male coworkers, at least the steady-paycheck kind. On weekends a couple of male volunteers come to walk the dogs, but we all breathe a sigh of relief when it's just us again. And we like it best—at least I do—when we're alone with the dogs, our private suffering drowned out by the very public suffering of twenty abandoned dogs.

A lot of dogs who come in have been abused by men, if I'm honest, so they're no different from us. We're all happier when they're off to new homes. I think we're all secretly afraid that someday the local men will realize the service we're providing and try to take the shelter away from us.

To be fair, we did have one dog who had been neglected by a woman. Having been neglected by all women, including myself, I could relate. The woman had been a drug addict, and I felt sad for both her and the dog, and I wanted Debs to let us have them both. Deb wasn't so understanding. She tried to use the whole incident as a cautionary tale for her kids, but the kids were too excited about the new dog. Those kids love every single mangy mutt that comes through our doors, oblivious to all the suffering around them. Whenever we have puppies, they can't wait to tell their friends. Sometimes Debs will let them have friends over, but usually she tells them it's not a good time.

That should be our slogan, I joked once: *Never a good time.* Debs doesn't do jokes.

16

I leave work and shuffle in to meeting #2, leaving my hoodie up until the very last moment. Everyone else is already seated. I'm always disappointed I'm not invisible.

With the grace of a hippo ghost, I sit down in the only empty chair. Karen welcomes us all. The pharma guy says, Hey, and then, I'm not here, but with jazz hands, which is confusing for us all.

How are we all feeling? Karen asks, because she's being paid to. It's her one job. The reason we're all here. It's sadness conversion therapy: they don't care if we're straight, they just want us happy.

Karen reaches in her giant disgusting bag again, and I think she's going to pull out some festive flash cards and ask us on a scale of one to ten how murdery they make us feel. When we don't feel murdery at all, they'll know the pill is working.

No one says anything. There are no words to describe how we all feel. I think about telling them all those words I know for sadness, but I know I'm not supposed to talk about sadness. It's our *We don't talk about the war.*

Okay, well, it'll take a few weeks, she says, believing in us all, bless her.

Then she starts telling us how we can get the most out of our pills. I can feel the entire room zoning out. We're all still in our heads. None of us can believe this is our life now.

Remember to let your doctor know if you have any side effects not listed, she says, but every possible thing a human could feel is listed. Then a silence fills the room, as if we're all silently revisiting the litany of dangers.

Ten minutes go by. How are we all doing? she asks, as if the pills might have suddenly kicked in. We all stare at her with the same glazed-over eyes. *We're not doing so great, Karen,* I want to say, but I don't. I know not to speak for other people, but it's pretty obvious. This is not how any of us imagined our lives would be. *You can't even enjoy yourself at Christmas,* the voice in my head says constantly. *What's wrong with you?*

You already asked us that, the girl next to me says. Her cuticles are all bloody. The thought of Christmas will do that to you, make you pick yourself to death.

The time does not go by. I really need to shit, which only adds to the magic.

Finally, the hour is over. No one is more relieved than Karen. I don't know what medication she's on, but she might need more of it.

As I pull my big coat on, I see a few people gathering by the door. They're going for a drink, it seems, not because they're friends now, just because they're all going to the nearest bar, because alcohol, and it would be weird for them all to go and sit separately when they're coming from the same place. I could go to a different, farther-away bar, I think. Better still, I could buy a bottle of something and go to a park, relive my youth.

No one asks me if I want to come. Nevertheless, I turn and smile and say, No, but thanks anyway. They all look at me like *Whatever*, which is the correct way to look at me.

Then one girl, whose name I can't remember, asks what my lipstick is. Usually I'd laugh, but I'm not feeling myself, so I tell her it's ChapStick and I bite my lips a lot.

I can tell she thinks I'm disgusting, but she says, Oh, I wish I could pull off that natural look, and I smile and nod and say nothing about her eyebrows, which are drawn on badly. For a moment I think I feel sadder about her eyebrows than about my life. It's a Christmas miracle.

I don't tell the girl I don't do makeup, because from the looks of her she might assume I'm somebody's outdated idea of a militant feminist, but really, it's because I can't be fucked. I used to wear makeup, when I was a teenager. Sometimes when people look at me with pity I want to shout, I was a teenage girl once! so they know I can survive anything. Anyway, one time a boy told me that he liked how I didn't wear a lot of makeup like the other girls, and I felt so cheated because I'd actually bothered that day. I had spent the little money I had on a bunch of cosmetic crap and he didn't even notice. Boys are fucking stupid. I still slept with him, but I was mad as hell.

I spent my whole teenage years that way, having too much faith that one day boys would no longer be so stupid. I always knew I would be.

I survive that second meeting by feeling sad about that girl's eyebrows and feeling like a boy-hating teenager again. Now it's just me and Karen and the pharma guy, standing awkwardly in the hall. You don't have to go home but you can't stay here, Karen says, and laughs at herself.

Then it's just me and the pharma guy, and we walk out together like it's the most natural thing, like we maybe came here together, and in the moment I like how it feels, so I keep it going, because I know these things have a habit of being fleeting.

I hear myself asking if he wants to get a drink, and he must say yes because my legs are moving now and we're walking to a bar and I can hear myself laugh at something he says and he tells me he has a dog and I hear myself ask if I can meet it, because of course he has to have a dog, doesn't he? Behind every okay man is a better dog. I watch myself leave the bar with him and go to his apartment and I tell myself it's for the dog, it's always for the dog. When life throws you lemons, remember there are dogs.

I do things like this and I don't know why. I pretend I don't want to be part of the stupid world and all its heterosexual bullshit, then I go home with some dude. Some bro. Not even for the sex, but for the feeling—something I pretend I don't need, because if I did, then what?

I'm drunk enough to not care, though. I've always thought I would make a great drunk. One of those ladies with droopy breasts and eyes who hang around bars in leopard print, terrorizing young men. I'm just not sure I could handle the commitment.

The sex with the pharma bro is weird—as it should be, because sex is weird, and if it's not, you're doing it wrong. I'm drunk enough to not care about any of it, except maybe about my body. I'll care later, maybe. Or just forget to. I have important Christmas feelings to feel, goddamn it.

The pharma bro is genuinely happy I'm going to stay over. I don't tell him it's so I can look through his stuff while he's asleep.

It came to me two drinks in, when my brain was still focused on Christmas, that this guy might have a file on me. He works for the drug company, after all; he's supposed to be monitoring us. Who knows what they know? Maybe I'll even find some dirt on Karen.

I don't find anything interesting. The only thing I find is his notebook, the one he pretends to be writing in when he's observing us. When I saw that, I remember thinking, Wow, this is some old-school shit, and being impressed. For all I knew he was recording everything we said. But when I open it, it's just ideas for a sitcom he's writing. I only know because of one note in the margin: like 30 Rock but at a drug company. I desperately want to add my own notes.

He has books at least, so I know he isn't a psychopath. I argued about this with the boyfriend. Mein Kampf is a book, he'd say, what if someone had that? At least they're reading, I'd say. I would argue anything with him for arguments' sake. But this guy has books I like, love even, old Stephen King novels, Philip K. Dick, a fucking Margaret Atwood even, and there is no Hemingway or Kerouac, no red flags. There is a *Screenwriting for Dummies* book, and I like that he knows what he is.

I flip open his laptop, but there's nothing on it, not even porn. This guy is weird. I guess he doesn't bring his work home with him, unless you count me.

The whole time I'm creeping around his apartment, his dog, a giant bulldog, is snoring away, like I could murder them both and they wouldn't even care.

His dog is pretty great. It didn't whine outside the door while we were screwing. I don't think it's because he's used to his master bringing women home; we're probably just not that interesting.

I like the pharma guy's bathroom. It's way cleaner than mine—cleaner than my whole apartment—so I keep going back there to admire it. He even has a plastic turtle that lives by the tub. Says a lot about him, probably—that he has a kid, maybe, or at least was a kid himself. Maybe that's what's missing in my life. Maybe if I got a little plastic turtle it would make me smile when I saw it by the tub. Not now, obviously; if I saw it I'd just think of the time I slept with the weird pharma guy. Which, to be honest, was a little bit like sleeping with my professor, because those meetings are basically school.

I am too tired for all these thoughts.

When I get back into bed, I tell him that turtles almost don't have a nose. What? he says. I think he's hoping I'll either grab his cock and say, Ready to go again, or start getting dressed awkwardly and make my excuses and leave.

No, I'm the girl who sleeps with you and then tells you turtle facts.

And they look pissed off about it, I say. Almost not having a nose, that is.

I'm sure they have noses, he says.

It's barely anything, though, I say.

What turtles have you been hanging out with? he says, still hoping this is foreplay.

Just that one in your bathroom recently, I say.

The plastic one?

Yes, I say, wondering if I'd missed a live one.

The one with a tiny nose? he says, not knowing me well enough to know I don't do cute.

So you did notice! I say.

Not really, he says.

He goes to pee and is gone way longer than it takes to pee—long enough to escape through the window, maybe, if it wasn't his place.

I think about stealing the turtle. Not to put in my own bathroom, because of the PTSD it might cause. Maybe to give it to one of the dogs at the shelter to rip to shreds. It would be poetic. A choking hazard, but poetic. While I was at it, I could steal his towels. We always need old towels to wrap up one sorry thing or another.

He eventually comes back. I sniff him to check he hasn't

showered, because if a guy needs to shower immediately after sleeping with you, he's a creepy jerk who doesn't deserve your stink on him anyway. I don't shower enough, mind you. I'm fully aware of that. Most of the time, these days, it doesn't matter.

I'll shower for Santa, if it comes to that, but I'm not shaving my legs.

What was that? he says, and I don't know if he means the conversation or the sex or if he heard someone break in. His dog is still asleep on the couch.

I don't know, I tell him. I talk a lot of shit.

Then he says he's not sure his friends would like me. Like I had any intention of meeting his friends. I tell him it's fine because I don't like his friends.

Right, you only like dogs, he says, like he doesn't believe anyone who says that. Which is surprising, as he has a great dog, so he should know that's a thing.

It always amazes me that there are people who have dogs but aren't really into them. Sometimes I think the reason I don't have one is that I'd never need anything else again. I would basically be married to a dog, and when one day that dog died, I'd have to kill myself and leave instructions for our ashes to be combined. It would be awkward for my family.

Sometimes, when I'm at someone else's house, I think about murdering them a little, just so I could live in their house. Like taking over their lives: This is where I live now, this is who I am now.

This guy I wouldn't even have to murder. I could just live in his bathroom. It's really nice. I have eaten many a good sandwich in many a shittier bathroom. They must pay him a lot. All the money is in drugs now. Everyone wants to be medicated. All those sci-fi writers I love predicted it, but no one did a damn thing to stop it.

I feel like I need to get more from this little encounter. I'm sure I had an agenda before I started drinking, and it wasn't just to get my rocks off. I gave up a part of myself for whatever this is, and I want something in return.

Is there really a Hanukkah pill? I ask him.

Yes, he says. I'm Jewish.

Holy shit! I say, and I'm not even trying to be funny.

Everyone's sad, Janet, he says, not just you. He missed the opportunity to say *Not just Jew*, which is pretty sad.

How much money is my doctor getting paid to push these pills? I ask. I need to know just how evil Big Dick Pharma really are. I mean, I know, but I want to hear it quantified.

A lot, he says.

Hmm, I say, still fishing. Can you find out the name of the first Janet for me? I ask, forgetting he doesn't know what that means. He looks at me quizzically.

The woman this pill was invented for, I say.

Oh right, he says, sure. I'll see what I can find out.

I don't say it's important to me, but he knows it must be.

And then all at once I realize I'm too sober for this and I need to leave. It's like my mother has stormed in and opened the curtains and the brightest sunlight ever is pouring in and she's staring at us in bed and his limp dick is just lying there trying not to look at her.

This was all a big mistake.

Sometimes I get desperate to get out, like I'm missing something urgent elsewhere, like I just need to remind myself that my legs work and I can go if I want. This happens even though, the minute I'm out there, someone does something to piss me off and I start wishing I was back inside. In this second, I want to be outside. Outside this room, outside this apartment, but back in my body, which is something I rarely feel.

I tell him I have to go to work.

He asks me how that is, work. Same shit different dog, I say, and he thinks I'm hilarious, which is better than broken, although I can be both.

I'm almost free when he says he'll see me next week, and I remember the meetings, and I realize that I've just made everything weird. Sure, I say, and I leave.

As soon as I'm outside his apartment, with him still ten feet away, I cut it all out of me. Him, the sex, all of it. It's the only way I can keep going. *Don't look back, Janet,* I tell myself daily, though I'm not really looking forward either. I'm sidestepping like some weird, uncertain crab that doesn't really know how to be a crab. *Am I doing this right?*

The sex wasn't bad. Even he wasn't that bad. It's me that's bad. Bad Janet.

I'm glad he doesn't have my number so he can't text me anything gross, like *I really like you Janet.*

When I see him again, I'm pretending this whole thing never happened.

The next day at work, I feel like Debs knows I had sex and is disgusted with me.

Rough night? she says when I roll up a little late, my hair greasier than normal, my eyes crustier. She can't see I'm wearing the same clothes as yesterday, thanks to my giant coat, but she knows.

I nod, grimace, look away.

Well, as long as someone's getting some, she says, and Melissa's ears prick up and suddenly there she is and I can't deal with her today.

This new pill is terribly exciting to everyone in my life but me. People love a novelty, especially at Christmas. Everyone wants to know if they work. I don't go around asking people if their meds work; I can usually tell without asking. But people love to tell you what works and what doesn't anyway, like they get a bonus for recruiting a friend, probably because they do get a bonus for recruiting a friend.

As I'm putting my stuff away, my phone rings. It's Emma, calling from Ibiza. Emma, my version of a childhood sweetheart, the one I pictured myself growing old with, comparing chin hairs with, my *one that got away.*

Emma knows the pills have begun. She wants to know if they work.

I only talk to her a few times a year now and suddenly all she wants to talk about is these pills. She's all about the drugs now that she lives on a party island. The rest of the time we email and text like normal people, but sometimes it's good to hear her voice to reassure me that she's not a ghost.

Emma was the first person I told about the pill. It finally happened, I texted her, they made a Christmas pill. To which she replied, Wtf, email me, my phone is literally melting. I wanted to reply, Well that's your own fault running away to a party island, which is not a thing, but I just said, k.

I sat up late writing her a long weird email, because that's our relationship now. *The pharma bros made a Christmas pill!* I wrote, keeping it upbeat to keep her attention from wandering.

Emma doesn't read the news, or anything anymore. She used to, but she's trying to live on the surface now with the shiny people, and the news only bums her out. Her whole life now is trying not to get bummed out.

I told her everything that happened with the boyfriend and my mother and my doctor, trying not to use too many swear words and exclamation marks. I threw in a general rant about the state of the world, so she knew I was still me, and at the end I rewarded her with news about a cute puppy I rehomed. That's a trick I learned a long time ago: When you sense that people are losing interest, just mention a puppy you rescued. It brings them right back.

The other day I saw some guy vomit out of his nose, she

emailed back. It reminded me of you at school. Which was sweet,
I guess.

But do they work? she shouts now. She shouts everything
now, because where she lives there's always an intense throbbing
beat surrounding her. I'm doing what I need to do, she told me
when she left for Ibiza, and I thought, *Me too.* We all do things to
make life bearable. Hers was to leave. Mine was to hide in the
woods with a bunch of dogs. Our relationship now is just shouting at each other, affectionately, from a great distance.

Yes, they work, I tell her, but I don't sound too sure. This is
what they tell us to say if anyone asks. They also tell you that for
weeks you might feel nothing, but then I'm used to that.

They wouldn't be on the market if they didn't work, I tell her,
but we both know that's not true.

I tell her they do what all antidepressants do, they take the
edge off. Enough that you don't want to stab your mother or sib-
ling with a fork at Christmas dinner. Enough that you don't have
to eat with plastic cutlery.

Your mother must be pleased, she says.

You know my mother, I say.

Will it make you fat? she says, because she thinks in biki-
nis now.

I tell her it might make you want to eat a shitload. Maybe
that's what actually makes you more tolerant of other people, not
the drugs at all.

Right, she says. You get so bloated and sleepy that you don't
mind that someone has put a hat on you and is singing at you and

there are children climbing all over you. You just sit there and take it, as long as the cookies and eggnog keep coming.

Emma has been to my house at Christmas, so she knows how it is. My mum puts on a show and you just have to let it happen to you. Christmas for Emma now is something she used to do but can't remember why. Something she did in another life.

How is this thing supposed to work, anyway? she says.

How does it work? I say, incredulous. They've worked out the chemical formula for holiday-specific depression. Has she really not seen it on TV?

No, I don't see much TV, Janet, she says.

Well, the internet, then! It's all over the internet.

Well, I mostly look at Instagram. Is it on that?

Probably, I say. I don't look at Instagram. Afraid I might see a glimpse of actual hell, or my mum.

Trying to talk to people about important things feels impossible, like there's a disconnect between my brain and my mouth. Like words don't mean anything anymore, because they don't.

I realize that I might have lost Emma with the phrase *chemical formula*. She doesn't do math anymore. So I try another tack. It's about the feelings, I say, hoping she still has them. The pill's all about what happens in your brain when it starts feeling like Christmas.

Like Santa and Rudolph and shit? she says.

Close enough, I say. So, this pill produces those effects in the body, apparently.

It's almost nine thirty, time for our daily check-in with Debs. I have to go to a meeting, I tell Emma, pretending I'm someone who has meetings now when really we'll just be huddling round a space heater in a damp office trying not to die of hypothermia arguing about who gets to pick which radio station we listen to.

You really have to go? she says, knowing how much I hate having to be anywhere.

Yep, I say. I try to be there on time, otherwise Debs has a fit.

So you're a new woman now the boyfriend is gone, she says.

Basically, I say.

She asks what I'm reading, which is our version of phone sex. I tell her the last ten books I've read, of which she has heard of zero.

You read too much, she says. My mother always says the same thing, like when I was seventeen and I read somewhere that women are twice as likely to be medicated as men.

You don't read enough, I tell Emma. Same thing I tell everyone.

I've read enough, she says.

They're still making books, you know. New ones every year.

I know, she says. You just told me a bunch.

I miss you, I say.

I know, she says.

So you're really doing this? she says, trying to keep me on the phone. I mean, I don't blame you. Christmas is fucking hard. You should see how many people come here every winter just to escape it.

Not everybody can just run away to Ibiza, I say, but it's not true. It's just not everybody wants to. As an example, I don't want to.

I tell her I slept with the pharma guy. But don't worry, it's over, I add pathetically.

Why do you always do that? she says.

I don't know, I say, but I do know. I wanted to be the one in control. I wanted to be the one making the first move, taking someone home. I wasn't going to be one of those girls who got fucked. I wanted to do the fucking.

You would have too, I say. Because she's the same way. She wants to make her own mistakes, not have anyone make them for her.

Probably, she says.

I really want things to not be about boys for once, I say. Or worse, men.

It doesn't matter, she says, they think it's about them no matter what.

I tell her I miss her again.

I guess I got tempted by the easy option, I tell her. Like daughter, like mother.

Then she lectures me on how antidepressants are not the easy option for a lot of people and I remember that she's always been smarter than me, and tanner now, and wears a bikini, even though her thighs rub, and she doesn't give a fuck about any of it.

Or you could just forget about Christmas, she says, and we laugh so hard, because how could anyone? It's easy for her to say, though, sitting up in her ivory lifeguard tower. She's forgotten about normal life. If you run away to live on a party island I can't even pronounce, where it's hot and loud and everyone is so dehydrated and off their tits all the time that no one knows what day it is—sure, then, I can see how it might be easy to forget about Christmas.

Do they even have Christmas there? I ask. I picture a DJ shouting, *It's Christmas!* and the crowd goes wild, the same way they do when he says, *It's Tuesday!* or *I found my car keys!*

It's like diets, she says, and I think about her in her bikini and I think about myself in my giant coat and boots and I laugh because together we almost make a person.

Huh? I say. How?

Once you say, *Fuck it*, you lose weight, she says. This immediately gets me worried that *she's* lost weight. She was perfect as she was, and I never think that about any humans, only dogs. Of course she's lost weight, I think; she's been spending every day dancing and shouting and swimming in the ocean and eating nothing but exotic fruit platters.

Right, I say, like I understand.

It will take me a while to process what she's said because she doesn't seem like someone who I should be taking advice from, but then she does seem happy, even if that's the heat stroke talking, and maybe the drugs.

I don't think Emma really does that many drugs. She just likes the sun and the dancing and all those bright colors. That's why she left. She's one of those people who's genuinely high on life. She came out of the womb tripping, seeing the world as one big psychedelic party, and all she had to do was see some color and wave her arms over her head and spin around, and the head rush and colors were amazing enough. I don't know how we ever became friends.

(That's not true. I do know. On the first day of school she took my hand and said, Come and see this gross bug, and who was I to say no? It was as simple as her touching me, wanting my attention. No one knew not to talk to Janet yet. No one knew I'd be the weird girl who liked books and dogs and not people, who was probably a lesbian or witch or psycho. Emma didn't care what the other kids were saying, she was too busy spinning round and laughing at how funny the world is. She may have also been dropped on her head as a baby; she's yet to confirm or deny it.)

Emma thinks I should say *fuck it*, that I should just give up wanting to be happy. I wonder if she means just for Christmas or forever. I suppose I should be glad she didn't say, *Just dance away your troubles*, or *Come visit me in Ibiza*.

Emma isn't stupid—she actually went to grad school, whereas I went to the woods—but sometimes I wonder if she's had something in her brain removed. The thing that worries. The thing that needs a rest. A proper meal. She seems more like a plant than a person. Only needing sunlight and water. This simplicity is what annoys me, more than her bikini body. It's like she's some secret existential Jedi master who knows all the rest is bullshit. And if complications are bullshit to her, I wonder if I'm bullshit too.

I tell her goodbye again.

Oh, I almost forgot, she says. Can you send me some emergency candy? The candy here is weird.

This is why I love her.

17

My mum thinks the pills are acid. She thinks I'll see elves everywhere, and I will, because there *are* elves everywhere. It's Christmas. I don't know how everything got so complicated, she says, popping a Xanax. When I was a girl, she says—never a good start—we were just grateful to have some time at home and a tangerine. Please, not the tangerine story, we groan. She used to put a tangerine in our stockings. One year I left mine in there the whole year and it turned to dust. I thought it was poetic, she thought it was disgusting, we were both right.

When I still had a boyfriend and we still liked each other, he'd come and see me at work. Debs didn't really like him just showing up, because it distracted me from my job, and also from my larger job of helping her smash the patriarchy. Mostly it reminded her that I wasn't as dead inside as she was, not yet anyway, but she said it was fine, cool beans, whatever, as long as he pitched in. So she gave him the crappy jobs she'd been putting off, like fixing the leaky kennel roofs and walking the monster St. Bernard in boarding. He didn't mind—he liked to feel useful, and he wanted Debs to like him, because I told him that she maybe murdered her husband.

One day, he showed up unannounced. I didn't even know he was there; I was too busy having my arm ripped off by a Staffie. The poor girl had locked onto my arm, which is something animals do when they're really pissed, and there's no way they're ever letting go. It's huge fun for everyone involved. It was a shame; she was such a sweet little girl when she wasn't ripping people's arms off. This dog was doing nothing to change public opinion about its breed. Melissa saw it all happen, but she just stood there screaming. If we'd been in a cartoon, she would have been on a chair with a broom.

I stayed calm, apart from trying to crowbar the dog off with my boot while telling Melissa to shut the fuck up. This is why women should always wear Doc Martens. You never know when you're going to have to defeat the Jaws of Death or kick a man in the nuts.

Eventually Debs appeared, like she'd heard something vaguely but was hoping we'd sort it out because people always needed her to solve stuff and what she really wanted was to let the dogs go and wash her hands of the whole thing. Like any good relationship, hers with the shelter was complicated, and a lot of it was wanting to run away or burn it all down. I think that's what love is. When you mostly stay.

Debs took one look at us all, then turned around and walked away. *I'm wrong about the love thing*, I thought. *She's leaving us.* But a few minutes later she came back with a frozen steak and the dog let my arm go immediately and went to the steak. Dogs are such fucking clichés. They've seen all the cartoons too.

The whole time, my boyfriend just stood off in the background watching. Taking bets, probably. It's not like I wanted him to save me or anything, but a *Hi!* might have been nice.

He did take me to the hospital. Melissa wanted to come with us, and I almost let her because I wasn't sure I wanted to be alone with him, which was a problem since we lived together, but thankfully I was in too much pain to think about it.

My arm was fine, but our relationship wasn't. The body has remarkable healing capabilities, while the mind is one big gaping wound that you keep touching until it gets all gross and infected.

On the way home, my boyfriend started going on about how I'd said I was just going to stay in this job till I figured out what I wanted to do, how I was supposed to be thinking about maybe going back to college to get my master's. He believed this because I'd lied and told him I was thinking about it, like you do in those hazy days of new love when you'll say anything to make yourself seem like someone else entirely.

I said I wasn't thinking about much right now, really, and could we stop for burgers, because I'd just had my arm almost ripped off and they'd given me some great painkillers that I knew I shouldn't have been given because I couldn't be trusted with things that made me feel like this, and he couldn't say no because of the whole almost-dying thing.

The whole time, I'm sure he was wishing I was someone else, but the joke's on him because so was I.

He got me a burger and a shake and took me home and helped me get in bed. Then he left me and went elsewhere, to look at his

porn probably, I didn't know or care, I was on awesome painkillers and had some fries left and *Supernatural* was on and sometimes all you need is some hot, demon-hunting brothers.

I still like drugs when I get to choose them. A bit of pot now and
then. A lot of alcohol. Speed a few times in college. No one wants
to be told to take anything even if it's a big, delicious bong being
shoved in your face.

The boyfriend was all about the pills—for me, anyway. He
pretended at first that I should do it for me, that I might even feel
like going back to school if I felt better. Then there'd be no stopping me—I'd get a real job and marry him and there'd be fewer
trips to the hospital. In my mind, we'd need just one last trip, but
maybe straight to the morgue, because all that normal stuff he
wanted would kill me.

My mother was just like him. She'd say things like, So-and-
so's daughter just passed the bar and it's all thanks to Prozac, because before that she didn't get out of bed! I'd tell her I've gotten
out of bed every single day, apart from those three days I had the
chicken pox when I was seven, and even then it was because *she
told me* to stay in bed.

My mother thinks I'm living a half life. Like I'm in the world
but just barely. And she's not wrong but she doesn't understand
compromise. She doesn't see me at night, curled up in front of the
TV laughing my ass off, or at work when I'm walking a dog I
really like and it's just the two of us striding out, not giving a shit

about anything and I feel the closest thing to happy. I keep my joys small and close to my chest. I'm not trading them in for anything flashier, not anytime soon.

Now that the boyfriend's gone, I'm alone with my thoughts too much. I keep trying to block them, but it's exhausting. TV lets me down constantly. If I'm watching a show and it's just not cutting it, I start trying to read something at the same time, and then I start eating, just trying to drown myself out, flood myself with something other than me.

I wish Debs would let me sleep in one of the kennels, so I'd at least feel contained.

I can't imagine what it's like living without self-doubt and its friend self-loathing. I can't imagine not questioning everything.

I read once that you're supposed to lather your hair for a full twenty seconds, and even knowing that specific information I still seem to do it wrong. Sometimes I step out of the shower and realize I haven't washed my legs and don't even know if I was supposed to. I read once that you're not supposed to over-wash your lady parts, so now I'm probably under-washing them. Showering, to me, feels like a tightrope walk: You don't look down, just stare straight ahead. Get in, get clean, get out. I'm like a shower ninja. Bodies are just another thing that can make us sad, the way they break, the way they slow us down, keep us from being free.

I imagine Melissa never thinks this way. She never takes a

shower and wonders, *Am I doing this right?* She's too busy singing some god-awful pop song. She probably gets her lady parts washed perfectly, by a flock of gentle cartoon birds.

I wonder if pills help people feel at home in their bodies. This would be a big draw for me. I don't mind feeling sad, but I don't like how my body makes me feel. If I was fully medicated, would I be the boss of me again? But then I've heard people say they feel numb, or disconnected, so I doubt it. It's as if people take things not just to make them feel better but to ward off feelings altogether. Like they assume the world will upset them. This is where I part ways with the world. It's people in the raw state—the state they're trying to block all the time—that I want to meet.

When I want to forget myself, I guess I'll stick to giant coats and alcohol.

By the third meeting there's a rhythm starting. Life can be that way sometimes, apparently, if you let it. We all know our parts, where we come in, where we stay quiet—only we're idiots, not musicians, so someone always fucks it up. Sometimes it's me. This week it's me.

These meetings have me regressing to when I was a teenager, when I used to have to prepare for what I would say in social situations. If I knew I had to talk to people, I'd stay up late the night before making notes. The first time a boy called me, I remember having a sheet of paper labeled *Stuff to talk about*, but in the end he never stopped talking, so I just made agreeable noises and laughed. That's when I learned that people are easier than you think, once you figure out how self-involved they are. I was healed by people's narcissism.

When I realized that I might be required to speak at these meetings, I wanted to have something to say. I wouldn't say it very well, there would be a lot of awkward pauses and *ums*, but I'd have a go. I'd try to be a little drunk, too, which would help.

This week, there's already an awkward silence when I arrive. Karen is in the front, sweating. Pharma Guy is sitting in his usual spot, over by the door, like a prison guard. If anyone leaves for anything other than to pee, we're going straight on the naughty list. I already feel different, and it's not because of any drugs. It's because I've had sex with someone in the room. I feel exposed but also carefree, like I give even less of a shit.

It's so quiet in the room that you can hear people in the street getting on with their lives while we're in here, stalled out entirely. Usually it takes twenty minutes or so for the awkwardness to start suffocating us all, like a scratchy sweater you're being made to wear because your grandma knitted it, even though she'll be dead soon judging by how many she still smokes and how she only eats Oreos, or at least nibbles off one cookie, licks out the middle, and leaves the other cookie by the side of the bath. The sweater she knit you is the size you were when you were twelve, but you must try to wear it even if it kills you, which it probably will. We're all dying in this sweater together. That's how these meetings feel.

Karen is rooting through her folder, trying to work out what we're supposed to be doing. Good luck to her. I'm not sure she even remembers if she drove herself here.

Suddenly I realize it's now or never, this talking thing I've been preparing for my whole life, and I open my mouth and suddenly—

So apparently February has the highest shoplifting rate!

I imagine it's quite jarring. This weird shuffling blob of a girl—at least they think I'm a girl—who mostly looks mad at everyone and rolls her eyes like a teenager, and she's definitely a drunk, or on her way to being one, and now out of nowhere she's doing some skit. I'm always surprising people, but not in a good way. Like when you weren't expecting someone to be lurking out behind the trash.

I have no control now. My mouth has taken over. I start spilling out a bunch of weird facts I read on my phone in the car before I came in. I wonder if I've been possessed by Melissa, who talks like this all the time. People are looking around, peering off into the middle distance. It's some kind of aftereffect of Christmas, I tell them, hoping the C-word will catch their interest. I'm such a freak. It would have been less embarrassing if I'd have done a striptease.

The room is quiet but prickly. I want to say, *Well, no one else was saying anything*, but I don't because someone else might start talking.

Why are you talking about shoplifting? says a girl whose name I can't remember. She's shifty looking, like she might have something concealed in her pants. I know I'm not supposed to touch anyone, but now I want to frisk her on the way out. The awkward silence is threatening to crush us all, as it does sometimes. Sometimes I wish it actually would. I should feel some kind of solidarity, an ounce of compassion at least, for my fellow happiness shirkers, but I just don't. Not yet anyway. I'm still in denial. I don't want this motley crew of miserable fucks to be my people. They probably don't even know who Mötley Crüe are.

November is the second-biggest month for shoplifters! I go on.

I'm wishing I had PowerPoint now and I fucking hate

PowerPoint. No one tries to take the floor from me, though, so I continue with whatever it is that I'm doing.

July has the lowest reported incidences of shoplifting! I say, feeling like a weather girl, only without a map to point at or good hair. I don't even know what I'm saying anymore. Never in my life have I encountered a nice chunk of silence and decided it needs filling. Usually I want to pry it open and have it swallow us all. But here I am, trying to rally the troops instead of pushing them off the cliff.

Where are you going with this? says the girl with the stolen lipstick, probably, in her bra. I've never taken anything! she says, guiltily. A guy I think is called Kevin, who looks a bit shifty, keeps staring at her, then sneaking a glance at the door. I wonder if he's actually a shoplifter and I've just rumbled him, but then again he probably feels special because a girl noticed him.

Shoplifting, medicating, it's all the same! I hear myself say, and I do a thing with my hand that I've seen other people do, like *Pfft*. I'm definitely possessed by Melissa.

A girl I think is called Sarah, and if she isn't she should be, starts to show signs of brain activity. I want to jump up and say, Yes, Sarah! You can do it!

So you're saying people are too happy in summer to shoplift, but before and after Christmas they're miserable? Sarah says.

Attagirl! I say, because I can't help myself. I'm suddenly feeling the fuzziest I've felt in here without sugar or alcohol. Anyone observing this meeting would assume my meds had kicked in, but I think I was just bored and looking to start trouble.

So . . . you're saying there's a link, Karen says. I'd forgotten there even was a Karen. Karen, the one who's supposed to be running this show but most weeks can't really be bothered, and no one can blame her, as this little gig is clearly punishment for something. I always know what I deserve punishment for, but what on earth could Karen have done? It's that tiny air of mystery that keeps me coming back each week. In an age when most people Instagram their vaginas, I like people who keep a little something back.

Is this school? says a guy called Danny or Dan or D—no, Brian, it's Brian, it says so right there on his backpack in Magic Marker. Because I hated school, he says, and this seems a lot like school. *Me too, Brian*, I want to say, but that feels like bonding, so I just glare.

Totally, someone else says—about the school thing, not about the fascinating statistical information I'd chosen to share.

For some reason, I'd thought this would be the night when I'd contribute. I just thought I would try something different. I was opening myself up to new things, just the way this whole thing was supposed to work. I wanted to see if there were any signs of life in these husks of people. I thought Karen at least would appreciate it. I was definitely not doing it to appear smart to any man. At least I know now people don't care about facts. Maybe next week someone could teach us how to break into a car.

I thought we could talk about anything we wanted in these meetings, I say. I didn't really think that, but things were getting desperate.

I look to Tim. Tim is one of the only people in the room I consider normal. He might even be a freak like me. Tim seems to come here because he wants to tell someone, anyone, about the latest thing his cat did or didn't do. He didn't shit once for a week, apparently—the cat, not Tim. I've been trying to get him to bring the cat with him one week, mostly so I could just sit in the corner and pet the cat instead of interacting with people. But Tim seems preoccupied. In desperation I look over at this other guy, a skinny guy with an almost-quiff who looks like prescription meds are the least of his worries, but he just shrugs at me.

But by now it's clear I've agitated everyone with my weird talk of shoplifting, and Karen decides to end things early. Seeing Karen grow some balls immediately brightens the mood, and people start gathering their shit and leaving, but not without throwing me plenty of dirty looks. I'm guessing they're all secret shoplifters and think I'm there to narc them out.

Just as I'm leaving, Karen corners me. Don't make this harder than it already is, Janet, she says. Some people want to be here. It's the kind of thing only someone getting paid to be there would say.

Okay, I get it, I say, holding my hands up.

If not for me, for the others, she says. And I understand. All she really needed to say was, Soon, Janet, you will be one of us and this will be easier. *One of us. One of us.*

We're all there for the same reason, I guess, which is that none of us wants to take pills. That's the official line, anyway: We're the resisters. We need to be rounded up and head-counted and monitored for at least an hour a week in some fusty church hall with stale snacks and the local Karen at the helm. But these people's sadness doesn't seem anything like mine. I feel protective of my own sadness, suddenly, as if it might somehow be under threat. I'm not dismissive of their individual stories; it's more that I'm bent on preserving mine. If I should let anyone in, open up about myself, I'll be one step closer to wanting the everyday pills—which of course has been their plan all along. Put us in a room with the people who would most irritate us, drive us to distraction, then offer us the everyday pill at our moment of weakness.

I button up—in a hurry, like I have someplace to be—and head for the door. I leave fast, before Pharma Guy has a chance to say anything. He'll probably go home with Karen, and I'm fine with that.

I'm almost safe in my car, back in my own world, when Pharma Guy approaches. I can't run him over, because then everyone will know I slept with him.

Hey, he says.

Hey, I say.

So I got the name of that lady, he says.

That lady? I say. What lady?

You know, *the* lady, he says, glancing back at the meeting, and I get it. I'd forgotten I asked him. I had erased that whole night.

Oh great, I say, hoping he isn't going to ask me for something in return.

It's Vyla Shirk, he says.

Thank you, I say. That's not a name, is what I want to say. I don't, but I'm thinking it. I still don't really believe she is a real person; it's all just some bullshit origin story created by some marketing team.

But now she has a name.

Maybe he made it up, the name, I think as I drive away. Because he knows I won't be able to find anything out about her. If he did, it was kind of a sweet thing to do. And I have to admit he's good at making up names.

When I get home, I lie on the couch facedown for a while, then watch *Home Alone*, because I'm home alone, and maybe a child. I don't feel Christmassy as such, but I don't feel not-Christmassy.

Watching movies now makes me think of my boyfriend. We fought about movies a lot. Not the way most couples do, about what movie to see or what a movie was about, and you don't tell him you're only there for the snacks, but he knows it anyway. We fought about old movies: he wanted to watch them, and I didn't. He loved watching old movies—from the eighties, not the fifties. Even movies from the nineties were somehow cool again, which is quite a trick since they were never cool to start with. The problem was, the movies made me cry, even ones that weren't supposed to, and I couldn't explain it to him. They all took me back to when I first saw them, when I was someone else, all those feelings I had back then about how I thought the world might be and who I might be in it. All of that was destroyed now, somehow, leaving only whatever I was now. One time he asked me why I was crying, and I said it was because I still didn't have a hoverboard, but I was lying. It was an extreme reaction, but I couldn't help it. I was sure things would be better by now. They tell you things will get better. They lie. Things will just be shitty in a different way.

Music is the same way. It makes me feel things I don't want to feel, so I don't listen to it much. I can't afford those kinds of thoughts if I have to get up every day, and I have to get up every day.

I don't like anything making me cry. I want to be in control of my emotions. I need to be in control at all times.

Before I go to sleep, I google the name *Vyla Shirk*. She doesn't exist, at least not on the internet, and instantly I'm in love with her. Hi, I want to say, I also don't exist on the internet. As opposed to my mother, for instance, who exists mostly on some online Jazzercise forum.

I add the words *mall Santa* to *Vyla Shirk*, but nothing. I try *mall Santa* on its own and I get all sorts of porn, which is my own fault.

Then I try googling the head of the pharmaceutical company, Mr. Big Pharma himself, Richard Grossman. A photo pops up: a middle-aged man who looks like a potato. He's a goddamn hero, the pharma bros are saying. Nobody says much about Vyla. She's mentioned in passing, but never by name. They only tell us the backstory so we're more susceptible, because everyone believes in love, or so they think.

I look at the potato-faced man, who looks like every creepy

man I've ever met, and I think about Vyla. She was right to run off with that mall Santa, I think, especially if the sex is anything like all the mall-Santa porn I just saw.

Sugar Plums would make a great male stripper name, I think, and fall asleep.

The next day at work I intend to walk the shit out of the dogs and get out of my head. The dogs don't know all the ways I'm messing up and don't care.

My favorite part of my job is walking the dogs. If you've ever seen a dog's face when someone says the word *walkies* or jangles a leash, you know what those sounds mean to a dog. It breaks my heart how excited dogs are at the mere idea of being taken for a walk.

Then again, imagine not being able to walk yourself. Imagine having to be walked.

Walks are always my favorite part of the day. Melissa tries to spoil them by trying to go with me, so I have to get around her by walking the dogs who don't play well with others. Which suits me fine, because I can relate. Also, the walks give me a chance to get out of my own head for a while. Usually I go too far *into* my own head, just to stay out of the world, so it's a nice change of scenery.

Today, when I get back, Melissa is standing there grinning. Did you have a good walk? she asks. As if you can have a bad walk. Maybe if you're being chased by someone, sure, but mostly walks are good. They're pure. Yes, thanks, I say, but then I realize she's talking to the dog.

The walks do give me some joy, but I don't see it as joy, exactly. It's closer to peace, maybe. Walking with a dog is the closest thing to free, for me and the dog. We forget about the leash and the clock and the fact that eventually I'll have to return the dog and go back to the world.

Melissa follows me inside. They were talking about your pill on my radio show, she says. My ears prick up naturally at this. She follows me to the bathroom, but I'm just washing my hands, so I don't tell her to go away. I want to hear more, obviously. I know my pill is all over the news, but I don't watch the news. Until Vyla surfaces, I'm not that interested.

There was some pastor, she says, and some man from the drug company. One lady called in and said, What will they come up with next, a birthday pill? She laughs, and I don't, because that was my idea.

And? I say.

And what? she says.

And what was the verdict? I say, worrying that she turned over to some Christian rock channel and I'll never know what the world thinks of me.

Most people think it's great, she says. I mean, don't you? We all just want everyone to be happy, don't we?

She's such a moron. I want to ask her all the obvious questions: Didn't anyone call in and say maybe pills aren't the answer? Is it possible that we just shouldn't care as much—not just about the holidays, but about whether everyone we know is happy?

Everyone's sad now, it's a fact, so why keep pushing us all to be something else? I don't ask her any of these things.

Sure, I say.

When I leave work that night, I don't want to go home—I'm too worried that I'll start drinking, or worse, thinking—so I take myself to the movies. The theater is filled with people who are out for the night with other people, and they look at me like I'm pathetic, but I don't feel pathetic. I just feel like a moviegoer.

19

The next day, Pharma Guy shows up at the shelter with his girl-friend. He's obviously shocked to see me; I'm obviously shocked to see her. He's uncomfortable at the sight of me, for a second—like most people; I look like how hard life is—but he quickly pretends we've never met, and I return the favor.

Later he'll probably say, *Remember, I told you about her.*

I'm not even mad, just numb.

He definitely didn't tell me. I would have remembered. I don't do sleeping with other people's boyfriends. I don't even do sleeping with my boyfriend if I can help it. So the fact that he's made me someone who sleeps with other people's boyfriends—without my consent—makes me super mad.

I feel sad for his girlfriend. She doesn't look awful. I feel sad for him that I'm the person he cheated with. I feel sad for all of us because we will never understand why any of these things happen, but they do, and we push them down and keep going until we can't anymore.

I really wish I'd stolen that turtle now. It was the only thing that hasn't made me sad in a while, and it's a lump of plastic.

We're looking for a dog, she tells me, his girlfriend, and I think, *No shit, because that's pretty much our thing here.* I wonder what's wrong with the one they have; I thought he seemed pretty great. I want to say, But you have a dog, but I can't, because then she'll know I slept with her future husband, which sounds like a rom-com I would totally watch.

Pharma Guy's phone goes off, and he excuses himself to answer it, so I start the tour without him. I think about making her take home a dog I know will probably maul her in her sleep, but I don't even like him enough to bother.

His girlfriend has great legs. I wonder if the dogs notice or care. I don't see real-life human-lady legs very often. We're always covered up here, even in the summer. I see them on TV, but I don't believe they're real. I don't trust anyone who looks like they don't have any stretch marks. This girl looks like she probably doesn't. She'll probably spend her whole pregnancy rubbing cocoa butter all over herself like she's meat.

As we're walking down to my block, she lowers her voice. This dog idea is just to test the waters, she says. You know, *before a baby.* You know, a lot of serial killers had dogs, I want to say, but I don't. I don't get it—she's acting like having a dog is a totally new idea to her. *But your boyfriend already has a dog!* I want to say. What is happening here? Has she never been to his apartment? Or did she make him get rid of it, so he can start over with her? The number of people who dump their dogs when they start a family is truly astounding.

Before we get to my block, she sees a dog in Melissa's that looks like the one she had growing up. I've lost a sale, but at least it allows me to palm her off on Melissa and sneak back to my hole, where I won't be seen again till they're gone.

Later, I tell Melissa who he is. I want her to know what sort of home she's sending her dog off to.

Did you know about the fiancée? she asks, confirming her low opinion of me.

I did not, I tell her, but I'm not sure she believes me.

Then she surprises me by saying he was good-looking, and I suddenly remember that we're like women on a prison island who haven't seen men for years, and sometimes just a whiff of Lynx body spray does funny things to us.

It's nearly December. Christmas is almost definitely happening. There's no backing out now.

Every year, around this time, I hope everyone will be as exhausted by the prospect of the holidays as I am and we'll just do a half-assed Christmas, where we mostly lie around in sweat pants, eating whatever's within reach, and there is no performance. Shouting at the TV is the new singing songs round the piano, anyway, and everyone knows it—even the mums who are always trying to get everyone to sing round the piano, like they've just watched *Little Women* but forgotten that one of them dies.

But it's never like that. Even when everyone seems like they're wilting and might fuck it off, they somehow spring back to life as soon as Christmas is in sight. Like Nosferatu in the shadows, ready to descend. Like a plant you think is dead because you definitely did everything necessary to kill it but somehow it's still alive. People came back from the dead for Christmas the same way. The same goes for relationships—even the ones you thought were dead and buried suddenly perk up and demand you water them.

When you're a kid, of course, Christmas is all laid out for you. You don't have to do shit. It's all about tradition and ritual, and you rely on the grown-ups in your life to make sure everything happens as it should. They tell you they're doing it all for you, so you'll have a great childhood, but really they're doing it because they *didn't* have a great childhood, but somewhere along the way all that sadness swells up, and you're not supposed to see it, but it's there. By then you're fifteen and it's suffocating you, so you start telling everyone it's all bullshit, and no one appreciates you pointing it out because *It's Christmas, Janet.*

Then, finally, you reach the age when you realize you don't have to do any of it anymore, if you don't want to. You were probably doing it for longer than you wanted to, just because you thought you should. And it seems like a flash of genius, of clarity, that you don't have to do it anymore.

But what if you do want to, it's just that you don't feel it? That's how it is with most relationships, and I think maybe that's how it is with holidays too.

All the things adults do—the jobs, the homes, the families, the organized activities—are things I just can't do. I want to, but I can't. The boyfriend, he thought I could. Maybe I should have appreciated that more—that he had this hope in me that I don't have. I genuinely don't think it was that he wanted me to be something I'm not. I think he thought that if he believed I could do it, then he could do it too, and then we'd both be doing it. I miss that hope he had in me. Other things—like the fact that he thought that lying down on my back in bed was my way of signaling that he could mount me—I don't miss. Now I sleep in whatever position I want, when I sleep at all.

But I still have to do Christmas somehow.

My mum's number pops up on the landline. I never answer the landline, but it keeps ringing, and then she texts me, Answer the phone Janet. So I pick up.

When the boyfriend lived here, he would answer the phone and it would annoy the hell out of me. It might be something important, Janet, he said. It never was. I always hated the idea of someone calling me at home because it meant they knew I'd be there. I want to be seen, but at the same time I want to be invisible.

Still, my mother always calls on the landline, and I know I should be grateful to hear her voice, but as soon as she speaks, I remember why I left.

Janet, you've poisoned your father, she says.

What do you mean, *poisoned*? I ask.

Not literally poisoned, she says. But you've poisoned him with your words. Or with your ways, I forget which. All I know is that she's angry because my father still hasn't thought about making the Christmas cake and somehow, I'm to blame.

It needs to age, Janet, she says, and I think, *You're aging us all*.

He said he doesn't feel like it yet! she yells at me. Like I'm the one who invented the idea that you could not feel like doing things. Where else does this come from? she yells. When has he ever not felt like it before?

I don't know, I say. I didn't say anything to him, if that's what you're getting at. He's his own person, I say, knowing full well this hasn't been true since he met my mother.

You need to fix this, she says before hanging up.

I call my dad. Which scares him to death, I'm sure, because daughters don't call their dads up out of the blue unless they're dying or pregnant or—worse—need money.

Mum said you haven't done the cake or something because you didn't feel like it, I say, throwing my mum under the bus. I do this to soften the blow, because I actually do need money, and if he's just mad at her, not me, he's bound to send me some money because he's glad I'm not dying or pregnant.

There's time, he says. I take this to mean he isn't unwell, as my mother thinks, and also I'm not the troublemaker, as she thinks.

It's okay not to feel like it, I tell him. Talking about not feeling is as close as we've ever come to talking about feelings.

It's not okay, he says, it's awful. I don't know how you do it. And I hear something in his voice that no daughter ever wants to hear in their dad's voice: The sound of despair. The sound of when you've taken on a sadness that isn't your own, one you don't have a place for. One you don't have words for. It's the kind of sound helpline volunteers must hear all the time, the kind specially trained dogs can smell a mile off.

Maybe I'm just bloated, he says, and to be honest he does sound a little gassy.

Maybe, I say, hopefully.

That next weekend I go over to my parents' to do some laundry, which I hardly ever do, but really I'm checking up on my father. I find him in the kitchen making the cake.

Felt like it? I say, kissing his floury forehead.

Not really, he grumbles, but your mother was nagging.

He did feel something, though, whether he liked it or not. I start to feel something too—only it's the opposite of festive, it's the desire to flee, to abandon them all. It's not their fault, it's just who I am. It wasn't their fault, it was never that bad living in their house, but live in someone else's domain for too long, and you're bound to suffocate eventually. I wasn't the daughter they wanted, in the same way they weren't the people they thought they'd turn out to be. Their solution was to put on a huge song-and-dance for the holidays and hope it was enough to convince everyone otherwise. Mine was to flee.

Week four of my meeting. You'd think I'd know people's names now, but I don't. I know Karen, and I know the pharma guy who likes his balls squeezed. That's about it.

Unless there's a war or an apocalypse, Christmas is happening, but even then, it would find a way. It's like Japanese knotweed, which we have at the shelter. It's the least of our worries, until it tries to strangle a dog.

The purpose of these meetings is supposed to be to give us a place to share our experiences, but really they're a way for the pharma guys to monitor us. They want to know the pills are working and not doing any weird shit they shouldn't be. We're constantly being encouraged to report any negative side effects because they don't want a lawsuit, but I'm pretty sure they're going to get one anyway. Not from me, though. I could turn blue, or wake up and not feel my legs, and I'd still keep it to myself.

There's a girl at my meeting who thinks everything is a side effect of the pills. It's exhausting but also amusing. She might be the only reason I keep going. She's told us all several things that she's also told the drug company—probably weeping into the phone in the middle of the night, after she got no joy from telling her mum and cat and the spider that lives in her shower, which she keeps there just to give her an audience. If she ever invites me over, I'll pretend I need to pee so that I can go in and free that spider.

Last week, she told the whole meeting that she thought her socks felt scratchier than normal. We all had to hear about her usual experience of socks, then her current experience, which was less than satisfactory. I offered that I was a fan of no socks at all, which didn't help, but then I wasn't trying to.

The week before that, she told us that she thought the blue M&M's tasted like the red ones now. Which she illustrated by bringing in a load so that we could watch her eat them and pull a face. She didn't even offer us any.

This week she tells us they've changed her hair dye, but she thinks it's Santa's Little Helper that's changing her color, not the dye, and she wants one of us to go to the drugstore with her to check. No one offers. Instead we just slump down into our chairs and look at our phones, wondering if there are any drugs whose side effects include making her disappear.

Karen is very tolerant of this girl—of me too, for that matter. I think that's why they hired her.

Sometimes I want to know more about Karen. I picture us in a bar one night. So, what's your story? I say. What makes Karen Karen? I am very drunk and maybe have my arm around her. She thinks maybe I'm coming on to her, and maybe I am. I'm lonely too, Karen, I might say. I know she's here for the money, but I suspect it's also for the company.

As for the pharma guy? He seems totally indifferent. Every time I glance over in his direction, he's looking at me.

I don't think the people at my meeting want to make friends, particularly. It's almost enough to make me want to make friends with them.

I get the impression they want to come here without anyone seeing them, and then go back to being invisible as soon as Karen says we're done. They aren't bad, as people go, but it's still weird to think of seeing one of them outside of group.

A week or two ago I did see one of them—Carl, I want to say?—in a store. We just pretended we hadn't seen each other. It was perfect. I've gotten in trouble in the past for doing that, because most people don't like it. Most people need acknowledging. I'm not so fussed.

Is that one of your friends from your meetings? Debs joked

once when we stopped for gas and some creepy dude in a bandana said hi to me.

Probably, I said, but he wasn't. I couldn't be in a room with anyone in a bandana.

When I was little, I loved to lie awake and hear life going on around me. My folks watching *Law & Order* and rowing about something I'd done. The woman next door stumbling in after another bad date. A bar down the road. The distant sound of the highway. The sounds of other people allowed to stay up late and live exciting nighttime lives, as I saw them. *One day that will be me,* I thought. I'm still listening to life going on around me, but now I want them all to shut the fuck up so I can sleep.

Another girl at the meeting keeps saying she feels worse than ever. The pills are never going to work for me, she says. She wants to stop taking them. Karen reminds her it takes a few weeks. I don't say anything. But I'm tempted to corner her, later, and tell her that she should definitely stop taking them, that I've heard they make you really fat. I want to see what happens if you stop taking them.

Karen just keeps saying it'll take time and distracting us with stupid questions. What's your favorite holiday movie? she says, and all the bros say, *Die Hard* and all the girls say, *Love Actually.* I tell them mine is *Santa Paws 4: The Revenge,* but they don't seem aware of it, maybe because I made it up.

Afterward, the pharma guy corners me.

I split up with my fiancée, he says.

Why? I say. I almost mention something about her legs, but give me some credit.

She wanted me to get rid of my dog, he says.

How about I take your dog and you keep the fiancée, I want to say.

Well, that's up to you, I say instead.

Melissa makes us hang lights in the office, and we know she's building up to us getting a tree. I get the impression that, before we came along, Debs barely acknowledged that other people existed in the world, let alone that they celebrate Christmas. When you're knee-deep in dog shit, it's hard to remember what time of year it is.

Melissa wants us to let her play Christmas music, but we like the radio. That way we'll know when there's an apocalypse. Please, god, let there be an apocalypse.

The theatrics of the season have started. It reminds me of my childhood, when I had to get on the Christmas train or get out of the way. I always opted for getting run over.

The lights are pretty, but they always are, it's not their fault. I'd love someone to switch me on like that and watch me be just what I was meant to be.

I'm standing there, looking at the lights with a funny expression, thinking about being a light and not a Janet, when Debs walks by.

She looks at me like, *You're so fucking weird, Janet.*

I make a face like, *What can you do? I'm trying.*

20

Debs tells her kids they should write letters to Mrs. Claus instead of Santa. That she's the one who should get the milk and cookies, because she obviously does all the hard work while her fat husband gets all the credit. Every Christmas movie they try to watch, she switches it off, wants to know when Mrs. Claus is going to leave that jackass, maybe run off with an elf, where's *that* movie? They snicker at her calling Santa a jackass, but they're used to it. I almost want to go see Santa at the mall with them, just to see if they tell him what their mum said.

The kids tell me they can't bring their friends home over the holidays. They say Debs is trying to ruin Christmas with her feminism, only they're too little to say things right, so it comes out as fenemism.

I like it that her kids think I don't feel the same way their mother does. I'm plenty feminist, but if I was their mother, I wouldn't ruin them in exactly the same way. Christmas does funny things to people—softens them—but not Debs. I'm half expecting her to wait up for Santa herself, shotgun ready.

On the first of December, I get mauled by a dog. Mauled again, that is, and this time bad enough to need stitches. There's no audience this time, thank fuck. Better us than some kid, Debs always says, and I know she's right, but the pain in my arm is insane.

The dog responsible is Jasper. He's a pain in my ass—he's my Janet. He's a German shepherd, though, and Debs will not allow anyone to trash-talk a German shepherd. He could bite my arm clean off and she'd say, What did you do, Janet? If Debs won the lottery, she'd tell us all to fuck off and retire to her own little German shepherd sanctuary, only none of the dogs would be up for adoption, they'd all be her babies and sleep in her bed.

This time, when I got mauled, for some unknown reason Melissa calls my mum and tells her to meet us at the hospital. I think it's because she knows there's no one else in my life anymore, so it makes me doubly mad. Once we find one another, the three of us just stand there agog, like we've just won the shittiest contest.

As soon as my mother's distracted by some woman with a crying baby—probably trying to steal it—I turn to Melissa. I'm a grown-ass woman, Melissa, why did you call my mum? Before she can answer me, my mum is back and talking. She talks constantly. Visit her house and she's already there in the drive when you pull up, talking before you get out of the car. When you leave, she'll be back outside, still talking.

You're a grown woman, Janet, why did you call your mother about this? she says.

We both look at Melissa, who's standing there smiling like she's just reunited a mother with her lost daughter.

I think we're done here, a nurse says, handing me some after-care stuff I already have at home because this has happened before and will happen again. Maybe next time we can invite a new boyfriend, or my dad.

I'm supposed to be getting my hair done, my mother says—to Melissa, I think, because she knows I don't care about those things. I need to go gift shopping, she says, and I'm looking for the exit. For your father, she says, knowing that's how to get me.

Yes, I say. Fine, I say. She is silent, but I know she is shocked.

She doesn't say, *It's Christmas, Janet*, because she knows she's not allowed to bug me about it yet. I have a few weeks before the madness kicks in.

I'm sure she drove home screaming.

When we get back, Debs is pissed.

Did you really all need to go? she says, looking at Melissa. She even invited my mum! I tell her. For fuck's sake, Melissa, what's wrong with you? she says. I feel bad for Melissa then, because there isn't really much wrong with her. It's the rest of us.

It's week five of my meeting. I know because people keep reminding me Christmas is coming, like it's something bad and I'd better hide. Only this year I promised I wouldn't.

It's the most wonderful time of the year, apparently, but when you work at a dog shelter it's hard to tell. Melissa has started humming carols nonstop; she tried singing them out loud, but we put a stop to that. So she settles for humming while she cleans up dog vomit. When we open to the public, everything has to be super clean and shiny and happy. This is a problem, but we know it's necessary if we're going to find homes for any dogs.

Sales is a huge part of my job, and I'm not good at it, but I still shift as many dogs as Melissa. She's so aggressive, most people leave wanting a cat. When people come, I'm supposed to greet them and show them around, like it's a store, try to get them to take a dog home with them, but I'm not great at people, so I mostly hide in the storeroom. I give all my dogs a pep talk before we open, encouraging them to sell themselves. It's hard to tell them not to bark at strange men, though, when I want to myself.

There's a warning on the staff room whiteboard reminding us that we must leave no dog turds visible to the public. As if ours are magical dogs who don't shit. I think if you want a dog you have to know you're going to have to pick up a lot of shit. For that matter, you should know that one day that dog will die and you'll need to come on back for another. I'm under strict orders from Debs to not mention dying in front of the customers, though, so they're on their own.

When we open for the public, any dogs who can't control their bowels or bark too aggressively are kept in their stalls. This only makes them extra stressed, which means we have extra shit to deal with. Sometimes we manage to get some unlucky volunteer to take them for a really long walk. I always hope they slip their collars and escape. I would.

Whenever we think we're on top of things, a litter of puppies comes in and fucks us over because they take so much work. They make Christmas harder, because people want puppies as gifts and we always tell them no. If you really want one, we tell them, come back after Christmas. Inevitably, they go and buy one from some janky breeder—and then we get that puppy too, when they realize it's wrong in the head.

The last thing I want to deal with today is a pile of puppies, but what do you know. This lot was found in a trash bag, apparently, which is nice. We have no space, but Debs takes them, and soon we're turning the office into a puppy pen.

Puppies have this smell. It's like all known bodily fluids mixed together and then left out in the sun. It's soft and hard, like sex and death. It's like babies, I guess. Puppies smell of life. It's somehow both disgusting and irresistible. We all get excited when we get a new lot—even me—because we've forgotten what hard work they are. Even Debs, the only person deader inside than me, gets excited for a millisecond before she remembers the horror, the horror! It's also impossible to keep her kids from falling in love with them all before she breaks their hearts by telling them they can't keep any of them.

The thing about puppies is, they can be little shits. They look cute, but until you've been in a room alone with a dozen of them all skidding around in their own mess, trying to clamber up your leg, biting and scratching you with their little razor teeth and nails, you have no idea. There's a desperation in them, a vulnerability, like they want to claw their way inside you, because out here is some messed-up shit.

I can relate.

Once, when I was mad at the boyfriend about something, I told him we had some puppies at the shelter and he should come by and play with them. They ripped him to shreds.

Puppies do get homes quickly, though—because every idiot loves a puppy—which just makes me feel bad for the old-timers. I always want to tell the dog-shoppers, Listen, if you want something that'll poop on you and bite you, look no further than Grandpa over here. The old-timers are my favorite. If they're missing a limb or eye, even better. These are my people. They are the reason I get up every morning, even if they barely know I'm there.

Still, puppies are a welcome distraction when Christmas has its hands round our throats. You will give in, Janet, it says, pushing harder, and I can feel myself letting go. And then a puppy scratches me in the eye and I'm back in the room.

I never want to go to my meetings, but I really don't want to go tonight. The puppies have taken every last bit of energy I had.

I thought I would have given in to it all by now, a little, but I haven't. The more the holiday pressure mounts, the more I resist.

It doesn't help that my mum texted me yesterday to ask how it was going. I made it quite clear from the start that she wasn't allowed to bug me about these pills, but she couldn't help herself. She even asked if I'd met anyone special. I was tempted to tell her about the pharma guy, but I knew she'd just say, Oh, Janet, why do you always have to complicate things?, and I'd say, because it's what I do best.

I hate that the meetings aren't so bad. I've become great at just shutting down when I get there, and when I get out I feel good because I've done something I fear. I'm like a dog, more scared of you than you are of me.

But tonight I don't want to go. I just want to go home, eat my body weight in potatoes and butter, and pass out. Who needs drugs when there are potatoes? I take extra long finishing my jobs at work, and Debs finds me brushing a dog within an inch of its life.

Death by brushing, that's a new one, she says, leaning on the kennel door. Haven't you got that thing of yours tonight?

I do, I say.

Well, I can't tell you where to go, she says, but you can't stay here. She takes the brush away from me and pushes me out of the kennel.

We walk up to the office. I can see she wants to lock up and get on with her evening, but she doesn't quite say goodbye.

So, how's that going? she asks.

Well, I say, how would you like to be forced to spend time with a group of miserable fucks who're supposed to be *people like you*? I'm hoping she'll understand—the whole reason we're both here is that the only people we like are dogs—but no such luck, because it's late and she's tired and her kids need feeding and she hasn't got the mindspace right now for anything else.

I'm not your mum, Janet, she says, but I'd just keep at it if I were you. We all need to get on with our lives.

I want to cry. I want to cry and follow her inside her house like a puppy and curl up by her feet while she does her mum duties, and maybe later when she's done she might stroke the soft spot behind my ears and it might be okay for us all.

But I'm a human woman, so I just say, Yes, boss, and head off to my meeting.

There is a definite change in the room this week. People are humming at a different frequency. Someone brought in sugar cookies, and they look like shit, but there's enough sugar in them to make your brain forget they're essentially little drug delivery systems.

There have been some developments. It's been five weeks now, so that's no surprise. I still don't know anyone's names, but some people have bonded. I wonder what's wrong with me, but only for a second before I remember how my brain is wired.

People really seem to be getting down with the whole Christmas thing. People are whipping out their phones, checking their calendars, talking about leaving early; it's as though everyone has somewhere else to be. Shopping or caroling or whatever it is that normal people do this time of year.

The only one killing the mood is Brian, who says he's been getting the shakes most mornings. Karen says that's just his body getting used to the meds. She doesn't ask how much coffee he drinks, but I'm guessing it's a lot.

One thing is obvious: we're all very sweaty. Some people think it's the drugs, but I know it's the sweaters, and the busted AC, and the stress.

Someone asks me if I've done all my shopping yet and I tell them I need toilet paper, which confuses them, so they laugh and say, Oh, Janet, you're hilarious, and I think, *Maybe I am?*

Karen has a new haircut, but no one mentions it. I feel sad for her, but not quite enough to say anything about it either.

The pharma guy is not here. For a second, I think it's because of me, but then I remember what my mother said once about how things aren't always about me, on my birthday probably.

Karen asks if anyone is having any problems, and of course the girl with all the side effects raises her hand. Only this time her problems are not with the medication but with her mother.

For once, Karen tells her that's not what she meant.

Everyone seems to be getting on well.

The pharma guy shows up late and waves and says sorry and sits by the door like he usually does, pretending to be writing stuff in his sitcom notebook. At one point I glance toward the door longingly, just as he happens to be looking up, and I think he thinks I'm looking at him longingly, but I'm not, and I feel bad for us both, but I don't smile because I don't want to be a tease, so I shrug and he just looks back down.

On the way home, I stop to get a double order of mozzarella sticks and I eat them in a car park and cry because it's all too hard. Tomorrow I'll get up and do it again.

The next day, my mother texts me.

Will you come to the mall with me? Mum x

I appreciate the x, I know it's hard for her.

She knows I'm supposed to be able to do this now: Go to the mall at Christmas with my mother without wanting to murder her. It was on the TV ad. The girl who was me, but with better everything, was shown out in the world with her TV mum shopping and saying hi to Santa. It was some fucked-up shit. *Good luck with that*, I remember thinking. *There is no pill strong enough.*

This is the first year my mother has ever even dared to ask. I'm starting to think this pill was invented by mothers to get their daughters back.

I text her back: when?

Saturday, she replies. I should have known.

It's the ultimate test: Saturday at the mall, two weeks before Christmas. I won't be surprised if this is all part of the experiment and I get a point for every holiday activity I complete successfully. Truth is, I like my malls abandoned. Even teenagers don't really want to go there anymore, they're drawn to them out of some bullshit programming about what being a teenager means.

There isn't enough space in a text box for me to remind my mother of all the failed shopping trips in our shared history. All those back-to-school outings that caused so much pain, just to find a sweater. I feel sad for all those sweaters. I assume parents today just buy shit for their kids online and save themselves the heartache.

My mother? She still believes in making memories in person, even the traumatic ones.

I didn't know why things were so difficult with my mother. The mall was always supposed to act as a buffer for us, but it only highlighted how impossible our relationship was. She couldn't make it either, which was why she took all those pills, but she'd pretend she could till she died. Sometimes I think she was secretly proud of me for resisting, for not even pretending. But not this time. Not when we have important gift buying to do, and Christmas right around the corner, ready to suffocate us all.

Melissa asks what I'm doing on my Saturday off. We only get one a month. I was never really that into them. People make such a big deal about the weekend, like it's going to save us all, and has it ever?

When I had a boyfriend, we spent Saturdays doing the usual couple stuff, as if we were obliged to. We always picked going to the movies, because they didn't require much of us, and it felt like we were together because we were sitting next to each other, even if we were miles away in our heads. Sometimes in the dark I would put my hand on his knee, because I could, but if he put his hand on my knee it would be too much. We would emerge bleary-eyed, like, *What just happened?*, and we'd go somewhere to eat, and then we'd go home and drift apart again. We'd done the bare minimum to keep us together another week. It was desperately sad.

I tell Melissa I'm going to the mall with my mother. Just saying it brings up bile in my throat. Melissa immediately goes all heart-eyes, telling me about every trip to the mall she's ever taken, not just with her mother but with anyone.

I took my daughter to see Santa there last week, she says.

I'm not seeing Santa, I say, but I know I can't avoid him forever.

She laughs because of course I'm not seeing Santa, I'm a grown-ass woman.

I want to say, *You can go instead if you like*, but I know I can't.

Saturday comes around too quickly.

As a joke, I root around in my closet and dress up like the girl in the drug ad, but it's all lost on my mother. She tells me to meet her in the pharmacy beforehand—she needs hand lotion urgently, like if she goes one minute longer with her dry old-lady hands she'll die. Right there in the drugstore there's a poster for my pill, with Model Me wearing the same shirt and jeans, and I stand right next to it, but even then she doesn't see.

Those posters shouldn't even be up now, I think. I mean, even if you do want in, at this stage it's way too late. Maybe they're trying to soften up candidates for next year.

My mother asks if I need anything. She means hand lotion, or tampons, and I probably do, but having her buy them for me is weird. The old me might have said something snotty, like, *A happy childhood*, but it's Christmas and I'm really trying not to be a bitch. And I don't really even believe in happiness, technically, so actually I'm good, thanks. Some gum, maybe.

Why did you bring that coat? she says, looking at my overcoat like it's made of an actual dead dog.

Because it's winter, I say.

But we're indoors, she says, then realizes that this isn't the time, that she's got me here now, and just shakes her head and heads out onto the sidewalk, talking about all the things she still has to buy and do before the big day, like it's a wedding.

She's walking and talking with tremendous purpose, but not going into any stores, and I'm just thinking about what I can scrounge up to eat to make this all worth it.

I made some Christmas cookies, I tell her.

She stops dead, and a woman and her child walk straight into us. You did? she says, mouth open.

I don't tell her that I ate them all that night, all by myself. I think I was supposed to take them to work, or to a neighbor, or to eat just one myself before giving the rest away, and I definitely think I was supposed to be listening to carols and not Metallica when I was doing it. But I made them, so take that, everyone who thinks I'm totally dead inside.

I start walking again, and she catches up to me. She starts telling me more shit she needs to buy and do, but this fails to hold my attention, so she tells me I look nice, which is a lie. I don't return the compliment, but it doesn't matter, because she volunteers that she thinks she doesn't look that bad for a woman of her age. I smile and think about food. If that's not getting down with the holiday spirit, I don't know what is. Christmas is working its magic, helping me to hold my tongue. I just wish it would hold my mother's shopping bags, which are full of crap she's bought for people I didn't even know were people, cousins I swear she's making up just to highlight how empty my life is.

We walk into the Gap, and I walk straight out. She doesn't

even notice. Twenty minutes later, she comes out with a bag and says, Underpants! For your father. I don't know why men can't buy underpants on their own but they can't. Then the Gap is the existential hole in all of us hiding in plain sight. I let her drag me into some women's clothes store. She pretends to be looking for something to wear for some party, saying, This is nice?, and holding it up against me, and I keep saying, For you, yes. Then she tuts and says, If I had your figure I'd wear all sorts of things. She hasn't seen my figure in years. She has no idea what's going on with it and never will. Finally I tell her a really ugly dress is great and she buys it and thinks we've bonded.

At one point, I ask her why my brother never has to do this kind of thing with her. My brother, a stranger mostly, who I see on holidays and at interventions, is smarter than I am, and moved a good few hours away, which proves it. He likes cakes, that's all I know about him.

Because he has his own family, she says, and it hurts because it's supposed to.

I help her pick out a sweater for my father. He'll like it as much as he ever likes a sweater, which is not that much. He doesn't want gifts. He wants a different family, perhaps, or better still, to be out at sea alone.

It feels like I've been there for hours—it's only been one—and I can feel Old Janet creeping back in, like the magic is wearing off. Finally I get her to buy me a disgusting Christmas pretzel, covered with red and green icing and glitter, which I proceed to get in my hair. My stomach makes a noise like, *This isn't food, Janet.* My mother watches me eat it and drinks her coffee. I think she's going to say she's proud of me, but she says, Do you even own a comb? At least I know what I'm getting for Christmas now.

We're breaking each other's hearts over and over, which is exactly why I avoid this kind of unnecessary interaction.

Then it's off to pick out some overpriced bath junk for her friend Jackie. You remember Jackie? she says. With the hair? Like I'm face blind but good with hair.

I need to leave soon, before I start ruining things.

My mother can tell I'm getting scratchy. I'm not done yet, she says, dragging me into another store.

Can I build a bear? I ask. Why? she says. I say, Why does any-one build a bear? She looks at me like, *What planet are you on?*, but then she just laughs, like I'm her hilarious gal pal and she can tell my father we had a hoot and I made a joke about a bear and he'll say, What joke, and she'll say she forgot but that Janet is doing great, she can see a real change, and my dad will sleep better knowing I'm less likely to murder my mother.

The last stop is a shop that sells only candles, which sounds like a fire hazard to me. Aren't you going to ask me if I need any candles? I ask, and she can tell I'm done.

I walk her to her car, because I'm a gentleman, and she says, Only two more weeks, Janet. It sounds like a threat, though, coming from her. Like, *Don't you dare go backward now, Janet. Stay in the light.*

See you at Christmas, I say, and kiss her on the cheek.

I get in my car, and I'm overwhelmed with relief. *That was al-most some Grade A mother-daughter bonding shit,* I think. It'll give me something to tell Karen at the next meeting anyway, if I feel like it, which I probably won't. More likely I'll do what I always do, which is pretend it never happened. Instead it'll lurk below the surface, so that whenever I see a mother and a daughter on TV I'll get a twinge inside that I'll dismiss as indigestion but really it will be the pain of what might have been, and what's still to come, and how I'll never find the words for any of it, with my mother or with anyone.

Love is like gluten, I should have told the doctor. I can't process it properly.

21

I knew my boyfriend would show up at some point. I knew someone would tell him what I was doing. All he had to do was read the news. Or watch the commercials on the news.

Our mothers have probably been texting each other this whole time, meeting for secret lattes under the guise of swapping books. I imagine my mother saying something like, Oh, she's much more manageable now, I've just been shopping with her, it's just wonderful. And she'd say, You know, I'm sure they can work it out, and his mother would say, I hope so, as I was really hoping to turn his room into a home office. Or maybe she's hoping for an exercise room, or whatever else parents do when their kids leave to stop themselves from turning the kid's room into a shrine. No one wants to cry on a cross trainer. I can, but you probably shouldn't.

I have to find a way not to think about it all. For too long I've let my mother's voice take up space in my brain—hers, and his mother's, and maybe all the mothers' voices, definitely a few TV mums. It's not my job to make them happy.

I'm half expecting him to be there at my parents' house on

Christmas Day. Hiding behind the door, maybe holding mistletoe or some bullshit. I'll have to swerve his kiss, tell him kissing is a symbol of the patriarchy and that I have no intention of touching him or any other man for some time, maybe ever. Then my dad will probably try to kiss me—on the cheek, relax—and I'll have to give in because he's my dad and probably holding a carving knife. My mother will say, Look, Janet! Look who's here! Isn't it nice? And I'll look at him and look at her and look at my dad's knife, and I'll have to leave.

Thankfully, though, he turns up before that. Gets it out of the way.

I've just gotten home from another long day at work. My body aches. My dogs are barking, I used to say when I got home in this state, and he'd look at me like, *What?* My dogs! My feet! I would say, but he'd already ruined it. My one joke. That's not a thing, he would say. It must be, because I just said it, I'd say, and it was like we'd forgotten how we even got here, how we ever thought this would work, but we couldn't say that out loud because both our names were on the lease and he'd just ordered a pizza.

Tonight I don't even have the energy to take off my coat and boots. I'm just lying fully clothed on my bed. It's technically still our bed, but I'm not going to be the one to remind him that his mother bought it for us. That is weird on too many levels.

I could easily fall asleep like this and then just get up and start again tomorrow, I'm thinking. Taking off clothes just to get up and put them on again—that seems stupid. So does washing off your makeup just to put it on again, so I mostly don't bother with that part. So I'm lying on the bed in my coat and boots, like a corpse at the beginning of *Law & Order*, when my phone goes off.

Are you home? he says. I'm outside.

I'm home, I say.

Can I come up? he says.

You can come up, I say. I'm already mad at him for making me get up.

Hey, he says.

Hey, I say.

We slept beside each other for three years, isn't that weird? I want to say, but I don't because I might not ever want to talk about that again. Cutting things out of my life is what I'm good at.

Our mums had coffee, he says, knowing it will make me uncomfortable, but to be fair it's also the only sensible way to start the conversation. I fucking knew they would, so I don't act surprised.

So, you're doing this pill, he says.

She told you, I say.

How's that going? he says.

Fine, I say. I'm full of joy now, can't you tell.

He lets out a big sigh then, like it's the one giant sigh that sums up our relationship.

Why are you here? I say, because I want him to not be.

I just wanted to see how you are, he says, and he tries to touch my arm. Maybe he thinks no one has touched me in a while. When we were together, he was always touching me when I was trying to pretend I was invisible.

How am I? You fucked me up big time and now you're sniffing around again because you think I'm taking something that might make me more like the girlfriend you wanted, I want to say but I don't. Maybe he knows it all already. I definitely remember putting all that in a text to him, but I can't remember if I sent it or not.

I'm fine, I say. Then, just to hurt him a little, I'm good.

I have never been good, my whole life. According to him, it's because I won't let anyone make me come. Boys are great.

I actually have to be somewhere, I say, partly so he knows I really am changed now, but also because I do have to get to my meeting.

So that's it, he says. You're just going to pretend none of this happened, all those years?

Yes, I say.

It's only been a few months, but I've already cut it out of me. I maybe started cutting it out of me while we were still together, but I spare him hearing that. In a few years I'll cut this stage of life out of me, and I'll probably keep moving that way until I can't anymore.

Once he's gone, I sit down in the hall with my back against the door.

I don't want it to be like this, he texts me. Well it is, I text back.

I feel sad. Which is fine. It's something I know how to do.

22

Week six. The penultimate week of meetings. Just one more and I'm free. If that's even a thing.

We're so close to Christmas now, but the people at the meeting already seem to be flagging. I worry that Karen is going to make us sing songs or something, or act out the nativity, just to liven us up, but she doesn't because she knows we'd all leave. I get the sense that she's bored of us, of all of this, by now, that she wants it to be over as much as we do. She has a life, it seems, one that doesn't include babysitting a bunch of killjoys.

The pills are working, in that everyone's here and we're not dead. Everyone in this room is trying to embrace this Christmas thing that's invading our lives, but mostly we're all tired, at least by the looks of it.

Karen reminds us that there's only one meeting left. Karen reminds us to report any problems. Karen tells us all we're doing great, but no one believes her.

I think Karen might be a robot.

As we're leaving, a woman whose name I've forgotten asks me what my plans are for the holidays. The usual, I say, and she nods. I can't remember her name, but I like her. She tried, and I tried, and that's enough. I wish all interactions were like that. Maybe there were other people in this room I could have bonded with. Guess I'll never know.

Maybe we were supposed to rise up or something, start a movement, take back Christmas, but we just sat here every week and listened to Karen tell us how exciting this all was, how we were part of something big, how drugs could really help people rejoin the world. I think she was trying to convince herself she made the right decision doing this, not us. I imagine she gave herself a pep talk in her car each week before she came in. Karen, you're doing something great, she'd say. You're actually helping people. Christmas is wonderful. Everyone should be able to enjoy it. You're giving people Christmas, Karen! And the Karen in the rearview mirror would blush at herself. Oh, stop it, she would say. And then she'd put on her coral lipstick from the eighties that she thought made her look more youthful, because she used to wear it in the eighties when she *was* youthful, and she would march into that church hall and see us sad sacks sitting there and she'd know that somewhere along the way she had made a wrong turn.

Maybe that's what we should have been talking about every week.

A couple of years ago, on Christmas Eve, I googled *how to be full of Christmas spirit.*

The boyfriend was already asleep. I'd told him I'd come to bed as soon as I finished wrapping gifts, because that sounded like something people did. It sounded better than *I'm so sad I can't even masturbate anymore and tomorrow will only be worse since it's Christmas.*

I didn't really think the search would bring up anything. Maybe some ads for alcohol, which I would click so fast. I wasn't expecting there to be a whole wiki guide. According to the wiki, all I had to do was follow their simple guide and I'd be full of Christmas spirit.

At ten steps, this plan was already two steps easier than Alcoholics Anonymous:

No. 1   was *Watch Christmas movies.* In case you were a moron, it even listed a few. They never mentioned *Black Christmas*, which is the best Christmas movie.

No. 2   was *Get in touch with family and friends*, which is a big leap from watching Christmas movies alone under a blanket that reeks of despair and Cheetos.

No. 3   was *Read Christmas books.* Like *The Shining.* It didn't say that, but it should have. Fucking Dickens, I mean, who can really be fucked?

No. 4   was *Decorate as much as you can*, which reeked of desperation to me, like a dead giveaway that you're really trying to avert people's eyes from the sadness underneath. It reminds me of those people who leave their tree up deep into the new year because the thought of taking it down is too heartbreaking. Some flirt with leaving it up all year.

No. 5   was *Make a to-do list of stuff you need to get done before Christmas.* So now, I thought, I'm reading a list that's telling me to write a list. *Fuck this,* I thought, I didn't get on the internet to be given a bunch of errands.

No. 6   was *Send holiday cards.* If someone got a card from me, they'd know I was having a breakdown.

No. 7   was *Make a Christmas list.* Wait, wasn't that number 5?

No. 8   was *Make sure everything is clean and uncluttered.* WTF. You just told me to decorate everything!

No. 9   was *Make a display counting down the days.* Or, as we called it when I was growing up, *Buy a calendar.*

No. 10 was *Get a calendar.* WTF? I just said that. It was one of those moments when you feel so seen that you're sure they're watching you. Was this all an elaborate ruse to sell calendars? Are the calendar people secretly evil geniuses? All those cute kittens and hot firemen a fiendish trap?

It was late, and I was sure the internet was playing tricks on me. I crawled into bed, defeated. He was fast asleep, dreaming of sugarplums or whatever boys are into, and I lay awake worrying how I'd get through the next day. The only way I could pull it off, I thought, was to forget it was Christmas at all and pretend it was just another day. A day I had to spend doing a load of things I didn't want to do. I would have gone to work if I could.

I knew there were people out there like me who felt the same way. That it was all so much pressure. Only no one else wanted to admit it, because Christmas is supposed to be nice.

Those pills couldn't have come soon enough, really.

A dog comes in two weeks before Christmas. A scruffy mutt we'll never shift, because these days people want to know what breed they're getting, but also because people like things that look rich. They want designer babies and designer dogs and designer vaginas. I introduce myself and he shakes a little and I think he might pee on my foot, but he just looks at me like, *You better not be my new mummy, I've read about girls like you*. Debs tells me his family couldn't afford to do both Christmas and a dog, which is sad on so many fucking levels. Debs is so good with those people. She told me years ago how to zone out when they're talking and think of the dog, so that's what I've learned to do, but this time I really want to go to their house and tell them they're scum and Christmas doesn't have to be expensive and they can have their dog back and just be together and that's when I know my mind is not my own.

Melissa is suddenly there, making a fuss over the new arrival. She's like a vampire, but a really bad one, the kind who can only appear out of thin air and has good teeth but does none of the killing.

They should have brought the kids instead, I tell Debs. We could shift those quicker.

People always want pugs, and we have never have any fucking pugs. They're all on the internet being celebrities. People don't give up fancy dogs like pugs, or treat them badly, which makes you wonder if people who have pugs are slightly better humans than people who don't, or if they just don't like risking their investment.

Sometimes people come in, look around, then say, Have you got anything else? As if maybe we keep the good shit out the back. I don't have time for these people. They're the same people who won't buy a wonky carrot and probably can't wait till it's Gattaca because they want a fancy kid. I hand them off to Melissa; she's more tolerant. Sometimes I think if it weren't for her, Debs and I would be in real jail instead of dog jail.

Some people come in looking for a very specific dog. They even have the name picked out. These are the same awful people who have lists of what they look for in a partner, who think it's all about checking things off: Job. Marriage. Car. House. Family. Like they really believe there's one right way to do things, and those of us who go off script are going to hell.

I'm supposed to be feeling Christmassy now, but mostly I feel angry and tired.

When I get home I accidentally flick over to the channel that's all Christmas movies all the time and I worry my hand isn't my own anymore.

Before Melissa, no one cared if we had a work Christmas party. There were only two of us humans anyway, so it would have just been me and Debs getting drunk and wondering what we were supposed to be talking about—TV, work, our feelings, even—but we didn't much feel like it, because one thing we have in common is that we both feel like everyone else does enough talking.

But Melissa expects something, wants something, and she feels it's her duty to rally the troops. A party will boost morale, she thinks, though she doesn't say it, because she knows we don't want our morale boosted any more than we want out breasts lifted. They're fine where they are. What we want is a long nap. We want someone to rub our feet. Well, not me—I don't really like being touched—but I suspect Melissa could use it, those puppies probably haven't been touched for decades. When the kibble delivery guy comes, I pretend not to notice, but Melissa goes a bit red and somewhere inside her brain a light saying *boy boy boy* starts flashing, and I know she's doing everything in her power not to throw herself on the ground and beg him to take her away. Debs barely raises an eyebrow. Every month he tries to hoist the huge sacks of food down to the cellar, and every month Debs elbows him out of the way and does it herself.

The guy who delivers the kibble reminds me of someone released from maximum-security prison who has lost all ability to engage with other humans, so I quite like him. He never even says hello, which gets him extra brownie points. Every month Melissa stands by his van twiddling her hair when he arrives, asking him what the world is like. I don't know what's wrong with her.

Debs would probably take a foot rub from Kibble Guy, but I think she keeps her shoulders stiff and hunched as a badge of honor. You can have my feet, but don't even think about touching any part of me I actually still care about, I imagine her saying. I'm afraid I'm starting to get a hunch like hers. I don't know if it's the work, or my way of mirroring Debs like lovers do, but our decrepit bodies do seem to be mirroring our decrepit surroundings. So far Melissa is resisting the forces of decay—she still paints her nails—but soon they'll be jagged and bitten like ours.

But Debs and I both want to keep Melissa off our backs, so this time when she asks about a Christmas thing, we tell her, Sure, whatever, Melissa, whatevs. A dinner, maybe, Debs says. Someplace dark with alcohol, she's thinking. No gifts. No paper hats. We don't say that, but Melissa knows by now when to stop pushing.

A week before Christmas, Melissa drives us to some restaurant she says she *loves loves loves*. Debs tries to back out, but Melissa says they have good margaritas, which pulls her back in.

I wear my most festive black shirt, the one with the least armpit stink, and Debs brushes her hair. (I only know this because one of her kids tells me.) She calls her folks in to babysit while we're gone. There has to be an adult on site at all times in case shit goes down. Debs rarely ever goes out, but that's how she likes it. People think she's saving those dogs, but really they're saving her—and not for any Hallmark reasons, just because they give her a good excuse to avoid most of the bullshit that normal life offers.

Debs's parents are really nice, normal folk. Good people. And it's awful for all of us. Her dad is always trying to get me to go back to college; Debs keeps telling him to stop trying to lure her staff away with empty promises, but he still does it when she's not around. He always asks me what I'm reading, like he's trying to check that my brain still works. My own dad doesn't know what to say to me, so I appreciate the effort, but mostly I just mumble that I've got stuff to do.

Call me if something happens, she says to her dad, who's already settled in to watch a show about war. Some people really love war. I'm not sure if it's the outfits or the shouting.

Like what, he says. He always says this. Like if you hear any sudden commotion, Debs says, like maybe a cat is dicking about down there or someone's trying to steal a dog or a dog escapes or if they start doing any *101 Dalmatians* shit. They're used to her snark because they made her.

Nothing ever happens at the sanctuary at night. It's surprisingly quiet. Even the best dogs are mostly idiots, but they know when bedtime is. There's no rogue canine trying to tell ghost stories while everyone else is trying to sleep, no hound farting under the covers and giggling. I've been to two sleepovers, and that's what happened at both. And we think girls are better than boys. Anyone who's seen inside a ladies' public bathroom knows we're monsters, same as boys.

Sometimes, a dog who's new to the shelter might cry a little, which can trigger some whimpering from other dogs, but mostly they're quiet. Debs always does a last check after she's put her kids to bed, to make sure one of her idiot humans hasn't left a bucket out where someone might trip over it (me), or forgotten to lock the food room (Melissa).

Then it's off to Melissa's restaurant. The place is rammed because people like to drink, but we're all on our best behavior. None of us feels like eating, or drinking even, and even less like talking, so we sit and people-watch. For as long as I can remember I've watched people. People want to be watched, after all. It's all a performance. Those people with giant TVs, so you can see what they're watching from the street? They might as well let us see their digestive tract, which they basically are now when they show us their dinners on Instagram. I keep my phone on vibrate, but that hardly matters because I usually leave it somewhere, so the only one who ever feels wanted when the phone vibrates is a sofa cushion. The ex-boyfriend was always telling me how irresponsible I was, how people needed to be able to contact me. I'm not someone important, I wanted to say. You know where I am, I wanted to say.

Another work party is happening across the room. It's like an office party from the eighties. The type Melissa has wet dreams about. The table is decorated with all sorts of festive tat and everyone is wearing a paper hat. One woman falls off her chair because she's already too drunk, and I watch as she tries to get back up, clinging to the table. But she has no upper-body strength, because she works in an office and doesn't shovel shit all day and walk massive dogs who weigh more than her that want to rip her arm off. She has normal lady arms that are no match for that table. If Dave from accounting fell down, he'd get back up no problem because he has those big arms from pumping iron and jacking off to whatever image of a female is available. I know he's Dave because a bald man says, Another beer, Dave? I was listening because I need to know how these people live.

This party is my worst nightmare. The more I watch, the more I see it's not an eighties party at all but something from the Stone Age, when the men were men and the women were tipsy and endangered. Right now they're all bitching about some lady called Melody who didn't come. I like this Melody already, if that is in fact her real name.

That people like this exist still fascinates me. I could study them forever. Part of me wants to follow them home, rent their back bedroom, learn what it's like to live their lives. It would be awful, but it would be different awful, and these people are so unaware of their awfulness it'd be like a holiday from my crippling self-awareness.

I know what their days look like. I had an office job once. Not a lot of people know this; they just see the big coat and boots and surly disposition and assume I've only ever worked at the shelter or down a mine. I'm surprised my mother doesn't lead with this when she talks about me: She did work in an office once, there's still hope. Because of course offices are places where important stuff happens, not just carpeted warehouses where people stare at their computers till they can escape and go home to numb themselves. I forget what the company I worked for did, exactly, or why I was there; the whole episode feels like a dream now. I don't know who that person was who thought she could fool the world into thinking she was that high-functioning. But I kept up the façade for two months, which is not nothing.

The Christmas party there was mandatory. At five o'clock they just switched the lights off, and some lady from HR shuffled out with a boom box and another lady whipped out a tray of depressing snacks and we were all trapped there for an hour that seemed like weeks. We just sat there in the dark at our desks thinking we were having a collective stroke. One brave guy from IT got up to inspect the snacks, but they were so depressing he just stood there, stranded, for a solid twelve minutes. I admired his bravery. I just stayed at my desk and kept working in the dark—the equivalent of bringing a book to a party, which is also my style.

Meanwhile, at my current Christmas work party, Debs is starting to get antsy. I catch her stealing a glance at her fake watch—fake as in she doesn't have one, but looking at her wrist seems to comfort her, maybe because she hopes it'll fool other people into wanting to leave.

I shouldn't leave them too long, she says. She means the dogs, not the kids. They like to be home for *Law & Order*, she says.

Who doesn't, Melissa says, and we all smile and nod.

After around seventy-eight minutes, we call it a night. We tried. I'm just glad to get out of the restaurant without the townspeople noticing us.

We all pile into Melissa's car. When she turns on the radio, Mariah Carey blasts out like she's been trapped in there this whole time. Melissa goes to turn it off—she knows how we feel about cheesy Christmas music—but I stop her. It's okay, I say. I'm suddenly filled with an unfamiliar feeling. I'm not sure it's Christmas spirit, pity maybe, but more the margaritas, which were not awful. Melissa looks at Debs, who just shrugs and says, What the hell, because margaritas. We aren't drunk, but we're fuzzy enough to choose our battles.

Melissa drives us home singing along to Mariah and she seems genuinely happy and we let her have it because it's Christmas and Christmas does funny things to people, like make people try to medicate other people who don't want to be medicated. I regret not driving myself, because I'm starving and have no food in my apartment, but I know that once I get in my front door, I'll lose any remaining desire to deal with humans. I'll probably just have a little cry and fall asleep to *Law & Order* like a normal person.

There was one good thing about Melissa driving, and that was that she couldn't try to hug us. I give a little wave and tell Melissa, That was—I hesitate—*fun*, and Debs looks at me like, *I don't know her*, but I know she'll forgive me by the morning.

See you both tomorrow, I say, and Debs salutes me and that's that.

Fumbling with my keys, I say, out loud, See? I can do it.

It's okay, no one hears me.

The next day at work, Debs makes me go to the bank. She doesn't do online banking because she doesn't trust the internet. She doesn't trust people either, but she likes to see who's fucking her over.

It's already getting dark out, and there are Christmas lights everywhere. All I can think is, *If you weren't epileptic before, you will be now.* I heard that some kids ripped down some Christmas lights in town, and knowing my mother, she'll probably think it was me. I wish I had that much energy.

Out on the streets, things are strangely silent. No one carrying piles of gifts, no carolers singing on the corner. No one is in
earmuffs, thank god. It's like someone's taken a regular doomy
Monday and strung it with lights. There's a feeling of anticipation
in the air, like something is coming. Of course, that's also true of
horror movies.

All the store windows are variations on the same theme—Look
at all this shit! You need this shit!—with happy elves and flashing
signs arranged so strategically your brain doesn't stand a chance.
Even the bakery is in on it. There's a giant cake in their window
with Santa's big red face on it, and I think about what it would be
like to bury my face in it, like men do to tits, but this would be so
much better. I get myself a Christmas cookie, and only when I'm
walking out do I realize I probably should have gotten some to take
back, but it's too late by then. I don't want my love to be an after-
thought; it's not even love, it's obligation, or medication.

Even the bank has a Christmas tree. I'm disappointed it's not a
money tree. Maybe I'll suggest it for next year. The teller is one of
those people who wears ornaments as earrings. She sees where I
work and says, Oh, we don't usually see you! I let her look at me
more than I would usually let anyone, because it's Christmas, and
because a long look at me in my big coat is a treat for all of us. It's
Christmas, I tell her, inexplicably. I'm allowed out once a year, I
tell her, but she doesn't know if I'm joking. She's heard the ru-
mors about the dog women in the woods.

Well, happy holidays, she says when we're done, but she says
it like she suspects I'll be dancing naked in the woods sacrificing
something while she's carving her turkey.

And to you! I say, and I want to laugh out loud, but I push it down. Laughter is so rare and precious that I want to keep it all to myself—later, in the car maybe, like I'm hotboxing myself but with joy. Punching myself in the face with it so I really know I felt it.

Before going back to work, I go and buy myself a shitload of candy. People will think I'm buying it for kids—or worse, a party—but it's all for me. I always stock up when I'm out in the world and it's nothing to do with all the ads for holiday candy. You can get it all year, you know! I want to shout at no one. You don't need permission! It's a shame I'm not online. I'd be great at the shouting-into-the-void bit.

Driving back, I see *It's a Wonderful Life* is showing at the Rialto. I saw it once, out of curiosity, because I thought a Christmas movie about suicide sounded right up my alley, but I couldn't take it. I thought, *I'd throw myself off a bridge too, if I had those annoying kids*. And Mary's worst fate is that she ends up a librarian? Everyone knows librarians are the best people.

Melissa sees me pull up and waves. I feel bad for not bringing her a Christmas cookie, but she probably has dog shit on her hands anyway.

Every time I go out in the world and venture into Christmas land, I feel like I'm being scored. Like Karen might be following me, taking notes.

Like the pharma guy is still staring, who knows why.

23

It's the last meeting. It's basically Christmas. I could easily just pass out now, fall into the old holiday food-and-drink coma, and it would all be over. I would wake up and ask someone, Did he come? Santa, I mean, or anyone? If I passed out at my parents' house, at least I could say I was there. What more do these people want?

Karen is beaming at us all, and it's making me nauseous. I'm sure she's just glad we're all still alive, that her head count didn't take any hits. Every week, I'm surprised that no one subjects us to a medical check, or at least a pat down to make sure we still have all our limbs. If I know anything about medical trials, it's that people are liable to lose a limb.

The pharma guy isn't writing in his notebook today. I'd like to think he's finished his sitcom script, but chances are he's abandoned it.

I am desperate for the whole meeting—the whole experiment—to be over before someone tries to hug me or give me a certificate or something. I've showed up every week, played along as much as I could. If you asked me what I liked best about it, it's just that no one else wanted to be here any more than I did—not even Karen, and she's getting paid to be here.

Karen tells us again how proud she is of us and wishes us all a happy Christmas. No one laughs. We are all assimilated now. The experiment seems to have worked. Of course, until we get through Christmas without murdering anyone, we won't know for sure, but everyone has their fingers crossed, the pharma guys most of all.

As I'm leaving, Pharma Guy taps me on the shoulder. Hi, he says, and it's too late to hide. Hi, I say, and it's awkward.

If you ever want to get together, he says, and his choice of words makes me laugh, on the inside. On the outside I remain composed because he has to know I'm not going to call him. The only thing I feel for him is bad, and I feel bad about enough things.

He's genuinely not awful. He has that great dog. But I don't want to get together with anyone after all this, maybe for a long time.

I can't tell him, Sorry, I just like being single, because it sounds like a declaration I don't feel I need to make. So instead I just say, Cool. Cool, he says back, and smiles, and I feel bad for him again. I mean, he works for some creepy giant pharmaceutical company whose mission is to medicate us all within an inch of our lives, he really hasn't got a chance. But what do I know? People like their drugs. Maybe he's a catch.

Bye then, I say, and leave him standing there. He could have gone home with Karen again, for all I know. That wouldn't be the worst thing, for any of us, really.

The next night, the volunteers all appear at the shelter, even the ones we barely saw all year. Melissa's kid is there. Debs's kids are off somewhere getting rabies.

On the night before Christmas, all the dogs get walked together—which is less fun than you'd think, because a lot of them are psychopaths and don't play well with others, like me. So the more experienced walkers, like me and Debs and this ex-marine, and the cop for some reason, get a head start with all the really difficult dogs. The volunteers follow us with their chosen dogs, all wishing Debs didn't have such strict rules against carols or joy.

The dogs all get a bone and a new squeaky toy with the squeak taken out, which is a metaphor for my whole goddamn life. There is mulled wine Melissa made, if anyone wants it. I usually wouldn't trust anything she made, but the alcohol in it puts my fears to rest.

I spend most of the night hiding from the kids, who think it's a hilarious game, but I just really don't want to spend my Christmas Eve swearing at kids.

After the last of the volunteers have gone, we close up shop and say good night.

I go home to my apartment. It's empty, but it's really not that awful. I can eat what I want, watch what I want, I don't have to pretend to feel anything I don't, and it feels like Christmas might not be so bad. People who moan about being single are doing it wrong.

It's too late to get a tree, but I find some lights and hang them around a dead plant. The lights are pretty. The plant is still dead but I'm not going to be the one to tell it.

Curled up on the couch, I don't feel excited, exactly, but I don't feel full of dread either. Mostly I feel relief. Like Christmas will happen and I'll be okay. I have options—isn't that what we all want?

I've come this far. I'd have to be stupid to mess it all up now.

24

Usually what happens on Christmas Day is, I roll in to my parents' place late, eat, and bounce. Keep it casual. Don't get involved. I only stayed over when I had to, when I was at college; even then I thought about getting a hotel, but I knew my dad would be sad about it. I slept a lot, emerged when there was food, then packed up and went back to my life. My mother was in her own world, popping the pills she needed to get her out of bed, putting on a show for the neighbors, and I left her to it. I was the absent daughter even when I was home.

This year, I treat it like a regular day. I get up and go to work, only work is my mother.

I show up thirty minutes before our customary—that is, *late*—dinnertime. If my mother chooses this of all years to be on time, well, I'm already going to hell anyway, so what does it matter.

Happy Christmas, can't talk, need to pee!! I yell, running straight up the stairs. They'll probably assume it's a side effect of the pill.

Just as I'm bursting into the bathroom, my brother bursts

out. What do you do, just hang around outside bathrooms now? he says.

I ignore him and push past. I shut the door, sit down, and think happy thoughts. There's no greater feeling than peeing when you need to pee. The relief is still washing over me when the horror of the day surfaces again, as the sound of Christmas music wafts up from somewhere in the house. *The killer is inside the house,* I whisper to myself as I wipe.

I wash my hands and dry them on my mum's robe; if she's dumb enough to leave it hanging on the back of the door, she must know I'm going to use it to dry my hands. I think about sniffing it, to see if it smells of my childhood memories of her, but sniffing things is weird and I'm trying to not be, so I resist.

My brother is lurking outside when I come out.

Happy Christmas, lurker, I say.

He looks me up and down like he's about to critique my outfit. Mum said not to mention it, he says, but I wanted you to know I think it's really great, what you're doing.

And what am I doing? I say, because the last thing I did was pee, in the toilet, like even some cats can do.

This, he says, waving his hands over me like a magician. I think she thought she might have to pay you, he says.

Wait—you think she would have *paid* me? What the fuck?

She's been paying me to not be a dick for years, he says, grinning.

And yet you're still a dick.

But less of one. I might even let you watch my kids now, he says.

How gracious of you, but don't forget I turn back into a pumpkin in a few hours, so you better get all your digs in now while I can't punch you in the face.

I'd love a pill that kept me from wanting to punch people in the face, he says.

Wouldn't we all, I say, starting down the stairs.

Oh, and Mum also told me not to tell you I got a promotion and we're having another kid. But I figure you can handle it, right?

Why wouldn't I be able to handle it? I don't want either of those things, I say.

Well, you know, he says, she wants us to . . . *tiptoe around you.* I mean, now that you're doing so well and all. Because you're doing so well, right?

Right! I say, remembering what day it is.

People want things, Janet, he says, because I need reminding.

My mother appears in the hallway. Are you two coming down ever? she says, even though we're literally walking down the stairs.

We're just bonding, my brother says, kissing her on the cheek.

Just make it through dinner without saying anything stupid, I tell myself. How hard can it be? I do it at home every night. Of course, I'm generally alone, but still.

Everyone is surprised and delighted to see me, but I can tell they don't want to show too much enthusiasm, lest I crawl back under my rock. *Don't startle her, whatever you do,* my mother must have said while I was peeing.

My brother and his family are all there, and one more inside his wife, which I find strangely comforting because I prefer strangers. My uncle and his family are there, grinning and saying hello over and over again, as if pleasantries will make this all easier. My aunt is there, with her second husband, who looks exactly like her first husband, so we just pretend that's who he is and that seems to work for them too. There are two additional women in sports casual, who must have something to do with my mother. They smile and tell me what nice eyes I have, which means the rest of my face needs work. If one of them had said it, I'd just have said thanks and resented her silently, but they both say it at the same time, which feels a bit *The Shining*, especially because of my mother's hideous carpeting.

My brother's phone starts playing Elton John's "Step into Christmas," and suddenly he's holding his phone in front of my face. I push it away. He restarts the song and does it again. I wonder if I've time-traveled back twenty years, when Elton John was always in the charts and my brother was always in my face.

My dad snatches my brother's phone. Quit it, he says, both of you.

I read somewhere, my brother says, that if you play that song at them it makes them go nuts.

Them? I say.

She's not a robot, my dad says.

She might as well be, my brother says, taking his phone back and starting the song again, like he is ten and it's a booger and I give a shit.

Enough, my dad says, grabbing the phone and putting it in his pocket.

It's fine, I say to my dad. You can go to hell, I say to my brother.

To escape my brother, I head to the kitchen and ask my mother what I can do to help. She looks shocked, then tries to hide it immediately and tells me I can write out name cards for the table. I want to write the names of their prescriptions instead, just so everyone knows what really brought us all together on this special day, but I don't.

At Christmas, throughout the day, my mother barely sits down. She hovers, one foot at the table, the other in the kitchen, for the entire meal. That poor kitchen has given her its best years. It makes us all unnecessarily anxious, and we've already had enough necessary anxiety between us for a lifetime. The mysterious ladies in Lycra are weirding us all out enough. If one of them starts cutting the other's meat, I'm going to have to ask them what business they have here.

I find my mother in the kitchen, peering at her open laptop on the counter. A recipe? I wonder naively. Some show she really has to watch? Maybe she's more like me than she lets on.

She sees me and slams her laptop shut.

I open it, hoping to see those pesky cowboy robots we all loved but didn't understand.

She was on Facebook, talking about me with her friends.

A woman called Brenda said she heard about someone on the pill who tried to have sexual intercourse with a Christmas tree. Has Janet seen your tree yet? she wrote. Did it arouse her? I imagine the real-life Brenda whispering *sexual intercourse*, maybe with a lisp.

My mother replied: She touched it, yes, should I be worried? (She's right: I did touch the tree and all its decorations. Fingered them, you might even say. I wanted my mother to see that I appreciated her efforts. Also that I was a bit high, maybe.)

Is she doing songs? someone named Joyce asked.

No, no songs yet, my mum wrote back, though I might have heard her humming. I'll let you know. (I was indeed humming when I arrived, only it wasn't a Christmas song, it was Lizzo's "Truth Hurts.")

She's an angel, my mum had said. It's Christmas, and they all want an angel, and she was trying to impress them.

I look at my mother.

She just shrugs. People want to know, Janet, she says.

You can tell Brenda your tree really isn't my type, I say. I like more bush, I add under my breath, heading back to the table.

Well, I'm obviously not going to tell her that, am I, my mother says, having heard me.

When we get back to the living room, we both smile our best vapid Stepford smiles.

My mother gives a short toast, to say how happy she is to have us all together on this happy day. If she says *happy* once more, I might not make it. As usual, she's trying too hard. I'm trying just the right amount. My brother's kids clearly need Ritalin, or horse tranquilizers, something, but for now they're free and I feel strangely protective over them and want to take them aside quietly and tell them they don't have to take anything they don't want to, but I don't.

Then it's time for gifts. My mother got me an Amazon gift card and a comb. She says it's an inside joke, but it's not really, it's very obvious I don't own a comb. I should have shaved it all off by now, but people have ruined that too, like they ruin everything. Old Janet might have rolled her eyes at the gift card, screamed something about capitalism, consumerism, some ism, anyway, but instead I decide to just buy books and pretend it's not awful. I'm used to that. Letting people slide on their ethical lapses is my gift to them.

Free books and a comb are a lot better than last year. Last year she got me a pair of weird pink yoga pants and I couldn't even wear them in the privacy of my own home because I didn't want the boyfriend to get the wrong idea, like I was someone who might do yoga. I didn't even try them on, out of fear that I might get stuck in them and then I'd have to be that person anyway. I was afraid they might infect me in some way. I sold them on eBay eventually, but that didn't stop me being haunted by them. I was sure I'd get them again the next year and find out my mother had been the eBay buyer and we'd be trapped forever in that mother-daughter loop, never wanting to admit who's the worst.

Truth is, I'd never really wanted anything for Christmas. Not even to be happy, really. When I was fourteen, I did ask for laudanum, as a kind of half-joke.

What's that? she asked.

I told her. I hadn't been reading all those gothic novels for nothing.

For god's sake, Janet, she said, if I had any of that, do you think I'd give it away?

Dinner itself? It was fine.

Everyone watched me eat, which I expected, so I put on a little show, chewing meticulously, like a camel who'd read something online about the importance of chewing.

With my mouth full, I quizzed the interlopers. I wanted to know what my mother was like as a person in the world, a person who spent her mornings bent over in a downward dog somewhere without us around to laugh. She was the same, it seemed, which was disappointing.

My brother kept saying how great everything was, because he had his promotion and another kid on the way, not because the food was actually great, because it was just food. The carrots tasted like carrots.

No one asked me about my life because my mother had obviously told them not to, probably in a mass email. One of the ladies in Lycra told me what nice teeth I had—first my eyes, now my teeth. Thanks, they're my own, I said, because my mother was watching me. I raised my glass at my mother. We did something right, she said.

We all ate a lot and drank a lot and talked a lot about nothing that mattered. We all liked eating food. Whoever came up with the idea of spacing food out throughout the day to keep us all distracted from ourselves? Say what you want about Jesus or Santa; that guy was the real hero.

After all that fuss—not from me, but from them—the day was fine. I think I smiled a few times. I laughed once—sure, at the TV, but it still counted. I listened to my uncle while he talked about sports, and made it through by pretending he was talking about books and thinking how much better the world would be if we replaced sports with books. All of this kept me from saying, Maybe read a book, dumbass!, like I wanted to. I didn't make anyone cry or call anyone an idiot.

After dinner—and my mother's customary warning that no one can help clear up, because playing the martyr is always her gift to herself—we all sit down to watch *Harry Potter and the Something of Something*, because that's the true meaning of Christmas somehow. We'll all be asleep soon anyway, so it hardly matters. I glance out the window, mostly to see if it's anywhere near dark enough to escape yet, but instead I see a flurry of white floating down from the sky.

I jump up. It's snowing! I shout. Who said I was dead inside?

This of course makes the kids scream, but in the good way. They all jump up, as only kids' bodies can, and follow me to the window. Even my brother comes along, probably convinced that I was luring them to their death or something.

I get to the window first and see my mistake, as soon as I spot the flock of birds overhead.

Is it snowing, Daddy? the youngest kid asks, looking at my brother like, *Please let it be snow! For I am a tiny child and I shall need these memories to keep me sane through adulthood.*

My brother turns to me and whispers, That's not snow, it's bird shit. Then he turns back to his kid, says, False alarm, and heads back to the table.

The kids stay there at the window with me, staring at the shit.

What is it, Auntie Janet? they all say, wide-eyed.

It's, um, *pre-snow*, I say.

What does that mean? the kids ask.

It means snow's about to come, I say, leading the children back to the safety of the grown-ups and their snacks.

I'm standing by the kitchen, hiding from my brother, but also trying to slip out the back door maybe, when I hear my mum talking to my aunt.

Those pills are a godsend, she says.

I bite my lip straight through. This is progress, me hurting myself over someone else.

Old Janet would have made my eavesdropping known, butted right in, said something like, *You say god, but you mean some pharma guy who got dumped by his wife.* Something to undo any good she thought I'd done.

New Janet takes a pass. I let her have the whole ridiculous day, the way she's always dreamed.

I'm getting really good at witnessing life like this now, letting it all wash over me. Not because I'm hard inside, but because I'm softer, almost comfortable. Not happy, you understand, but at peace with it all, or at least that's how it feels.

Around eight thirty, when everyone is all nice and sleepy and cozy in front of the TV, I slip on my gloves, wave goodbye to their eyelids and light sheen of drool, and that's that.

I head off to my next Christmas, which is also conveniently where I live.

There's no stopping me now, I think. If I can handle my mother, I can handle anything. I could turn up at a stranger's house and be sociable. I feel gutsy. I feel like a fucking god. Maybe I'll hit two or three Christmases! Go all night! Crash every party in the neighborhood. I'll be Fun Janet. Crazy Janet. People will high-five me, shout my name in the street.

JANET! You LEGEND!

By the time I finally pull up outside my apartment, the buzz from surviving my family has gone. If I had a sponsor I'd call them and say, I'm thinking of fucking up again. I should have taken some eggnog for the road. I need topping up with Christmas spirit and fast.

But then it hits me: Min-seo.

I imagine her waiting for me on the stairs. *So you survived*, she'd say. *I was on my best behavior*, I'd tell her. And then I'd follow her up to her apartment and my tiny world would open a crack, just a crack, enough to let a little light in. Her family would welcome me into their fold in a way that suited me. No one would get up, no one would try to touch me or ask me anything, but everyone would smile or nod or do whatever they do. Her brother would be at that age when you don't smile for anyone less than a Victoria's Secret model or pizza, so I'd appreciate that he didn't just look at me with disgust and immediately call his buddies to come look at the freak. No one would ask who I was or what I did. No one would ask me to leave, more important, like my mother had on more than one Christmas.

I wouldn't ruin it all by saying something stupid like, I didn't know you did Christmas, because I'm not a racist and this was clearly a party and that was enough.

But Min-seo's not waiting for me. No one is waiting for me. I can hear noises coming from inside her apartment. Not holiday noises, just life noises. Footsteps. Fridge doors. The TV. The white noise of family.

I could go in, I think. I could knock and say, Hi, thought I'd stop by, hope this is still okay. Because can I really imagine it feeling okay, however much either of us said it was? Does she really want me there? I don't know. It's too hard to imagine. Maybe she's great and I'm missing the opportunity to start a new friendship, but does she really need a new friend? I think she just wants to know the person across the hall isn't going to stab her in her sleep.

Just because I'm now the type of person who gets invited to things, it doesn't mean I'll ever be the type of person who goes to things.

I keep walking.

Behind every door, I hear versions of Christmas happening. Some of them are silent apartments. Empty rooms. People gone for the holidays, off to be other versions of themselves for other people. This is what life is about. If you can do it. I can't even be a version of myself enough for me.

It's those empty apartments I want to crash the most. To knock on the doors and have a friendly ghost let me in. Let me stay a while, but not haunt me, just let me be.

I could knock on Min-seo's door and at least wish her a happy Christmas. Apologize. Say I'm tired or sick. But for some reason I don't think I could lie to her. Any more than I could lie to Debs.

That's the thing about Min-seo. The girl, this stranger, seems to get me.

She'd know I didn't really take the pills. Not a single one.

Debs already knows, I'm pretty sure. Everyone else thinks I've finally fallen in line, joined the rest of the world. Finally given in. For now it's our little secret.

But I suspect Min-seo is too cool for secrets, because she isn't a schoolgirl. She'd probably be like, Oh right, yeah, well, that was obvious or whatever. Wanna get frozen yogurt and laugh at everyone getting it non-ironically? And I'd say, Yes, always.

One day I'll tell her I'm sorry I didn't speak to her before. She'll say, Well, you had to get there yourself, and by *there* she'd mean past the narrow little world in my head.

One day, too, maybe I'll tell my mother.

But you went to those meetings, she'll say, confused.

Yeah, I went, I'll say. I wanted some of this, I'd say, gesturing at the holiday-heavy air. Just not *all* of it.

I might even tell the boyfriend, if I ever see him again.

You always have to be in control, don't you, he'll say.

Yes, I'll say, don't you?

The truth was, I liked the meetings. Having someplace to be that was weird and mine. Something I knew was temporary. Sometimes temporary is good. I was stepping outside myself, outside my sadness, into a room of other people and their sadnesses, forgetting my brain, breathing different air. One with less dog stink. Less Janet stink.

I was opening myself to something, to feeling something different. Ever so slightly, but it was a start. An offering.

A few days later, I pass Min-seo on the stairs. She's wearing a shirt that says, Dogs Are Delicious, with a picture of a dog on a plate.

I like your shirt, I say.

Thanks, she says. No one gets it.

Because she's Korean. It's funny as fuck.

I work at a dog shelter, I say.

I know, she says.

How was your Christmas? she asks then. She doesn't say, Hey, you totally blew me off, my dad made pizza bagels because he didn't know what kind of weird sad-girl shit you eat.

What I want to say is, Ugh, these days between Christmas and New Year feel like death, don't you think? But I can't, because we're all supposed to be enjoying the holidays. Even if you're not really enjoying life that much, you still have to enjoy the holidays.

My tongue is tied. I can't think of a thing to say.

Mine too, she says, before I can recover. Shits and giggles, she says.

Shits and giggles, I say. I thought I was the only one who said that.

If all human interactions went like this, I might not avoid them so much, I think as I tell her good night and go into my apartment.

The day after Christmas, you take half a pill for a week and then you're done. Tapering off is very important, they tell you. Let the magic seep out of you slowly, like when you walk to the bathroom after sex.

The one hitch is, you have to go back to your doctor one last time, to confirm you're alive. I leave this till the very last possible moment, just to keep him guessing.

When I do finally go, he doesn't even remember why I'm there.

What can I help you with today, Janet? he says.

I'm pregnant, I say, and he remembers me. He doesn't find it funny.

I'm supposed to feel like I've accomplished something, apparently. I'm part of a new world. A world where everyone can be happy at Christmas. But I don't feel like that. I'm starting to miss my sad, thanks. I might be ready to go back.

He opens a big drawer and finds my file—the pharma company's file. I don't know what it says. It might say I slept with the pharma guy. It might say I should be committed. I lean across the desk and try to read it.

So, he says.

So, I say.

I do have other patients, Janet, he says, and I admit it hurts.

He should know I'm not a talker. I'm the stone you can't get blood from. It should say so in my file.

So you survived, he says, relaxing in his chair, hoping I will too, but I'm a stone.

I did, I say. I want to say, *Ta da!*, but I'm not giving him what he wants. I don't want him thinking I'm all, like, *fun* now.

It was fine, I say, letting out a large amount of air, so he knows this is killing me.

Have you thought any more about the other pills? he says. Those little beauties could make this year different for you. He uses the word *different* because he knows that's my sweet spot. He's known me long enough to know that words like *better* don't work on me. I don't want better. What does that even mean? I only ever wanted different.

Didn't you like the support you had over the holidays? he asks. The meetings, he says, in case I've forgotten the last few weeks entirely—which I might have, for all he knows, as I've supposedly been off my head on drugs.

He never asks directly how I liked the pills.

I tell him I haven't thought about the pills yet, which is true. The whole conversation is making me very tired, but I thank him so he'll think I've made progress.

Then he ruins it all. What does your family think? he says. Your partner? People always say *partner* to me because they assume I'm a lesbian, and I'm okay with it. I don't tell him I don't have a boyfriend now because it's none of his business.

It's really nothing to do with them, I say.

He takes off his glasses, the way people do when they're about to get serious, as if seeing might hinder whatever greatness is coming.

I won't give up on you, Janet, he says. Which is probably a lie because he looks old as hell and is probably on the verge of retirement. I imagine myself running into him years from now, in some grocery store, and trying to hide. Janet! he'll say. Hi, I'll mumble. I'm not a doctor anymore, he'll say, and I'll assume he was fired for something until he remembers to tell me how much he's loving retirement. Then I'll remember the golf thing, and because I'm trying to be more positive, I'll think, *At least it keeps his sort in one place, so we can find them should we need them, which we won't.* We'll probably be in the potato chip aisle, the whole conversation will be interrupting my pursuit of potato chips. He'll notice I'm distracted, and instead of thinking it's because he's not that great at conversation, he'll scratch his head and apologize to me. I'm sorry, he'll say. It was my job. Drug companies, you know, he'll say, and shrug like that makes it okay. Right, I'll say. He'll look at me almost imploringly, like he wants me to forgive him right there in the grocery, and I might if it means I'll get back to my potato chips.

I hope you like your new doctor, he'll say as he pushes his cart away. I won't have the heart to tell him I've vowed never to go back, even if I'm clearly dying. I'm done with going back. I only want to go forward now. If I ever really need to see a doctor, I'll do what I should have done all along, which is go to the nearest woods and find a witch, someone who understands how danger- ous men are, someone who'll offer me something other than pills—a potion, maybe, or even just a lotion. I'd even be willing to dance in the moonlight a little if it meant I'd get to keep my head the way I like it, muddled and a bit sad but knowing who I am.

Well then, Janet, the doctor says now, I'll see you next year, if not sooner. Either way he's written me off. There's a sadness about *him* now, I can tell. It's like they'd all pinned their hopes on me, like they thought I'd do this thing and make them all pioneers. That I'd be the happy vehicle for their dreams of a new era. Per- sonalized Regimen! Boutique Pharmaceutical Care! Bespoke Happiness! Whatever bullshit slogan they were hoping to slap on it. They'd never found the pop star or model or actress they wanted to front it all. One time, at meeting, I suggested Mrs. Claus. You know, she never gets any credit, she'd probably work for cheap, I said. It didn't go down well.

What really stings is that the doctor said *if not sooner.* Like he thinks I'll never be able to go back to my old ways now that I've seen the medicated life. But I've known from the start that that's what they were aiming for, that they wanted to make this little diversion into a gateway drug. They'd taken the purest thing, Christmas, and tried to make it a dirty come-on. All I ever wanted was to take a few days off from myself, to pretend.

All these people who were supposed to care for me didn't give a fuck what I wanted.

What *they* wanted was for me to be happy enough with the drugs that I'd recommend them to my friends. I forgot I was supposed to be grateful. And they forgot I had no friends.

Aren't you happy, Janet? the doctor asks. Didn't you have a happy Christmas?

Well, I didn't stab anyone the whole time, or even want to, really, I want to say, but don't. It was fine, I say, which is the wrong answer.

Good! So you're in for the regular pills, then? he says, getting out his prescription pad. They've really turned out a huge success.

Where'd you hear that? I say. *Not from me,* I think.

The whole world's talking about it, he says. The internet, he means.

I look skeptical.

It's changed people's lives, he says.

I'm not so sure. I've seen a few testimonials, new footage in the last week of TV ads—*I never thought I'd be able to wear a Christmas sweater again*, or, *I don't even scream when someone sings Wham! at me anymore!*—but it's clearly all paid for by Big Pharma. These are not real people. My superpower is seeing through bullshit. The problem is, people love bullshit, so I make it a practice to shut up.

I don't really read the news, I tell him.

A lot of people like how it makes them feel, he says. They want to keep that feeling going. Don't you want to keep going, Janet?

I'm starting to think the pills are crack.

I haven't seen anyone from *my* meeting in the news, I say. They could be dead, for all I know. It's like they've all mysteriously vanished, if they ever existed at all. Maybe Christmas is all just a collective hallucination. Maybe this is all part of it.

Everyone in *my* meeting seems missing, Doctor, I say. Missing, presumed dead.

Maybe they're happy now, Janet, he says, but I don't buy it. Just as likely they're all kept out of sight, like missing limbs.

They've moved on with their lives, he tells me.

I do want to move on, but I don't want to be told when.

Before I leave, he tries one last time. His pen hovers over the prescription pad.

It's that easy, Janet, he says.

For you, maybe, I say, and get up to leave.

My door is always open, he says as the door shuts behind me.

I work New Year's Eve and New Year's Day, not giving myself much room to do or feel anything, only sleep and eat. I sleep through the world cheering in the New Year and I don't feel like I missed anything.

Happy New Year, I text Emma.

New Year, she texts back, because she knows how I feel about *happy*.

I feel desperately sad and weird that she only lives in my phone now, and heart. I wish I'd sniffed her more when I had her. Dogs know how important that is.

25

It's the first week of the new year. Christmas is behind us, or ahead of us, maybe, if you want to mess with my head already.

It feels like something we're all trying to forget, pretending it didn't happen, but the roads are still dusted with pine needles, with flecks of tinsel that act as ghosts. All that excess, all those decorations, no surface spared, vomitous glitter, mad-making light displays, garish sweaters whose owners think they're hilarious. Grown-ups in onesies, for fuck's sake. It made fools of us all, and for once I wasn't the only one. We were possessed by something—the devil, maybe, but also Big Pharma. Which is the big thing no one's talking about. In a few months someone might dare to bring it up, say, Wasn't that weird or whatever, but right now everyone's pretending it didn't happen.

Everything goes back to normal quickly. December turns to January like the most disappointing caterpillar. My mother is in mourning for her lost daughter. *Hi, I'm Janet*, I want to say, *I'm still here. I was always here.*

I fall right back into my old life. I wake up, check that there's still no boyfriend, old or new. I go to work—my one constant, even when my job takes it all out of me and I start wondering if I might finally be over dogs, until a new one comes in and it's never known kindness and it breaks my fucking heart and I try so damn hard not to think about how disgusting humans can be until I can get home and drink myself to sleep.

At least I always remember to brush my teeth.

Everyone is quietly disappointed in me. I tried, but the change they saw over the holidays didn't stick. Debs is the only one who's glad it's all over. For now, anyway.

Melissa hangs on as long as she can. She keeps saying how pretty the lights are in the office and what a shame it is to take them down. Even after the tree comes down she pretends to forget to take down the lights, and Debs lets it slide for a week before reminding her.

I am fine. I am getting back on track. It's not the track anyone wants me on, but it is mine. Sometimes just moving is okay, even if it's not in any particular direction.

Then the cop shows up. The one I think Debs is secretly screwing.

He always checks his hair before he gets out the car, as if that's what we're thinking about when we know he has a dick and a gun, two things we don't approve of.

I'm mopping the office floor because a dog got so excited that it was going home that it peed everywhere, which froze us into fearing that the family would say, Oh, we don't want him now, because people are idiots, but they just thought it was cute and took off with him, and now here I am holding the mop.

Debs is already there to greet the cop, but not in a welcoming way, waiting at the door and checking her lipstick, more in a *Stay back, he who dare enter* way. She never snarls, exactly, but she does do this thing with her eyes like, *If you mess with me, I will rip your face off.* She makes him nervous, but he still likes her.

Melissa and I are openly eavesdropping now. I put my finger to my lips, and she almost explodes with joy that we're doing something together. We can't hear shit from where we are, though, so we just watch and imagine what they're saying.

Melissa thinks he's asking her to marry him, because Melissa will never learn.

I think she's telling him to leave and never come back.

We watch him drive off. Debs sees us standing there as she walks back up, and we're sure she's coming to shout at us, but she just says, Some lady died and they need us to go and get her dog.

Spoiler alert: Sometimes people die. Even people with dogs die, and if they're left too long, there's always a risk a dog will eat its owner. Cats will just ignore you when you die, same as they did in life, but if you have a dog, you'd better plan ahead.

When old people die, and they don't have a family member who wants a dog, they bring it to us. The old ones get new homes quick, because old people like old dogs. Only sometimes the new owner dies and the dog comes back to us again, and it goes on like that until the dog dies. One day, just for kicks, I told Melissa that maybe the dogs were killing the old people, and now she doesn't like dealing with them.

This dog today won't leave the apartment, though, and the cop didn't want to cause it any trauma when it's already had a really shitty week, so he told the family he knew some ladies. He always calls us ladies, which makes me vomit in my mouth a little.

Melissa wants to go and get the dog, but Debs says I have to do it. She hands me the keys and the address. Suddenly I start worrying that it's a setup, that when I get there he'll be waiting in a robe, in candlelight, and it'll put me off men more than I already am.

Clearly I've watched too much trash TV.

I try not to think about it as I pull up at the apartment. I don't need any more weirdness in my life. I'm just now relaxing back in to my usual low-grade discomfort.

When I open the door, I expect to find a gross old-lady apartment, like from *Hoarders*, but it's not. This woman wasn't old, for one thing. From the pictures on her fridge she looks in her thirties, maybe.

This is the part in the movie where you find out it's me and I've been dead all along, but it's not me and I'm not dead, I don't think.

The apartment is really fancy. Nothing is from IKEA. I feel

underdressed, even though technically I'm overdressed in my
jeans and two sweatshirts and giant coat.

The woman is dead, but I'm still jealous of her for all the nice
things she has—including her face, even in death probably. The
dog is this little gray furball, a Pomeranian, I think. It's not yappy,
though. It's just sitting there on the rug—in the spot where they
found her body, I'm guessing—looking at me like, *What took you
so long?* Hey, I say, and give it a ruffle. I'm sorry, buddy, I say. The
dog doesn't show any signs of aggression, so I figure this is going
to be easy, I'll just have a quick look around, then pick the dog up
and get out of here. I don't know how long someone has to be
dead before they're allowed to haunt a place, but I don't want to
hang around and find out.

There's a Christmas tree in the living room. There's no better
excuse for leaving the decorations up than dying. It's a perfect
tree, expensive-looking, the kind you see in magazines and store
windows. Classy, my mother would say. Not like the kind I was
used to, that looks like someone just threw shit at it. There's a box
of fancy chocolates open on the coffee table and I close it because
dogs aren't supposed to have chocolate, but the dog doesn't seem
to be frothing at the mouth or anything. It was probably too
bummed out to think about candy.

The dog hardly seems to register that I'm there. It lets me pet
it, but it's not begging to be picked up or fed or let out. It just sits
there. For all I know that's just what this dog is like. It's what they
call *aloof*, if you're a dog or a supermodel. I couldn't be aloof if I
tried. A boy said I was mysterious once, but it was just because I
wouldn't tell him if I was underage.

I look around the apartment. I was wrong, it *is* IKEA, but it's the good stuff. And it's clean. She must have had a cleaner. She probably also had a real job, one that didn't involve dog shit. I wonder if she even picked up her own dog's shit.

I'm relieved to see she has books on a shelf, but I wonder if they're show books, books to make her look smart but not nerdy, cultured but not a bore. I run my finger over them all. I finger every book I come in contact with—I'm perverted that way. I bet she has a book on her nightstand because she wants to read but never gets around to it. Something with the word *girl* in the title, something some magazine said was *the* book to read.

I go to the kitchen and find the dog food and put out a fresh bowl, but the dog isn't interested. I'm not surprised; dog food is vile.

I take a closer look at the photos of the dead girl on the fridge. She was maybe five years older than me, but I never know how old people are—the adult acne I have on my chin keeps me feeling youthful. She had good teeth, as in they're all still there. In one photo she's kissing some guy up a mountain. She was one of those girls, then, girls who kiss boys up mountains. She'd probably gone kayaking too or something else awful.

I open up the fridge. Looking in people's fridges is important. I've never been in someone's house and not looked. My conclusion is always the same: people are disturbing. There isn't much here to report. Some hummus. Some celery. One depressing yogurt, the kind that helps you poop. Diet Coke. Nothing that a Janet would eat. No large pizza I could wear as a sheet mask.

In the freezer, I find a liter of vodka. I don't just neck it straight from the bottle—this is a classy establishment, remember—but I find myself a glass and pour myself one. I'm trying to be respectful. She would have wanted me to have a drink for her, I'm sure, the dead girl. Okay, so it isn't for her, technically, it's for me, but I am doing her a favor, after all, or at least doing one for her dog.

Before I even get to the bedroom, I know that this is the type of girl who owns multiple dresses and has regular hair appointments and manicures. I wore a dress once. It was traumatic for everyone. A peek in her closet confirms it: full of handbags, not backpacks. If I started carrying a handbag, I'd feel like I was having an out-of-body experience, like my hands weren't my own anymore, then my arms, and soon my whole body would be gone. I imagine the same would happen if I ever got behind a pram.

I was right, there is a book on her nightstand. *Marlena*. Which is a *girl* in the title, after all. There's a bottle of Xanax by the bed and I think, *yawn*. If only instead of pills we could go back to taking spoons of magic. I bet the hipsters would like that. I don't look in her drawers because I made that mistake once before, at a boy's house, and I can never unsee his mother's monstrous 1980s vibrator. It's like Schrödinger's cat: If I don't look, this dead girl may or may not have been able to get herself some pleasure in life.

On the dresser, I spot a photo of her as a child, sitting on Santa's knee. I know it's her from her teeth. And then my vodka-splashed brain does a funny thing: The photo makes me think of Vyla Shirk. The first Janet.

It's not that she looked like Vyla. I have no idea what Vyla looks like. It's just that this could have been Vyla's life. Nice dog, spotless apartment, go up the mountain, leave the pharma mogul, sit right here on Santa's lap. I wonder if she always had a thing for Santa.

What if that's why she ran off with the mall Santa?

What if it wasn't that the pill made her horny after all?

Debs texts me, Where the fuck are you?

This was supposed to be a quick job—get dog, get out. I don't know what to tell her, so I don't reply. I can't say, Sorry, but I'm about to have a breakdown, because I'm only fifty percent certain that's what's happening.

I head back to the kitchen, pour myself another vodka, then sit myself down in the living room to stare at the perfect Christmas tree. My mind is spinning. My eyes light on a pile of Christmas CDs by the stereo, on the tree, on the Santa photo. And in a swirl of reds and greens and vodka, I decide: this dead girl was definitely Vyla.

Poor, sad Vyla.

After the pharma boss got tired of her, I decide, Vyla must have come here and tried to start over, but it was too hard. She was already taking all the pills people take to keep going, only she *couldn't* keep going, and then somehow it was Christmas again and it all came rushing back to her: how sad she was, and how this man had wanted to fix her but he hadn't, he had just broken her more.

The first version of the pill made people horny for Santa, you see, I say to the dog, who I'm now lying next to on the rug. Your mum, Vyla, got horny for a mall Santa. He's your dad, I guess. So she ran away with him, or so the story goes.

The dog just looks at me like, *Humans are a fucking mess.*

Then Vyla came off the pills, I tell the dog, and she wasn't horny for him anymore. Poor Santa, I say. I wonder if he murdered her.

I get nothing from the dog. I was only joking, I say, but still not a sound. Tough crowd, I say. I hope she wasn't murdered, but it makes a juicier story than just saying she died of sad, though, right? Which kind of looks like what happened, don't you think?

The dog does not think. Instead it farts, which I guess is something. I fart back in reply. It's my attempt at bonding. I get my phone and show him this website I found for people with a Santa fetish. The dog sniffs and turns its nose up, which is the correct response.

So Vyla still wanted to be horny for him, the mall Santa, I tell the dog. She'd already told her family he was the one. Ignore the Santa outfit, she said, I'll make him shave for the wedding. Because the pills were making her obsess over weddings and babies and shit. Only when she came off them did she realize it was the pills talking—but she didn't want to look stupid, so she started taking other pills to make up for them, and Santa was all for it as long as she was still horny.

It sounds like every relationship, if I'm honest. You think it's going to be one way, then it's not, but you're invested now, so you do crazy shit to hold it together.

But then Vyla spiraled out on all those pills, and Santa decided he didn't like her anymore, and then he was offered a real job with normal clothes and he left. Poor Vyla even tried going back to the man who made her the Christmas pill, but he wouldn't take her.

It was sad for everyone, I say, stroking the dog's ears.

Which is what brings me here, I say, clambering to my feet, pouring myself another vodka, and resuming my snoop of the dead girl's apartment. All the nice stuff she had—the apartment, the furniture, the dog—it looks like she was trying to carve out a little space in the universe for herself, after all that mess. And then she crawled into it and died.

And then it hits me: Vyla is dead. She might have been the only person in the world who could understand me, and now she's dead. And here I am, somehow, in her apartment. It feels like some bullshit Ghost of Christmas Future moment. Like I'm being shown what will become of me. But I'm not sure any of it really makes sense. All I know is that I'm very drunk, and I'm grieving some girl I've never met. Two girls, maybe. Three, if you count me.

If poor, dead Vyla is my Christmas Future, the dog is my Christmas Present, and I'm my own Christmas Past, because I've been haunting the shit out of myself for years. This makes me laugh out loud, but still the dog doesn't care.

I look in Vyla's closet, and I find those dresses I knew she had, the ones I won't wear. I try one on over my jeans and sweater, but I don't look in the mirror. This isn't about how I look, never was. The world would be a better place without mirrors. I am very drunk, but dumb TV party girls have no monopoly on being drunk, you know. At least I'm not whooping or wearing some ridiculous outfit. Okay, so I am wearing a dead girl's dress, but I'm not flashing my tits at anyone.

I put on one of the Christmas CDs and dance with the dog. I somehow manage not to trip and kill it, though if I did at least he'd be with his mistress. Poor, sad Vyla, who thought a dog could save her. I have a bunch and they haven't yet.

I put on another dress over the dress I'm already wearing, over my own clothes, and I say to the dog, Could I *be* wearing any more clothes?, but the dog doesn't get it, and I don't want to live in a world where I have to explain *Friends*, even to dogs. Don't tell Debs I watch *Friends*, I tell the dog, or I'll never hear the end of it.

It's okay, Janet, the dog says.

But it's not, I say. It's not okay. None of it.

The first Janet is dead, and I'm falling again, only this time a chair catches me. The dog jumps up on my lap. I'm his mistress now, and he doesn't need to know I almost tripped and killed him. Or that I made up all that stuff about his mum. Vyla wasn't his mum, I know that. This wasn't her apartment. His mum was just some dead girl with better shit than me.

Next thing I know, Debs is standing over me, shaking my shoulder.

What the fuck, Janet?

I can feel her lifting me up and putting me in her car.

I knew you were screwing the cop, I mumble into the seat.

I thought you thought I was screwing the cat lady, she spits. Which is it, Janet?

Debs had no problem getting the dog to leave the apartment. Now he's sitting on the other side of the car, pretending he doesn't know me. Everyone does what Debs tells them. She's the boss of everyone. Of course, the dog probably would have followed me if I'd even tried to leave, instead of staying there forever, playing dress-up, playing *Psycho*, only with me playing all the characters in one weird, sad mashup where everyone is running away, where I am both the killer and the victim.

26

I wake up on Debs's couch with a dead arm. I've yet to figure out how to sleep without waking up with a lifeless limb. It's like our bodies don't want us to ever forget them.

I expect one of her kids to be sitting on top of me watching cartoons, or kneeling in front of me, their little face smooshed right up to me, ready to ask me if I'm alive, to which I don't know the answer. When they were small, they were always going through my coat or my bag, pulling out tampons, asking me why everything was, and it was too much, like if I knew, why would I be here? Wouldn't I have transcended? Or at least have my shit together? I know this is what kids do, but for a while I thought they were sent here to test me. Just ignore them, Debs always says. She ignores her kids, and they love her more for it.

Today, though, the house is quiet. The kids are all gone. I can't even hear any barking.

I want to go back to sleep, but I need water. Several cats have died in my mouth somewhere between leaving the girl's apartment and now.

I stumble to the kitchen. Hello? I call out. Nothing.

I can see down to the kennels from the kitchen window, and there's nothing unusual other than it's very quiet and there's a stillness that I'm not used to. The crappy old doors that usually rattle in the wind are silent. Even the roofs that usually drip aren't dripping.

Maybe I'm dead, I think for a second, but my arm is still a bit dead, so the rest of me must still be alive. I'm the right amount of dead.

Where the fuck is everyone? I say to no one. I look at the clock on the wall. It's eight thirty. Melissa will be here soon. For once I might be glad to see her, assuming we're not the last humans on earth, which I'm not so sure about. I'll have to try extra hard not to murder Melissa if we are. Then again, if I can't help it, who would know or care?

I call Debs, but it goes to voicemail. I don't leave a message because I know it will piss her off.

Melissa pulls up and waves. I watch her walk down to the kennels to start her day. The first gate creaks, like it's supposed to, to let the dogs know someone is coming. The barking starts up, and it won't let up till we close for the night. It's better than the silence I woke up to, though, and the one that threatens us all, the one that comes with giving up on yourself, the one that drops you into someone else's abandoned house, a place that's mostly ghosts and dust.

I take Melissa's lead and start my day. When I get to the office, there's a note pinned to the door. On the front it says, JANET. *Hi*, I think. *That's me. I exist.*

I open it.

Janet, it says, *I'll be gone awhile. Look after the place till I get back—Debs.*

That's it.

I am so mad. Not that she's dumped this on me, not that she didn't say where she has gone or why, not even that she didn't say *for how long*. What is *awhile*? An hour? A month? A lifetime? I'm mad because I didn't see this coming. Because I was so in my own head that I didn't think about hers, which is always the way in relationships with humans.

I am mad because people change, and they forget to tell each other.

It must be because of last night, I tell myself. Finding me like that, having to clean up my mess—it must have pushed her over the edge.

I'm sure it wasn't really just me. For all I know, Debs had a genuine emergency. But I get the feeling she just had to leave, and she knew that I, of all people, would understand.

I don't know what to tell Melissa. She'll ask so many questions I can't answer. I'll have to be firm with her. Tell her she has to listen to me, because I'm Debs now. She'll just ask, Then who am I now?, and, Where's Janet gone?, and I won't know what to say.

In the end I say, It's just us now, kiddo. Even though we're the same age.

Sometimes people have just had enough—of other people, yes, but also of themselves. We all spend our lives pushing and pulling in a million directions, until we're too tired to push another inch. Whatever's left is the life we all share. A new life of sorts, but built on the ruins of the old one. It's change, at least, and sometimes that's enough.

I'm not sure it's quite enough for me, though. Not yet, anyway.

27

For a solid week, I do my best impression of Debs. It's the hardest, longest week of my life. I move into her house, because someone always has to be there, and that someone is me now. I barely sleep, because when it's noisy I worry that something's wrong and when it's quiet I worry that something's wrong. It's like having a new-born. I'm convinced that everything I do is wrong, that I've missed something, that I'm not doing enough. Debs has made a terrible mistake in thinking I could do this. Maybe she knew I couldn't but didn't care. We always think people care, but sometimes they really can't anymore.

I'm too tired to miss Debs. Too tired to be mad at Melissa. Too tired to worry about whether I'm happy or sad.

On the seventh night, the cop shows up. I thought he might. He's looking for Debs.

I'm the right amount of hostile you should be when talking to a cop.

I don't ask him in. I'm a young woman alone in the woods.
Anything could happen. Including, I could suddenly get horny
and complicate things even further, as I tend to do.

He says he just wanted to know how the dog was.

Fine, I tell him, considering.

I ask him what her name was—the girl who died, I mean.

Louise something, he says, and he looks on his phone, like
that's where he keeps his list of all the dead girls. Louise Chapman, he says.

Not Vyla? I ask, just to make sure I was definitely having a
breakdown.

Nope, Louise Chapman, he says, looking confused, like there's
another dead girl he should know about. Why? he asks.

And I can't tell him what happened, how I drank a dead girl's
vodka and decided she was the first Janet. No reason, I finally say.

As he's turning around to leave, though, I stop him.

How did she die? I ask. So I can tell her dog, if he asks. Dogs
need closure too.

She slipped in the tub, he says.

Not drugs, then?

Nope, just your regular slipping in the tub. So, you be careful
now, he says. And I know he's picturing me in the tub, and I want
to tell him I only take showers, but I don't want to encourage him.

I say good night and fake-tip my fake hat at him. He looks at
me like, *You're a strange one*, and I am, but I know he's still thinking about me in the bath.

I watch him drive off, and I realize I'm losing my mind a little.
I always thought I might, but not like this.

About an hour later, Debs's brother shows up. *Seriously?* I think. Maybe I'm in heat and they can smell it, but inside I'm the coldest I've ever felt.

You're my second gentleman caller of the night, I joke.

Really? he says, lighting a cigarette.

She's not here, I say, Debs. I don't say I'm here alone; for all he knows, the kids are here with me.

I cross my arms so he knows I might bite.

He laughs at me then. You're not that fuckable, Janet, he says, and leaves.

I am, actually! I want to say, but I don't even understand what I'm trying to say.

It's almost impossible to be a woman. All I really want to be is a person anyway.

I don't drink that night or sleep. If madness is coming for me, I want to be ready. Instead I sit out on the porch all night like a hillbilly, but with a Twix instead of a gun.

I nod off for an hour and dream that Emma tells me she's never coming home and I wake up crying. I try to call her, but she doesn't answer. No one ever does when I need them.

I watch the sun come up, thinking it'll make me feel better, knowing I can count on something. But it's not as pretty as people make it out to be. It's just the sun doing what it does. It's trapped like the rest of us, tethered to something it doesn't understand.

I go down to the kennels. The dogs aren't expecting anyone this early, so they're all half asleep. I'm not anyone to bark about. I'm just funny old Janet. The lady with the kibble.

My phone goes off. It's my mother, like she knows I'm up to something.

Did you know he has a new girlfriend and they're having a baby? she says.

She doesn't say who. She doesn't have to.

I hang up on her.

I'm not surprised. It's a thing. You split up with someone, and straightaway they meet someone else, and suddenly they're getting married and having babies and their smug faces are all over Facebook. You can't help but feel bad for them, that they need to do all that, because they're afraid of the sadness.

He must have been seeing her already when he came back to see me. He hadn't wanted me back, he'd wanted closure. At least I gave him that.

I'm not sad because I wanted it to be me, I'm sad because I'm glad it's not. I should feel free, but instead I feel like my brain is collapsing. I feel like I need to do something dramatic, to stop me from doing something stupid to myself. I want to do what men do all the time—externalize my feelings, instead of internalizing them and making myself sicker.

Before I do, I think about Melissa. About what it would do to her.

I imagine Melissa pulling up. Melissa getting out of her car.

Melissa walking down to the kennels and seeing the gate open. I imagine her cursing me, shouting my name. I picture her on her knees weeping, saying, What have you done, Janet?

But really, I know she's stronger than that. In a crisis you see people's true character, and this whole week Melissa has been great. She can handle whatever I throw her.

So I unlatch the kennel gate, get in the car, and drive away.

Afterward, I feel no desire to go back to my apartment. I need to keep moving forward.

I drive to the next town over and sit outside different cafés, but I don't go in.

I drive to my parents' house and sit outside for an hour. I think I see my mother come to the window, but she doesn't come out. When she doesn't text Janet, are you stalking us?, I figure she doesn't know I'm there.

So I go to a shitty motel. Just for one night, I tell myself. I need some neutral territory. I'll take it one night at a time, I tell myself. The motel is very murdery, and it helps keep my mind off things.

I turn on the TV. The usual January ads: gym memberships, furniture, beer.

Then comes the news. *The so-called Christmas pill has proven a huge success*, the shiny host says. *That's right, Alex, people are already counting the days till November!* her cohost agrees.

That's my pill! I want to say. But I never took it, so how could it be mine? The day we were supposed to start taking them, I opened the bottle, shook one out into my hand, and I thought about it. I poked at it, even nudged it a bit with my nose. But I couldn't do it.

I'll go to the meetings, I said to myself. I'll convince them all I'm doing it. I *will* be doing it, just in my own way. So I sat in that room with those people for seven weeks, and to be honest, they seemed as sad to me by the end as they had on day one.

The news cuts to a commercial, and it's an ad for the pill, which seems a little on-the-nose if you ask me. *More people than ever had a happy Christmas, thanks to this groundbreaking new drug! The holidays are closer than you think—ask your doctor today!* They even mention an all-new formula, an add-on for people who are already on other drugs. My mother would love it.

I wonder if all those people in the meeting really were happier, or if they just liked having someone acknowledge they were sad. The same way I wonder if none of them really took the pills either, if they just went along like I did, because they didn't want to let anyone down.

And so it all begins again, with a new batch of guinea pigs, and it's likely to continue until everyone is medicated. New Janets everywhere will find out that their families have put them forward as the perfect candidate. I just hope at least some of them will realize they don't have to if they don't want to.

This is a lot of feelings for a filthy motel room.

Someone in the next room is having sex, but they might be alone.

I fall asleep looking at grad programs on my phone. Ones that are far away, and more money than I could ever afford, but I can look at them, and it's something.

28

I wake up to my phone going off. It's Debs. I don't answer.

What did you do? Janet? she texts me. I don't answer.

Tell me where you are, she writes, I'm coming.

She knows I'm not okay, because who would do something like that and be okay?

I tell her where I am.

Twenty minutes later, she rolls up with a six-pack of beer.

You have to talk to me, Janet, she says, sitting on the bed.

So I talk to her. I tell her everything. About how tired I am of trying to be okay—not even happy, just okay—when I'm not. About how I never took the pills. She says she guessed it, because I was still the same pain in the ass as always.

I tell her about how I thought the dead girl was Vyla, the first Janet. She says she's sorry she didn't go to get that dog herself, but that I'll always be her first Janet.

She doesn't say anything about the dogs, but I'm too worried to ask.

Everyone leaves me, I tell her. Physically or mentally. I haven't got anyone in my life who can give me everything I need.

No one does, she says.

She says she's sorry she left, but her ex-husband was in a car accident. She says she hates him but she loves him, you know? And I do know.

I tell her I thought he was buried under the floorboards somewhere. That would have been easier, she says.

Then she says, Janet, what do you need? And she's not the one who should be asking, but at least someone is asking, and now I'm crying.

I need to have had a different mother, I tell her, which is the truth but not fair.

What about your dad? she says.

He's never really been there either, I tell her.

And she's quiet then. I think she's going to lecture me about how some people don't have parents but she doesn't. Instead, she just says, I'm here, Janet, and I let her hug me. I've never seen Debs hug anyone, but she must, I realize—she has kids, great kids. I guess she just does the important stuff privately.

Debs? I ask. What about the dogs?

It was pretty funny, actually, she says. When she got there, she almost lost it, but then she heard a bark and looked around and realized they were all there, out in the woods, leaping around and chasing one another. The kids all piled out of the car and helped round them up, like it was a big game. It was the most excitement any of us had had in ages, she says, the dogs, the humans. You missed a real treat, she says. It was like fucking Christmas.

Sorry, I say.

No one got hurt, she says. Turns out all our dogs are good dogs after all. It's just the humans who are assholes.

And Melissa? I ask.

Melissa's confused, she says. But she'll get over it.

I do have to fire you now, though, she says. I say I understand. I shyly tell her I've been thinking about some grad programs.

That sounds great, she says. You were always too smart for us.

It might be, I say.

She says, I have my kids and my own shit, but you've got me.

No one has ever said that to me before. I thought no one wanted me—the way I am, anyway.

Just stop being such a pain in the ass, she says, spoiling it all. But I forgive her.

The way I look at it is, you have a purpose now, she says, handing me another beer.

I do? I say.

Hell, yeah, she says. You have to take down Big Pharma.

I laugh. I can't even get off a bus at the right time.

I'm not joking, she says. It's that or some hugs-not-drugs thing, which I don't think is really you.

I don't know, I say, smiling, I'm changed now. She punches me in the tit playfully. Yeah, you are, she says.

Things to think about anyway, she says, but I have to go because I left the kids in the car and I didn't crack a window.

Before she leaves, she looks at the stain on the bed. Are you really sleeping here? she says. Off to conquer Big Pharma, and I can't even hold a glass.

I thought *my* house was depressing, she says, clocking the hole in the wall.

I like it, I say.

Of course you do, she says.

That night I masturbate to a blurry picture of an actor I used to like. I imagine him kissing my neck and telling me it's going to be okay, and when I'm done I cry and stroke my own hair.

The next morning my phone wakes me up. I figure it's Debs checking I wasn't murdered.

Have you seen the news? she says. Put the news on, Janet.

I do as I'm told.

Richard Grossman is all over it. He's been arrested. The details are confusing, but it seems someone has leaked internal data suggesting that his pill was actually a chemical blend of ingredients I've never heard of. *Magnesium stearate,* the host reads, *microcrystalline cellulose, pregelatinized cornstarch, and sucrose.*

Wait . . . sucrose? Isn't that—

Isn't that something, Alex? says the host. *The pill they called Santa's Little Helper was a placebo.*

There was no scientific study. No chemical cure for holiday-specific depression.

The Christmas pill was a fraud.

Are you watching this shit? Debs says, still on the line.

I don't understand, I say.

It was all a scam, Debs says. I'm falling again, but this time it feels like I've been pushed.

The full story unfolds quickly, in a wave of scoops, press releases, and breaking news. I sit in my dirty motel room, glued to the TV, shaking with anger.

After the leak is confirmed, the company has to admit that the whole story, all the research—all of it was fabricated.

It was all a scam, just like Debs said. There never was a Christmas pill. We were the only untapped market, so they tapped us—with a sledgehammer. Once we were out cold, they figured, we'd take anything they wanted us to.

I flip the channel, and there's Pharma Bro himself. *My* pharma bro, Grossman's local rep. The reporter has caught him outside his building, looking disheveled and ashamed. We were just giving people what they wanted, he says, not looking for a minute like he believes it. People wanted to buy a happy Christmas, so we made that possible, he says.

His name is Jason, according to the chyron. I'd never bothered to learn it, or maybe I'd just chosen to forget it.

For the first time in my life, I feel a solidarity with the talking heads. They're outraged, they say. People have been duped, they say. It isn't right, they say. And I just sit there, watching and nodding furiously, before I finally fall asleep.

But it doesn't last long.

Overnight—*literally* overnight—the narrative changes.

The next morning, I wake up and turn on the TV. The first thing I see is Richard Grossman, somehow out of jail already, holding a press conference.

The world needed something to bring people together, he says. And we did that. Does it really matter how? He looks around, waits for that to sink in.

Don't you see? he says. *It worked*. People all over the country had a happy Christmas. They found the real Christmas spirit— right there inside themselves. And it was all thanks to our pill.

I wait for the talking heads to roll their eyes with me.

I can keep waiting. They're lapping it up.

Richard Grossman has done something amazing, Alex, hasn't he?

Suddenly it's not a scam but a holiday miracle. He's basically saying he saved Christmas, and the world is buying it.

It's enough to make me vomit, which I do, a lot.

I see a girl I recognize from my meeting giving an interview. She says she always suspected it was a placebo, but she doesn't mind. It helped her see what she was missing—and she's already started taking Prozac! Yay!

No one seems to feel cheated but me. And I didn't even take the damn pill.

The next day, the tabloids run an exclusive tell-all from Dickie boy. I don't even have to go outside to get it, the news is still covering it nonstop. He says he started out by trying to make the Christmas pill for real—for the love of his life—but it was just too hard. It wouldn't work. And he couldn't figure it out. So he made it all up. For Vyla.

Turns out the only true part of his story was Vyla Shirk. He goes on and on about Vyla, about her depression and her listlessness and how sorry he was about her life. And I can just hear what the people are thinking: *What a caring man. He loved this girl so much he made her a pill. Or, you know, maybe he couldn't, but he wanted to.*

All I see is a man speaking for a woman and telling her she needed to be fixed.

He even digs out old photos of the two of them to help his case. See, he says, I was just a man in love. I just wanted to make her happy. I just wanted to make the world happy, he says, and everyone weeps and cheers.

Everyone sees in this exactly what they wanted to see. What I see is that Vyla is alive. This is what I focus on. I don't give a shit about Dickie boy and his bleeding heart. He's just like my boyfriend and my mother. Wanting to fix us all. I care about Vyla.

Where is Vyla? the reporters ask. I don't know, he says, it was a long time ago, I just hope she's happy. And he fake-cries a bit, and everyone buys it.

All of this is followed by an announcement from Grossman's

company. They're sorry for deceiving everyone, but they're so gratified by the groundswell of public support that they're committing to a new plan that they hope will redeem themselves: they're making this new Christmas pill available to everyone.

The world rejoices. My mother gets her wish. Fake it, meet make it.

I'm screaming at the TV. For a minute, I stop, to see if anyone else in the building is screaming too. Crickets.

They've found the spirit of Christmas! say the heads on the TV. *Without the pills!*

But no one is listening, mostly because I'm alone in a motel room. It doesn't really matter what I say or where I say it. It's already starting over again. Only there won't be any meetings this time, just the pills.

You'd like that, wouldn't you, Janet? my doctor will say.

My mother keeps calling me, but I ignore it. All the crying and masturbating and shouting and vomiting has made me more hollowed-out than I've ever felt, like a scraped-out potato skin no one has any intention of stuffing with anything delicious.

It doesn't even matter that I didn't take the pills. It still feels like something has been taken from me. Not taking the pills was the only bit of control I had, and it turns out I never had it at all. And now the world is a bigger mess than I could have ever imagined.

I can just hear my mother's voice: See, I knew you could do it! You just needed a nudge. A nudge? It feels more like a big hard shove. I want her to see how ridiculous it's all gotten, but I know she'll never see it that way. All she'll see is me being difficult.

They made a pill just for you, and you wouldn't even take it, she'll say.

I need to get out of this motel fast, before I punch a hole in the wall, to go with the ones that are already there. Maybe motels are where girls come to punch walls. Who knew?

Stepping outside, I'm surprised how calm the world actually is. It's only my head that's full of noise and chaos. There are no news crews or reporters hounding me for my take on all this. I'm still no one, and I'm glad.

I drive to my apartment, and it feels like I'm going backward.

On the stairs, I see Min-seo, her phone to her ear. Hey, she says.

Hey, I say, hoping I don't have any vomit in my hair.

I saw the news, she says. Sorry, she says.

What are you sorry for? I say.

Because people keep dicking you around, she says.

I sit down next to her. I have no idea what I'm doing anymore, I say.

Never have, never will, she says.

I'm done with being touched again for a while, anyway, but I wish I knew her well enough to lean my head on her shoulder. I don't, so we just sit there, and it's fine.

I just wanted to feel different for a while, I say.

And did you? Min-seo asks.

I felt relief, I say. Hope, maybe. I don't know anymore.

Well, I see they're actually doing it for real now. So you have a few months to figure it out, right? she says.

Or not, I say, a tiny moment of quiet private joy that can only be felt by a Janet.

She doesn't say *I'm here if you need me*, because she doesn't really know me, but she does say, Maybe we should get a drink sometime, and I say, Sure.

I go into my apartment, close the door, and curl up into a ball on the floor, rocking a little. What yoga move is this? I say to no one.

Then there's a knock at the door.

I think it might be Min-seo needing that drink already, but it isn't. It's a woman I don't recognize.

Janet? she says.

Yes, I say.

Sorry to just show up like this, she says. Jason gave me your address. He thought we should meet.

Why the fuck is Pharma Guy sending random women to my apartment? I think.

And then, just like that, I know who she is.

I'm Vyla, she says.

Hi, I say, smiling. I'm Janet.

Hi, Janet, she says, and smiles back. Her smile is a little crooked, like it might not be the most natural thing for her—it looks like mine—but she's giving it her best shot.

She's real. I'm real. I don't know if anything else is, but it doesn't matter.

Before she left the motel, Debs told me there comes a time when you need to stop thinking about the people you don't have and start thinking about the people you do.

I have Debs. I have Melissa, whether I want her or not. I have Min-seo, maybe, and now I have Vyla. Together we have three hundred and forty-seven days to work out what to do about Christmas and all the stuff in between.

We're women. We'll work it out.

Acknowledgments

To be honest, I wrote this book on my own. It was only toward the end that my lovely agent, Stacy Testa, found me and probably saved my life, and then Cal Morgan and Riverhead gave it a home, and I still think I'm being punked. Thank you, Stacy and Cal, for believing in me, when I still don't. Thanks to everyone at Writers House and Riverhead.

Thank you to the following people and places for supporting my writing and general nonsense over the years: George Saunders for always saying the right thing; Rachel Fershleiser for being my early cheerleader; Jade Sharma for being an early reader and helping me find my voice; I miss you. Marcy Dermansky for her friendship and TV updates; Cynthia D'Aprix Sweeney for her wisdom and kindness; Adrienne Celt for inspiring me every day; Kerry Cullen for her general awesomeness; Tobias Carroll and *Vol. 1 Brooklyn*; Carol Ann Fitzgerald and *The Sun* magazine; Tracy O'Neill and *Epiphany* literary journal; Catapult Story; *Five:2:One* magazine; *Split Lip Magazine*; *The Millions*; *Tincture Journal*; Barrelhouse; *Glimmer Train*; *Jellyfish Review*; *Synaesthesia Magazine*; *Tammy Journal*; and *Bird's Thumb*.

Thank you to my family, especially my sister, Ruth, the first person I ever wanted to make laugh. I never would have finished anything if it wasn't for you.

Thank you to Alex for making this life bearable, even fun sometimes.

Thank you to you for reading if you still are and didn't give up at my first fart joke and go and read something else.